Hope you Enjoy!

YALC '15

SIGIL OF THE WYRM

INTO THE WEIRDING BOOK ONE
A.J. CAMPBELL

Xchyler Publishing, an imprint of Hamilton Springs Press, LLC
Penny Freeman, Editor-in-Chief
www.xchylerpublishing.com
1st Edition: July 2015
Cover Illustration by Emma Michaels
Interior Design by M Borgnaes of The Electric Scroll
Edited by Sarah-Beth Watkins and MeriLyn Oblad
Published in the United States of America by Xchyler Publishing

For Judith Clare and Jean Greenwood
Two extraordinary women who first taught me I could
write.

SIGIL OF THE WYRM

INTO THE WEIRDING BOOK ONE

A. J. CAMPBELL

PROLOGUE

The Northern sky had shaded to a deep blue velvet, punctured here and there with the last of the summer stars. The final shreds of the day's warmth were steadily being pushed back, and a sharp tin edge to the wind spoke of September's arrival. In the dark and the chill, the huge pillars atop the hill would have been foreboding, even without the faint green crackles of light which pulsed across their surface. Like a pillar herself, the woman stood waiting a few feet from the plinth that formed the base of the columns, white robes whipping round her ankles.

The green light flared and died like a candle flame blown out, and in the afterglow a man stumbled heavily out from among the tall stones. One hand was wrapped around his side, pressed to his ribs, while the other, groping in front of him for support, let fall the long steel blade he had been clinging to. It dropped to the stone floor with a dull clang. In a few steps, the woman was there at his arm, supporting him as he crumpled forward like a dropped cloth.

'Is it done?' she asked, propping him up on the damp grass against the plinth. 'Tom? Is it done?'

The man coughed. 'My shirt's wet,' he said matter-of-factly. He tugged at the side straps holding his vest together. 'I don't think the Kevlar made much—Ah! Damn it!' He winced as he peeled the black material aside. Beneath his hands, a dark pulsing stain spread up and across his chest.

'You're hurt.' The woman's brows furrowed and her eyes flashed with pushed-down panic.

'No, I'm dying,' Tom replied. He coughed again, damply, 'and I'd really rather not be. Look, there's a phone in my car. Driver's side door pocket. Call someone?'

'We had a plan, you have to—'

'You have to call someone. First. Before it's too late.'

'Then . . .' for a moment she looked about to argue but then nodded. 'There is still time. The important part is done.' She stood and hastily swished away through the wet grass.

In her brief absence, Tom sat, gazing across the countryside below, the lights of the city twinkling and growing fuzzy in the distance. He tried to wipe the blood from his hands, and as he did so, he felt something loosen from around his finger.

'I've called Kate,' the woman said as she returned. 'She's on her way. Now, before it's too late.' She knelt and looked imploringly at the broken figure. 'Please. You know what you have to do. Where is your sword?'

He shook his head.

'It doesn't matter now. I'm sorry. Kate won't be here in time.'

'You can't know that. We need to finish this.'

'I am finished. Even if I tried, it's already moved on.' He uncurled his fingers, showing her the little gold band that had slipped from them moments before. 'The ring's off. I've not got long.' Impulsively, she wrapped his hand in hers, closing his fingers again on the ring.

'There's still time. What if you're wrong? We could end it, here and now, forever. Like we planned.'

'Stop.' His free hand reached out limply for her face and came to rest on her shoulder. 'Even if it would work, I'm not doing it. Not with my last moments. I couldn't face it.'

'And I can't face doing this all over again.' Her face looked infinitely young, fragile, as if it would crack.

'Richard's not like me. He doesn't know you, doesn't know any of us. Listen, you've got to—' he crumpled as a spasm of pain shot across his features. 'You've got to take the key. Get it to Richard. Perhaps . . . he can . . . be the hero you've always wanted.'

'But he doesn't know me, doesn't know—'

'Then don't tell him. Trust me, it'll be easier if . . . if he doesn't know you.' His breath was slowing, coming thick and rasping now. 'Easier . . . easier if he doesn't . . . doesn't love . . .' Tom's hand dropped from the woman's arm. The harsh wheeze died on the wind, and the first spots of a September rain began to fall.

CHAPTER 1

THE FUNERAL OF TOM LAMPTON

Saturday morning was grey and overcast. Richard had almost expected it to be. It seemed the right kind of weather for funerals—not a thunderstorm, not pouring rain, just dull grey clouds, no sun, and a misty drizzle. He picked his way past the tombstones which stuck out at odd angles, leaned over drunkenly, and generally didn't appear to know how to behave on an occasion of such solemnity. He paused for a few moments in front of a granite angel, hands outstretched and wings spread, who, thanks to the careless ministrations of some bird, appeared to be crying.

The years had not been kind to her. Green and white lichens had begun to creep up her skirts, the rain and the wind had weathered her features so that the feathers on her wings and the detail of her face were now lost to time, and she was missing a finger and a lock of hair where the stone had crumbled away. Nevertheless, you could still imagine that her face wore its expression of hope that perhaps the

Almighty would look kindly on Agnes Grey, beloved wife and mother, 1849–1910.

Richard followed the pallbearers on through the cemetery to where the graves began to look better tended. The grass became shorter and there were pots of flowers—some fresh, some artificial, some drying out and mouldering to just stalks and a few wrinkled petals. One headstone had a small blue teddy bear leaning up against it, half perished in the damp. The inscription said simply 'Emily Musgrove, 2002–2005.' Richard shivered and moved on quickly.

Right at the far end of the field, furthest from the church, was an open grave. Other black-clad mourners stood around in groups of two or three, none of them saying much, as the coffin with its white wreath of lilies was set down by the side of the hole. Next to it stood the stone slab with the name 'Thomas Lampton' carved into it. The priest, stark in his white surplice, shuffled through his notes and began the final part of the litany.

Richard had been sitting at the front of the church with his Aunt Ellie during the service, so now he took a moment to scan the faces around him. He recognised very few of them. He had never been very close to his father's side of the family, so he didn't know if the assembled were family or friends. Aunt Ellie, Uncle Tom's wife, was standing quite stiffly, staring straight ahead and gripping three long-stemmed red roses so tightly they shook. A girl with mid-length, mousey-brown hair and glasses had come up to hold her other hand and had put one arm around her, as if to hold her up.

It was an odd looking bunch gathered by the graveside. Several figures in particular caught his eye, among them a tall woman, dark-eyed and ebony-skinned, who looked far too good to be attending a service for the dearly departed. Her hat had a black lace veil, her hair was perfectly curled into a flawless chignon, and she was wearing dark plum lipstick. She was tapping what looked like a short, black stick against her front teeth, which were startlingly white. Richard felt the hairs on his neck start to prickle at the sight of her.

She was also looking at Richard. He suddenly realised he was staring and quickly looked away. After what he considered a safe time had elapsed, he glanced back to see if she had noticed him staring at her. She winked at him. Richard cringed and tried to concentrate on the service. When he next looked back, the woman had gone.

'I'm gagging for a smoke,' whispered a husky female voice about three inches behind his right ear. It was a pleasant voice, silky and full of amusement, but the sudden proximity of it and the realisation of who it might be was like a bucket of iced water down his neck.

'I'm going to slip away for a bit,' the voice continued. 'Alone, before you get any ideas—I did see you staring. But priests do go on a bit long for my liking.'

'Who . . .?' Richard started to turn round, but the voice stopped him.

'No. Not yet. Poor man is still talking. Someone should indulge him. Just not me. Listen, just in case I'm wrong—not that I am, often—and the droning is over before I'm finished, I need you to stick around. I've got something for you.'

Richard didn't look around, but he could feel the woman turn and walk away into a quieter area of the churchyard. After a few seconds he heard, or thought he heard, the metallic flick of a lighter opening and a long, satisfied exhalation of smoke.

The rest of the service passed in a blur. Richard spent most of it looking at either his feet or the end of his nose, but eventually the vicar put down his service book, and Aunt Ellie threw her roses into the grave with a stiff little jerk. They made a soft, whispering thump as they hit the coffin lid. Other people quietly lined up behind her to deposit their offerings of flowers, cigars, coins and an odd assortment of bits and pieces. Finally, they began to shovel the earth back in.

Aunt Ellie turned away, not wishing to watch the rest, and the mousey-haired girl was shaken off. She shrugged and wandered off to talk to a thin woman with shockingly red hair. Richard felt it was safe to look up. As he had suspected, the tall lady in the veil was standing to one side smoking a cigarette in the long, black holder he had seen her tapping against her teeth earlier. She jerked her head in a motion suggesting he join her.

Up close, she was even more stunning than he had first realised, with a flawless complexion and huge eyes like the blackness at the heart of a star.

'Katherine Avery,' she said, extending a hand. 'Though I go by Kate. And you're Dick Lampton, am I right?'

'Richard, please.' One perfectly shaped eyebrow arched skywards, and Richard felt the blush returning. 'But Dick is fine . . .' he muttered shamefacedly.

'Not to worry. I always call people by names they don't like,' smiled Kate. 'It saves time. Do you smoke?'

'No.'

'You should. You'll die younger.' She blew out a mouthful of fog. Richard felt like he was reading off a script that was completely different than everyone else.

'Die younger?'

'From cancer, cardiovascular disease, respiratory problems, emphysema, not to mention yellow teeth, fingers, and walls. Pick one.'

'Do I have to?'

'No. You could live a long and healthy life and die of old age, but where's the fun in that?' Kate took a last drag on her cigarette before knocking it out of the holder and grinding the butt into the ground with the toe of a black patent-leather stiletto. She opened her handbag, and Richard thought for a moment she was looking for another cigarette, but instead she drew out a small box such as might contain a ring. She handed it over.

'What is this?' asked Richard, hoping it wasn't too stupid a question.

'It's a box. They're traditionally made for opening.' Kate's face never softened, but she added in a gentler tone, 'It was your uncle's. Now it passes to you.' It was an odd choice of words. Richard might have expected her to say how much his uncle would have wanted him to have it, whatever it was. 'It passes to you' sounded rather more formal, and the way she said it, more ominous than a simple bequest should. He opened the box. Sure enough, it contained a ring. A simple, gold signet ring.

'Odd symbol,' muttered Richard, examining the seal. 'Is it a snake?'

'Try it on,' suggested Kate. 'I want to know it fits.' Gingerly, Richard lifted the gold circle out of the box and slipped it onto the middle finger of his right hand. It was a perfect fit. She smiled.

'Good,' she said, taking the now empty box from

Richard's unresisting hand, and turned to go.

'What, is that it?' asked Richard, watching her retreating back.

'Hopefully,' she replied without turning round.

Dawlish was standing at one side of the cemetery, leaning back on the iron railings, playing with her hair. She was a scraggly kind of girl, barely into her teens, with limbs thin as jointed broom handles. Gingery roots were beginning to show through under her black hair, and her black nail-polish was beginning to chip. Three black feathers, half-hidden because of the similarity in colour, had been braided into her hair on the left-hand side. She nodded and stood up straighter as Kate approached her.

'He took the ring?' she asked when Kate was close enough.

'Yes,' replied the older woman, passing over the empty box. 'Do something with that, will you?'

'It fits?'

'Mmm . . .' She peered into the dark glass of a car window, parked just on the other side of the fence, and adjusted her hat.

'It is him, isn't it? What with Tom not having children and all?' insisted Dawlish.

'Yes, but it's a hard thing to predict. Inheritance. You know. The wrong grandchild always gets the furniture and all that.'

'We aren't talking about a set of bookcases though, are we? This is just slightly more important.'

'Slightly, yes. I have some very valuable bookcases.'

Dawlish sighed and started chewing on a clump of her hair. Kate noticed and frowned.

'Must you do that?'

'Mmm . . .'

'Well, don't. You'll make me ill.'

The girl obediently spat out the hair.

'What now, then?'

'We wait. Either things work out or they don't. In which case, I may have to give them a gentle nudge.'

'When will we know?'

'Estimates suggest a week. Probably less. Is everything alright? You're looking a bit peaky.'

'Hmm?' Dawlish looked up. 'No, I'm fine. Just thinking about things.'

'You're doing a lot of that lately. It's obviously bad for you. Anyway, we'd best get moving. Don't fancy hanging around here too long.' And with that, she began to make strides towards the car that was, in accordance with instructions, idling at the church gates. Dawlish hesitated for a moment before following her. A jackdaw floated down from the top of a nearby sycamore and landed silently on her shoulder.

'Tell the Baron I'll see him soon,' she said, scratching its head with the edge of a fingernail. The bird clicked its beak a few times, then took off again. The girl shivered and peered up for any sign of the weather lightening, then with some reluctance got into the waiting car.

The drive back to the wake had been uncomfortable. Richard had accepted the offer of a lift from the mousey-haired girl he had seen talking to Aunt Ellie earlier and as a result, found himself crushed into the back seat of an old, black Peugeot behind a small boy, about five years old, who had insisted on having the seat pushed as far back as it would go. The rest of the back seat was taken up with a large pile of the same white lilies that had been at the cemetery. Their scent was heady and cloying, and so Richard had spent the entire journey with his knees up round his chin, fighting the urge to sneeze.

The girl's name, he had discovered, was Jennifer Lomax, and the small boy belonged to one of her relations; he hadn't quite caught which. It seemed she was staying with Aunt Ellie and helping her organise things until she 'felt better,' whatever that meant in the context of losing a husband. Apart from introductions, however, the journey had been made in silence. Richard, still thinking about the lovely Ms Katherine Avery and the delicious way her hips moved when she walked, was happy to let his mind wander.

Now he loitered in a corner of a large chintz-filled living room that supposedly belonged to his Aunt Margot, eating cardboard that was masquerading as sandwiches and small cocktail sausages on sticks. The atmosphere was understandably subdued, and people stood around in little groups talking in hushed tones. Richard felt awkward and out of place. He hadn't known his uncle very well and felt that he was intruding on other people's grief. A set of French windows backed out onto the garden, and from outside came the sound of children at play, which was soothing if he didn't listen too closely to what they were yelling.

Richard wandered over and took a look. A small, serious-looking girl wearing a black dress was wallowing in the flowerbed and doing her level best to get it blacker. Another girl was alternately wailing because of the small boy hanging from her blonde pigtails and attempting to rectify the problem by hitting him over the head with a Barbie doll. Richard turned away, afraid that he might see something that would upset him.

'Janine, stop that!' yelled a voice from the house. 'You'll break your doll!' A large woman appeared behind Richard, wearing a black and grey two-piece suit which matched the furniture.

'Awful little brats,' she said charitably. 'How are you, Dick?'

'Richard, please,' said Richard. 'And I'm good. Well. Considering.'

'Dreadful business this,' said the woman who Richard realised must be Aunt Margot, Ellie's sister. 'Poor old Tom.'

'I am sorry,' said Richard.

'What for? Wasn't your fault the old boy snuffed it.'

'I mean, I'm sorry for your loss.'

'Oh.' Margot sighed. 'Well, thanks. Bad business though, bad business. Forty-two's no age to go.'

'What happened, in the end?' asked Richard. 'I don't think anyone ever said.'

'I think they decided it was a heart attack, eventually.'

'They're getting more common these days, I believe.'

'Yes, well, people not taking care of themselves, drinking, smoking, too much cholesterol. You know the drill.' The mention of smoking brought back the image of black patent-leather stilettos, and Richard felt for the ring

13

resting oddly on his finger.

'So you got the ring,' said Margot with a knowing look.

'Yes.'

'Used to be Tom's,' continued Margot. 'And your father's before that, and their father's, and so on and so forth.'

'Family heirloom?'

'In a manner of speaking.' There was an awkward pause.

'Good food,' said Richard, for lack of anything else.

'No, it's not,' replied Margot. 'Tastes like cardboard. Last time I use those caterers. Which reminds me, must go and have a word with Audrey. Lovely to see you again, Dick, pity about the circumstances . . .' And she wandered off absently. Richard was left standing at the French windows clutching his drink and wondering if it was something he said.

It might have been the sandwiches, but Richard was beginning to feel a bit queasy.

'Are you alright?' asked a little old lady with blue hair at his left elbow.

'Fine, fine . . .' he muttered.

'You look tired, pet,' she continued. 'You need a large scotch.' And she raised a small glass of amber liquid to her lips, drained it, and then tottered off, presumably in the direction of the rest of the bottle. Richard decided he'd done his bit and that no one would miss him if he just snuck away quietly.

'Leaving so soon?' Richard froze in the act of digging his coat out of the huge pile that had formed when the overloaded hooks next to the door had given up and dumped an avalanche of over-garments on the carpet.

'Umm . . .'

'It's alright.' Jennifer, the girl who had driven him to the wake, was coming out of the bathroom. 'I'm not your mum or anything. I'm not accusing you. You can go if you want to.'

'No, no . . .' Richard tried to cover, 'I'm just not feeling too well.'

'Like I said, I'm not your mother.' Jennifer shut the bathroom door behind her.

'Honestly, I'm not feeling well.'

'I believe you. Well . . . it was nice seeing you again.'

'You, too, Jennifer.' He reached out to shake her hand.

'Jenny, please.'

'Jenny. It was nice to meet you.' And something prompted him to add, 'I hope I'll see you around some time.' She smiled at that, and it was as if someone had just switched something on behind her eyes.

'I hope so,' she said. 'Goodbye, Richard.' He was halfway to meeting Andy at The Blackbird before he realised that she was the first person all day who hadn't called him Dick.

CHAPTER 2

THE FLEDGLING WHO CAME
FOR BREAKFAST

Every little town has a square like this. Stone troughs overflow with red geraniums, war memorials stand festooned in plastic poppies, and old fashioned ice cream parlours are sandwiched between the new chip shop and the dry cleaners. Sometimes there's a statue to some local dignitary who, in spite of everything, no one really remembers. There's often a clock tower. It's made of tall, grey stone and looks like a miniature Big Ben, only without the Houses of Parliament stuck to one side. It has a door in the front with a huge rusty keyhole. And it's always locked. But in this particular square in this little town where the geraniums are a slightly more orange shade of red, the clock door opened, ever so slightly, and Dawlish slid out into the street. She looked up at the clock. It was ten minutes to twelve.

Across the square, a tall woman in white was watching

the scene unfold. 'Pay attention.' A little jackdaw, perched on her shoulder, was more interested in the girl who had just appeared than in his surroundings. 'I didn't bring you here to see her,' the woman continued. She pointed at a street leading out of town. 'That's the one. You're looking for Richard Lampton. His flat is at the end of that road. Do you think you can find it?'

'Aak,' the bird replied and took off in the direction indicated.

'I'm counting on you . . .' the woman whispered as she watched the retreating speck of black.

Richard couldn't be certain that he wasn't still drunk. The room was spinning like one of those fairground rides that stick you to the walls with G-forces, and all he could do just at that moment was cling to the bed and hope that it would stop soon. His mouth and throat were dry and tight, his tongue sticky and gummed-up. He felt as if there was a steel band around his skull, over his eyes, squeezed too tight so that whenever he moved, he could feel just how heavy and dull his head was. Each noise was louder than ball-bearings rolling around in the taut, hollow space where his brain used to be.

He tried to sit up and regretted it instantly. He felt dizzy and sick. The muscles over his ribs were cramping and aching, each movement a further jab in his side from last night's stiff alcoholic fingers. He flopped back down on the mattress as carefully as he could. Instead, he tried opening his eyes. Just for half a second, as the flash of light sent shards of pain stabbing through his temples, but that limited glance let him ascertain that he had made it home, and he was lying in his own bed. A bed that was warm and comfortable and yielding as cotton wool. It was like lying on a cloud. He drifted back to sleep.

When he awoke for a second time, he was marginally more prepared for the onslaught to his senses. He opened his eyes gradually and just about managed not to throw up. The ache in his sides had begun to lessen, but the headache, if anything, was worsening. Very, very gingerly, and with his eyes only half open, he got out of bed and felt his way along the walls to the kitchen. Leaning over the sink and trying to catch his breath, he ran himself a glass of water. The first gulp went to rinse the fuzzy taste from his mouth, then the rest he tipped down his throat. It helped. Barely, but it helped. He ran another glass which went the same way as the first, then a third which he took with him as he staggered back into the bedroom. He clambered back into bed and lay there, waiting to feel better.

Lazily, and in no particular order, the events of the previous night began to present themselves in Richard's brain for inspection. They had been to the wine bar. And before that, he'd met Andy at The Blackbird and they'd had a few. Two pints. No, three—they'd had one for the road as well, after Richard had explained everything about the funeral and about Kate and the ring—though not all of it, just the bits that sounded normal.

Then Andy had suggested they go on somewhere, and there had been girls. Three of them. No, four. Three. Four. Three girls in very short skirts who laughed a lot, drank an awful lot, and fell over almost as much.

And one . . . She seemed very familiar. Richard wasn't

sure if she had been with the other three or not. She didn't look like she fitted in with them; she hadn't been wearing a skimpy dress or laughing quite so much. She had given him a drink though, something red and sticky that might have tasted of pomegranate. Or it might not have. There had been an awful lot of alcohol. And some vile pitcher of stickiness tasting of blue, and everything after that point was a bit blurry round the edges. He didn't remember how he got home.

By this time, Richard had reached the stage of his hangover when, though he was still tired and aching, any attempt to go back to sleep would be futile. The duvet that had felt so warm was now hot and stifling, so he kicked it off. He also began to realise that he was hungry. Perhaps it was time to see if he could manage some breakfast.

It was a place beyond, half a shadow's breadth away, where the breath of this world could almost touch it. Cold and deep, brushing up against dreams and nightmares, a constant pressure on the edges of life. And in scattered places, where the rivers ran deep and the blood pulsed quick beneath the skin, the taut, air-thin membrane between the Here and Elsewhere was growing thinner. In the darkness and the waiting, something stirred.

The River Wear flowed steadily beneath the wings of the birds, swooping like black and white kites in the patchy blue sky. Caught by the wind, the magpies bobbed and dived, weaving in and out of one another like a skein of feathers and air currents. A casual observer might have thought their movements random, playful, but over time their pattern of sweeps across the riverbanks and fields beyond started to take shape. One would think they were combing the area, methodically searching for something, but as any rational observer would know, birds don't do that.

Beneath their rush of wing beats, the shadows over the river grew darker, and just beneath the surface, something—perhaps it was waterweed—rippled. A sense of pressure was growing in the air, like a too-full balloon being gently squeezed. One magpie, gliding low over the water, let out a cry, and in a rush the whole flock suddenly coalesced into a shrieking, shattering mob that wheeled around and sped off all at once in the direction of the sunset.

After a discrete pause, a smaller cohort of birds—jackdaws—hopped furtively down out of a nearby tree. All of them seemed to be watching the flight of the departing magpies. One gave a short resigned croak, then, at a more sedate pace, they all took to the sky, too, and glided off nonchalantly in the opposite direction.

The smell of cooking bacon did something to revive Richard from the fug in his head. The fridge didn't offer many options, but there was always bacon, and it wasn't difficult to locate a frying pan and set it on the gas ring. As it started to sizzle, Richard found that he was hungry after all. At first all he could manage was to stick his head over the pan and inhale, the warm, salty smell being almost as good as a meal in itself. But as the rashers began to crisp up and blacken round the edges, he found himself reaching for a fork and eating them straight out of the pan. The taste, and the warmth as it reached his stomach, went most of the rest of the way towards waking him up, though it wasn't quite enough to make him feel human again.

While two more rashers of bacon were crackling in the pan, Richard flicked the kettle on for a cup of tea. A second examination of the fridge not only revealed an in-date carton of milk, but a pack of sausages which he had overlooked the first time around. Two of these went into the pan next to the bacon as Richard continued looking for anything else he could conceivably fry. He couldn't find any eggs, and though there was some bread, it was stale enough that frying it was about all it was good for. He cut a slice anyway and put it to one side for soaking in the bacon grease when he could.

A quick trawl of the cupboards turned up a small tin of baked beans as well, though no tin-opener. Richard contemplated putting the beans back, but there was so little else and he was hungry enough that he felt he couldn't. The thought came to him that his Swiss army knife probably had a can-opener attachment, though where he could find that was anyone's guess. He tried the pockets of five different coats before eventually locating the offending article at the bottom of a bag that he couldn't remember when he'd used last. He returned with it to the kitchen, where the bacon was burning nicely. As he grabbed a plate to transfer the bacon onto, he spotted the recalcitrant tin-opener glinting at him from the draining board. Muttering quietly to himself, Richard reached for it and set about warming the beans through. All in all, it was hardly the perfect English breakfast, but to a man with a hangover it looked like paradise.

He was just about to start his final sausage when the telephone rang. Hastily he snatched at the instrument, just trying to silence it before the noise scrambled his brain again, but ended up knocking it halfway across the kitchen floor. By the time he'd retrieved it, the voice on the other end was wondering where he was.

'Hello?' he said, trying to sound in a better state than he felt.

'Ah, there you are!' It was Andy, sounding far too cheerful for someone who had shared the fate of last night. 'How are you feeling?'

'Terrible, thanks.'

'Just checking everything's okay with you?'

'About as well as could be expected. How exactly is it you're alive at this time in the morning?'

'Dick, it's nearly half one. This isn't morning any more . . .'

Richard groaned quietly. 'Yeah, well . . . oh, shut up.'

'I take it that girl saw you home all right?' Andy continued. 'Or did you go back to her place?'

'What girl?' Richard asked, a wave of panic hitting him. 'I assumed you got me home.'

'I didn't realise you were that hammered. Don't you remember?'

'Not much. Andy, what girl?'

'The weird looking one from the club. You and she left together just before I did, and you were pretty far gone by that point.' He must mean the fourth girl. So he hadn't imagined her.

'The one who bought me a drink?'

'Yeah, that one. She get you home all right?'

'I assume so.' Richard briefly wondered why anyone would ask that, since they were talking on the landline.

'All right, then. Just wanted to check,' he said. 'I know what you're like. I'll let you finish the post-alcohol fry-up.' And he hung up. Richard stared at the dead receiver with a resigned expression. He was getting too old for this. Was he? That was a depressing thought. But the old sense of enjoyment just wasn't there. He felt empty. Thankful that Andy had called to check up on him but also bemused by his friend's enthusiasm. He couldn't see the point any more of an evening he couldn't remember. He didn't feel any better for it—if anything he felt worse. Hollow.

He wondered, without any particular interest, what had happened with this strange girl who supposedly saw him home. Even now that he knew she was real, he didn't remember a lot about her, just that she had seemed oddly familiar. She'd been wearing black, and had . . . dark hair? The memory of her seemed to be disappearing with the remains of his headache. Strange, he couldn't even picture her face now . . . Could she remember what happened either? It seemed such a waste.

Richard's musings were broken off by an unexpected thump on the window. He sat up suddenly but, looking about, couldn't see anything that could have caused it. He walked cautiously over to the glass and peered out. There was no one in view, no swaying tree-branch or recalcitrant ball, only a faint grey mark on the pane, with an edge like the shadow of a feather. He undid the catch and peered downwards into the rosebushes under the sill.

Sure enough, a small bundle of black fluff lay spread-eagled in the dirt of the flowerbed. It was a young jackdaw, stunned and lying very still. Richard hoped it wasn't dead. He leaned down amongst the thorns and gingerly picked up the bird. It was still warm, and he thought he felt, in his palm, the tiny flutter of a heartbeat. He wasn't sure what to do about comatose birds, but since it was his window that it had accidentally flown into, he felt somehow responsible for its welfare. He took it into the kitchen to see what he could do for it.

It was only a fledgling. Up close, Richard could still see the tufts of down sticking out at odd angles in between the adult feathers. It should never have tried flying so soon. With great care, he put it down on the table and waited for it to come around. He put the kettle on for a cup of hot, sweet tea, then realised that baby jackdaws probably didn't like tea. Nevertheless, he had the feeling that something warm might be a good idea. A quick search in the back of the wardrobe yielded a slightly decrepit hot water bottle and an old shoebox which he lined with a face flannel.

When he got back to the kitchen, the jackdaw had come around and was staggering drunkenly across the table. As Richard came in, it looked up at him and said, 'Aaark?'

'Hello to you, too,' said Richard. The small bird fell over. He tried to pick it up and got pecked for his trouble.

'Aaark!'

'Independent little sod, aren't you?' Richard frowned, shaking his wounded fingers.

'Aak.' As it got to its feet, Richard took the time to examine his new guest. Other than being a little dazed, there didn't appear to be much wrong with him. It hopped over to the cardboard box and began pecking it hopefully.

'I wouldn't eat that if I were you,' said Richard. 'I expect it tastes filthy. It's been in the bottom of my wardrobe for I don't know how long.' As if it understood, the jackdaw left off attempting to eat the box, wobbled over to Richard, and pecked his finger instead. It looked up at him and opened its beak.

'Well, don't look at me,' said Richard. 'I don't know what you eat.' The bird kept staring at him, beak open. Obediently Richard got up and retrieved a bit of leftover sausage from his hangover breakfast. He cut it up into slightly smaller pieces, which he then presented to the jackdaw. The bird looked at them quizzically, then sat back on its haunches with an expectant expression. Richard dropped a piece of sausage into its upturned beak. It disappeared in a fraction of a second. Richard offered a few more pieces, then eventually the whole sausage to the little bird, who wolfed it down in a matter of gulps and returned to staring expectantly up at Richard.

'You want more?' he asked. The jackdaw remained motionless. 'I don't have any more cooked, you know.'

'Aak?' It tilted its head to one side.

'That was the lot.'

'Aak?' It blinked and cocked its head the other way.

'So it's no good, you staring at me like that. I haven't got any more.'

'Aak?'

'I'll put some more on, shall I?'

Three sausages later, the bird seemed full. It hopped over to the shoebox and began to make itself comfortable by ripping up Richard's flannel to make a nest. Richard gave it a pained look but decided he was too tired to argue.

'I suppose we'll have to give you a name, then, if you're staying,' he said. The bird again cocked its head on one side. It seemed to be a favourite gesture and managed to convey an awful lot.

'Aark?'

'I suppose you are a boy, aren't you? I don't know how you tell with birds. Maybe we should stick with something that could work for either. Like Spot or Blackie.'

The jackdaw remained suitably unimpressed. As it returned to shredding the bits of cloth, Richard noticed a tuft of down sticking up on the top of its head, right in the middle of the darker black patch that jackdaws have. It was quite comical, in a way, and he was struck with how much this made it look as if the bird were wearing a bobble hat.

'I know,' he said, 'I'll call you Bobble.' There was a short pause while the newly christened Bobble stared up at Richard as if he had gone stark staring mad, then he fluffed up his feathers, gave the bird equivalent of a shrug, and buried his head under one wing.

CHAPTER 3

THE RING AND THE RIVER

Deep in the nothing space of Elsewhere, something pricked its ears. A scent was rising on the wind, a singing scent, golden as sunlight, tangy as copper. The scent of blood. The creature reared its massive head. Somewhere on the other side new prey had emerged, and it was calling. Across the void, across that soap-sheen light-flicker barrier, thin as breath and shadows, it was calling. Irresistible, inexorable, un-ignorable, pulling the creature like a wire. And there were places where the walls of the world were growing fragile as fallen leaves. If there were enough need, perhaps something might just be able to slip across. And the creature needed this prey very badly.

After Bobble's appearance on Sunday, very little of interest occurred for Richard. He hadn't felt up to doing much, so he watched a made-for-telly movie in the afternoon, then ran a long, relaxing bath. It hadn't lasted. Bobble had joined him, fallen in the tub, and Richard had spent the next half an hour with an old hairdryer attempting to get him dry again. He was beginning to think that the young bird had a screw loose somewhere.

As the day drew to a close, Richard found enough in the kitchen to cobble together some pasta and tomato sauce. His new companion watched semi-peaceably from the top of the fridge, occasionally swooping down onto the floor to chase a dropped teaspoon, jangling and clattering around the kitchen. Richard found he was warming to the little bird and his antics, occasionally shuffling the spoon out of awkward corners or giving it a kick himself, just to watch Bobble react.

The food didn't take long, and once it was cooked, Richard took a plate outside into the garden. He was in two minds about taking Bobble with him but needn't have worried. The jackdaw made no attempt to run off, and this way he wasn't shedding down all over the lino. Richard sat back on the grass and began to eat.

There was something overwhelmingly peaceful about the evening, just as Sundays ought to be. It was warm and still light. The half-circle of a waxing moon glowed pale and orange in half-hearted competition to the sun, low on the western horizon. A slow breeze tousled the grass. No sound of cars or people interrupted the quiet of the world turning. Done, Richard picked up his plate to take it back inside, and as he straightened up, he thought he caught a glimpse of something—a black smudge against the setting sun. A figure that was there one minute and gone the next. He blinked away the vision, clearing the shadow that had momentarily fallen across his mind.

To his surprise, Bobble responded to his whistle and obediently flew inside with him when he opened the back door. Expecting a fight, or for the bird to merely fly off, Richard felt rather gratified. Inside, he moved Bobble's shoebox to his bedroom windowsill and hoped that he'd have a good night.

Richard felt less enamoured of his new houseguest when the next morning he was woken at six by a sharp pain in his ear. Somehow Bobble had got hold of a peanut still in the shell and was attempting to ram it into the first available orifice.

'Get off, you daft bird!' yelled Richard, making the transition from asleep to firing on all cylinders in approximately ten seconds.

'Aark?' Bobble fluttered up to the top of the wardrobe, where he peered down on him with a hurt and bemused expression. Richard sighed, rolled out of bed, and staggered into the kitchen.

'All right, what do you want for breakfast?' asked Richard, pouring himself a bowl of cereal.

'Aak.' Bobble glided over to land on the fridge and pecked at it.

'You can't keep having sausages, you know,' said Richard. 'We'll have to find something else to feed you on.' But he obediently opened the fridge and got out the sausage packet. Bobble hopped onto the table in a very self-satisfied way and settled himself down to eat.

'Aak.'

Having accidentally stolen a march on the day, Richard left a plate of sausages out for Bobble and headed off for work. He worked the front desk at a small IT firm whose offices were located just outside of town, a short drive away along various green-fringed country roads. It usually took half an hour when it was quiet; there was never any traffic to speak of.

About halfway there, as if for the first time, Richard's eyes wandered out of the window and noticed the way the sun hit the hillside. He pulled over on the side of the road, got out of the car, and just stopped, looking out over the fields, the small copses of pines, watching the way the early morning sunlight gave everything a corona of white gold. He felt good about life, full of a white-hot energy and a stirring feeling deep in his chest as if something wonderful was just starting.

An odd urge to start singing came over him, but the tune he wanted remained just out of reach. The world around him was quivering with a song, just beyond hearing, and he ached to join in. For a full twenty minutes he just stood staring at the view, then he got back in his car and drove the rest of the way to work.

'Everything all right?' It was Maddy, one of the partners, sitting on the edge of his desk with a stack of files, a coffee mug, and a concerned expression.

'What?' Richard looked up.

'You look half asleep. Did you not sleep well last night or something?'

'I'm fine,' he stretched and rubbed his temples. 'Sorry, was I drifting off there?'

'Just a bit.'

'I'm sorry,' Richard sighed. He'd been finding it hard to concentrate all morning. Little things, like the sunlight on his computer screen, the sound of birds outside—two magpies fighting over a scrap of something in the bushes—everything seemed far more interesting than the piles of filing still to do or the list of clients to ring. He kept losing his train of thought and coming to, certain there was something he ought to be doing somewhere else but unable to remember what.

'Come on, buck up,' Maddy said, squeezing his shoulder. 'It's only five more days 'til the weekend.'

'Thanks. Sorry, I've just not been feeling with it this morning.'

'Coffee?'

'Would be fantastic.'

'Get me one while you're at it?' Maddy smiled cheekily. 'Then there's all the ad space on the Bryant website to get sold if you can manage it?'

'I'll see what I can do,' replied Richard, accepting the stack of files and proffered coffee mug.

'Atta boy,' said Maddy, hopping down off the desk and back into the office.

The river wound through the city like a vast garden hose snaking through grass, deep and dark as a crack in the world. Seagulls screeched and wheeled above the water, snapping and fighting over pavement scraps. In overlooking offices, bored desk-jockeys would occasionally glance out over its grey expanse for a moment before returning to their computer screens. It was a dull day, so perhaps some of them let their gaze linger a little longer whilst hanging around the office photocopier or coffee machine. Perhaps they even noticed the way that the gulls' shrieking was just slightly more harried today, or the way shadows passed over the water with nothing to cause them.

Perhaps, for just a moment, one or two of them thought they saw something stir beneath the surface. They would take it for a trick of the light at first, or something quite small. Then it would move and they could suddenly get a sense of its scale, far bigger than first thought. Something vast and dark that twisted and contorted but never broke the surface. The kind of thing they would forget, or try to. And if any of them did see something, or thought they did, they put it out of their minds quickly.

But the seagulls saw, and they noted, and they didn't forget.

'Good afternoon, E-Tempe Systems, how can I help?'

'I need to speak to Mr. Lampton please,' asked a thin, fluty kind of voice. Richard wasn't sure if it was male or female.

'This is Richard Lampton. Can I help you?'

'It's coming.'

'Excuse me?'

'The rumours are true. It's coming already.'

'I'm sorry?' There was a pause and a crackle on the line, so that for a moment Richard thought he'd been disconnected. Then the voice continued.

'Where am I calling exactly?'

'E-Tempe Systems? We're an IT security consultancy?'

'Never mind. I must have the wrong number.' The phone clicked as the caller hung up. Richard removed the receiver from his ear and looked at it with confusion.

'Everything all right?' asked Maddy, popping her head out of the back room.

'I think so,' said Richard. 'Just some wrong number. 'Scuse me.' He picked up the phone, which had begun to ring again. 'Good afternoon, E-Tempe Systems, how can I help?'

'I need to speak to Mr. Lampton, please.' It was the same fluty voice.

'This is Richard Lampton—I think I was just speaking to you a moment ago.'

'Oh.'

'Yes.'

'You're the computer firm?'

Richard rolled his eyes. 'Computer consultancy firm . . .'

'But you're Dick Lampton?'

'Yes, but I don't see . . .'

'Odd. Very odd. My sources must be mistaken somewhere.' Another click as the caller rang off. Almost immediately as Richard replaced the receiver, it began to ring again.

'Good Afternoon, E-Tempe Systems, how can I help?'

'It is coming. If you're the wrong Lampton, this won't mean anything to you, but if you're the right one, then it could save your life. You have about a week. Goodbye.'

The phone went dead in his hand.

In a little jeweller's shop just off the Green Market, Dawlish was mooching around the shelves, making no attempt to be useful. Most of the things this shop sold were second hand, and though she'd never admit it, Dawlish liked going through the stock and inventing stories about where the pieces came from and who had once owned them. The thin sapphire ring, its main stone bracketed by two diamonds, for example, was obviously someone's engagement ring from back in the eighties when there was a vogue for that kind of thing. She had turned him down, Dawlish had decided with her usual pessimism, else why would the ring be back in the jeweller's? Unless she had died soon after the wedding in a tragic accident, and he couldn't bear to have such a poignant reminder of her in the house. The moonstone broach with E.H. on the back she knew used to belong to an old lady, now sadly deceased, named Mrs. Harrison. Her son had sold it to them in a job-lot with a box of costume jewellery, three strings of seed pearls, and five huge pairs of earrings set with semi-precious stones. The other pieces had been sold, snapped up by vintage-hungry browsers, and the moonstone broach was all that was left.

Some of Dawlish's favourite pieces were kept in a large, velvet lined cabinet at the back of the shop. No one seemed to buy anything from there. Pieces occasionally disappeared or moved, but for some reason no one ever requested even to look at the contents more closely while she was there. The prices weren't even marked. Sometimes she wondered if customers even saw the cabinet when they came in and why the owner seemed perfectly happy about that.

At the moment there was a large, rather gaudy, diamond choker in pride of place, but it was the smaller pieces which interested Dawlish. A long rope of black pearls that she was sure must have been some pirate queen's, a ring set with three yellow diamonds, a broach in the shape of a golden bird with a fine filigree tail, a locket whose mystery only increased when it rattled but wouldn't open, a silver charm bracelet with three of the charms missing, five signet rings of different shapes and sizes, all bearing the same crest, and many more. Dawlish had not been let in on the secret of where they were from or who they had once belonged to, but she was certain that there were secrets to find out.

The shop door rang expensively, and Dawlish looked up from the ledger she had been idly flipping through. A tall, elegant woman with dark eyes and a long black cigarette holder stepped into the shop. Dawlish quickly straightened.

'Seen anything interesting?' Kate asked, skipping the 'good morning.'

'Not much,' shrugged Dawlish.

'Just lurking for no reason?'

'Nowhere else to go.'

Kate deposited a chic leather handbag on the front counter.

'And here I thought you were actually taking an interest in something for a change.' Dawlish didn't reply. Unusually for Kate, she seemed to soften. 'I know this life isn't easy for you, but there's nothing wrong with enjoying the things you still can.'

Dawlish sniffed petulantly.

'Gold isn't my thing. It's yours.'

'No, and as I recall, deals were never your strong suit either.' Dawlish coloured at that and seemed to develop a sudden interest in her shoes. Kate glanced at her. 'No use in pretending. But there's a lot more to this business that I do think you like.'

'Like what?'

'Stories?' Dawlish's head came up again. 'Finding lost things? I imagine that would be right up your street.' The girl gave a noncommittal shrug. Kate leaned over the counter and took her chin in one hand, pushing it up so their eyes met. 'Listen to me,' she said. 'In this world, like any, things happen because someone makes them happen. You can sit around and wait for your opportunity, which may never come, or you can go and look for it, and if there isn't one, you make one. It's your choice.' She dropped her hand and turned away, leaving Dawlish to replace her usual sulky expression.

'Now, I'm opening up in a few minutes, and I have to get some things put away. So are you in or out?' Kate continued. Dawlish realised a shrug would not be an acceptable response this time.

'I'm in,' she said, after a moment's consideration. 'I suppose.'

'Good.' Kate reached for her handbag and brought out a small black box.

'What's that?' asked Dawlish.

'A few more things for the back cabinet.'

'Anything exciting?' Kate merely raised her eyebrows and produced a small golden key from a chain around her neck. 'What? You want me to take an interest.'

The black box made no noise as it opened. It, too, was lined with velvet. Inside was a small paper packet that Dawlish assumed would contain an uncut stone, but lying next to it were four rings and a bracelet. Three of the rings looked as if they were part of a set, for they were all made in the same style—basic gold blanks, like signet rings without signets. They looked inert, slightly dulled, waiting. The bracelet was different again. It was silver, too, and shaped like a snake biting its own tail. The eyes were made of chips of jade, and every scale was picked out individually. It twisted and looped back on itself quite alarmingly and almost looked as if it were moving. The last ring, tucked in one corner of the velvet, looked different. It was made of silver, unlike the others, and the stone caged within the thin metal strands glowed with an inner fire that didn't quite seem to follow the usual pattern of light and shade. Something about it felt strangely familiar and somehow compelling. Without really thinking, Dawlish reached out to examine it further.

'Don't touch that!' Kate snapped.

'What?'

Kate regained her composure swiftly.

'No, not that. I'm sorry. You mustn't.'

Dawlish knew better than to ask why. Too many of the things Kate bought and sold were dangerous or forbidden. There was rarely sense in messing with things she didn't understand. Instead, her attention turned to the snake bracelet lying on top.

'How about that, then?'

Kate lifted the bracelet gently out of the box.

'Commission piece,' she replied smoothly, 'for an old family friend.'

'You have family friends now?'

Kate ignored the jibe and pocketed the trinket.

'At any rate, I still need to take it, and all of these pieces, to be valued, so there's no good asking me about them.'

'Valued?'

'I have a contact,' Kate said, holding one of the blank rings up to the light. 'If she can't tell me what something is, no one can.'

'Hard to believe there's someone who knows more about gold than you, isn't it?' asked Dawlish with a hint of sarcasm.

'Indeed,' replied Kate, archly. 'Still, it does happen.' She returned the pieces to the box. 'There are, however, plenty more things in this shop I can tell you about, should you wish.' She picked up the box and, unlocking the cabinet, left it on the empty bottom shelf. She quickly turned the key in the lock and straightened. 'But first things first,' she said brightly. 'Coffee.'

CHAPTER 4

A MOTHER AND A MESSAGE

The house backed onto the river. Richard's mother was wont to complain that it made the place cold, and she had to spend far too much on heating, but she wouldn't move to somewhere a bit smaller or a bit less remote. It also didn't stop her enjoying the little garden which sloped towards the water's edge nor from throwing stale bread to the ducks which occasionally bobbed downstream. Since her stroke two years prior, the wheelchair she was forced to use, and which she bitterly resented, prevented her from doing much by way of gardening herself, but it certainly didn't prevent her from barking imperious orders to the gardener twice a week about exactly how she wanted the bedding plants laid out or complaining about the state of the rose bushes or the hedge.

When Richard arrived, after a quiet afternoon and an early finish, she was sitting out in the garden, wrapped in a scratchy woollen blanket in a vile shade of mustard yellow tartan. The burnt umber September sun was warming the garden enough to make such a precaution unnecessary, but perhaps she was planning on seeing out the evening outdoors.

'Just come from work?' she asked, peering over her glasses at him, her speech even now slightly slurred.

'Yes, Mum, nice to see you, too.' Richard bent down to kiss her forehead.

'You're wasted there, you know,' she continued, accepting his brief token of filial devotion.

'Please, Mum, don't start.'

'You're going to have to make your mind up at some point what you're going to do with your life.'

'I know, and I will, I just . . .' He sighed and ran a hand through his hair. The old argument had been done to death, and he was tired of it. 'I'll get it sorted. Can we not talk about this now?'

'All right!' His mother held her hands up in mock surrender. 'But you can't blame an old woman for worrying.' She waved a hand at the wooden garden chairs. 'Now sit down. You're making the place untidy.'

Richard did as he was told, and an uneasy silence fell over the garden.

'I went to Uncle Tom's funeral,' he said. It was like he'd dropped a lead weight in an empty church. His mother examined the back of her hand with studied nonchalance.

'Did you?' she asked.

'Yes. It was a good send-off, I suppose. There were a lot of people there.'

'I sent Ellie some flowers. Lilies. Expensive, but then he was family, I suppose.'

'I barely knew who was family and who wasn't.'

Richard glanced sidelong at his mother. 'It's a shame—there were a few people there I'd have liked to have known better.' His mother's retort was unexpectedly sharp.

'No, you wouldn't.'

'Why not?' Richard challenged, as a sudden image of Kate's dark eyes flashed into his head. He certainly wouldn't have minded knowing her better. His mother developed an equally sudden interest in making sure that her blanket was tucked in properly all around.

'You just wouldn't,' she said, when it became clear Richard was not going to carry on the conversation without her. 'Take my word for it.'

'Is this for the same reason you and Uncle Tom fell out in the first place? You never told me what happened between you two.'

'That hedge needs another trim. I shall have to tell George when he comes around on Thursday . . .'

'Mum . . .'

'Don't you "Mum" me. It's personal.'

'Then why should I have to live with it?' Richard knew he was sounding childish, but he felt himself bristling at her stubbornness. It was the hot, heavy feeling that precedes a thunderstorm. 'It's the only reason I don't know all those family and friends—some of whom I might have liked to know. What can it matter now anyway? He's dead! What was so important that you couldn't bury the hatchet?'

She turned her face away from the outburst. He couldn't tell if she was more angry or upset. She seemed to be studying the waterline, where the reeds had started bowing to a chill wind. The water was covered with ripples, waves like the creases of a worried frown. He softened a little.

'I'm sorry, Mum, I just . . .' he reached over and took her hand. 'It's just hard feeling I'm missing out, and I don't even know why.' Her fingers, slightly puffed and arthritic, turned to squeeze his, and she seemed about to smile. Then her head suddenly whipped down, and she stared in horror at his hand.

'Where did you get that?' she demanded. 'Where?'

'Get—?'

'The ring! Your father's ring!'

'That? It was Uncle Tom's. He left it to me.' Richard stood up, brow furrowing. His mother didn't get scared. Angry, but not scared. Only now she was as pale as a ghost and seemed to be filled with a twitchy, panicked energy, as if she were desperate to leap from her chair, cross the lawn, and hold her son 'til danger had passed. It frightened him. A creeping cold clambered up the back of his neck, and the garden suddenly felt like an unfamiliar place.

'Take it off,' she said. 'Now. Richard, please, take it off.'

'What? Why?'

'Just do as I say. Please, take it off.'

'No.' Richard scowled. He'd had enough of being bullied that afternoon. 'If you won't tell me what your little feud was all about, I don't see why I should be part of it.'

'But—'

'Mum, stop it, please. This isn't up to you. Let it go.'

She sighed and somehow deflated. She looked smaller, older, sadder. She put her face in her hands.

'My God . . .' she breathed. 'You looked so much like your father just then . . . There was no changing his mind either.' She looked so very crestfallen that Richard almost relented.

'Mum . . .'

'I think I'd like to go back inside now,' she said. 'I have to make a phone call.' She turned away and began to drive the electric wheelchair back up the path towards the house, leaving Richard standing in the cold.

The sun had gone in. Richard stood, fingering the gold band. He wasn't sure what had made him fight for it the way he had. He was tired and overcome with an inexorable sense of something missing—not lost, but forgotten. The water by his feet was growing dark. Inky, with an oily sheen like spilled petrol. Something splashed a little way upstream—a duck? But all the ducks had gone, along with the rest of the birds from the trees along the waterline, leaving an eerie silence, filled with nothing but the whistle of the wind. Richard thought for half a second that he could see something moving, some here-and-gone flicker as if something were passing underwater or as if the riverbank itself had shifted slightly with the current. He was aware of a strange, acrid smell, just on the edge of perception, bitter and sweet at the same time, like rotting fish. It must be the drains, he thought to himself. He should remind his mother to get them seen to. And he turned away and headed back into the house to see if his mother was ready to make peace.

Even after he left, Richard found it hard to shake a

nagging sense of frustration. He drove back to his own place with the windows rolled all the way down, and an old Dire Straits CD playing on repeat. The fresh air helped to clear his head. He felt like a weight was lifting. Not entirely, but enough so that he could breathe. He flipped down the sun-visor and leaned back on the gas.

Remembering the barren state of his kitchen, he made a few stops on his way back to replenish the fridge and to try to find something more suitable for Bobble.

'Good evening!' he remarked, sounding cheerful as he walked through the front door, scanning the room for the bird.

'Aark,' replied Bobble genially, gliding through from the sitting room to land on the back of a kitchen chair.

'Guess what I got.' Richard dumped his briefcase and a small tub on the table. 'I had a look online while I was at work, tried to find out what you actually eat.'

'Aak?' Bobble toddled over to the tub and began pecking at the lid. Richard removed it for him, then stood back to let him get at the contents.

'They're mealworms. Apparently you should like them. Good source of protein.' Bobble peered into the tub at his still squirming dinner, then slowly looked back up at Richard. He looked unimpressed.

'Aark?' he asked, which Richard interpreted as meaning 'you expect me to eat that?'

'It's what the internet said you would like . . .' he tried, a little disappointed with the bird. Bobble shrugged. 'Would you at least try them?' Bobble firmly turned his back on the mealworms and started investigating Richard's briefcase. 'There's nothing interesting in there, and you don't know the combination to get in anyway.' Bobble had begun to inspect the lock. Richard sighed and continued to unpack the rest of the shopping into the fridge. He left the mealworms open, just in case Bobble could be persuaded. A click came from behind him. Richard turned round. Bobble was standing in front of Richard's briefcase, one lock of which had just flicked open.

'How . . . what . . . did you do that?' He pointed an accusing finger at the bird.

'Aark!' Bobble jumped up and down, flapping excitedly.

'It must have been set to the right combination anyway,' Richard thought aloud. 'You just pushed the catch. Anyway, clever-clogs, there's two locks on that thing.' He glanced over at the other side of the case to note that the combination was definitely not set. He turned back to the fridge. He heard another click. Bobble was sitting proudly on top of Richard's briefcase, which was, against all probability, unlocked. Richard was rendered temporarily speechless, but before he had a chance to react, the telephone rang.

The sun had just dipped below the horizon, and the River Wear was dancing with the fading light as it wound its way through Durham. It looped lazily around the twin beacons of the castle and cathedral, their imposing stone solid, the work of past centuries standing like grizzled Norman knights or chess-board rooks, a bastion against the darkness of the world. But down by the waterline, the mists were rising, and the grey-green waters of the Wear lapped at the roots of twisted trees. Water, ever-changeable, running like thought, dancing in the dappled light like dreams, flowing and rippling like the edge of reality. Water has ever been a conduit. And just here, in the shadow of a bridge, where the smell of wet grass and forming dew was slick in the wind, the water became a long, dark hole in the night.

The creature was very close to this world now, frustrated and fierce. It had been so close before, it could have reached out and snapped it, but the prey had moved on, and it was no closer. It lurked still, prowling the edges, mad with that scent, that golden prickle itching at its mind. It leant its vast bulk against the barrier. It needed. It needed so badly. It pushed.

The blackness beneath the bridge deepened to the matte richness of brushed velvet, then buffed to an oily sheen. A greasy scum began to coalesce and ride on the surface of the blackness, and slow, thick black bubbles began to rise and burst around it. There was a sense of heaviness, of the pressure that comes before thunder, and a dry crackling in the air. Then a spark.

The creature thrashed in the watery green light. Something was standing in its way, something sharp and bright and stinging. It bared stiletto point teeth and screamed.

'Hello? Be that Dick Lampton?' a rough, growly voice confronted Richard on the phone. The thick burr of the accent wasn't one he recognised.

'It's Richard, yes. Can I help you?'

'I needs to leave a message for Dick Lampton.' Rich-

ard glanced briefly over at Bobble, who was having diffi-
culties prizing the briefcase open. The lid half was just too
heavy for him to lever off, but nevertheless, he was having
a damn good try.

'Yes? I'm listening.'

'Confirmed sighting,' growled the voice. 'In the Wear.
Durham area. It's back, and it looked like trouble. That be
all.'

'All?'

'Yes.' And the phone-line went dead. Richard replaced
the receiver. He was completely at sea as to what the message meant. What had been seen? And why was it any of
his concern?

'Another total loony,' he muttered to Bobble, who was
now jumping up and down on the briefcase, flapping his
wings, and digging his claws into the leather in an attempt
to lift it. 'Will you stop that!' he snapped.

'Aak?' Bobble looked up at him with a hurt expression. Richard tapped him gently on the beak.

'I'm not mad, just don't mess up my stuff, understood?'

'Aak.' Bobble bobbed his head. It looked to Richard
like he was nodding.

'Right. Well, as long as that's settled. Are you sure
you don't want these?' he asked, picking up the mealworms again. Bobble paid him no interest, so Richard put
the lid back on the tub and heaved it into the bin. Instead,
he turned back to the fridge and began hunting for something that would placate a hungry jackdaw. There was a
thunk behind him. He whipped round, a pack of sausages in
one hand. The briefcase was open, and Bobble was sitting
in the middle of Richard's papers looking sheepish. He

cocked his head to one side and looked up imploringly.

'Aak?'

No more odd phone calls came for him that night, and Bobble, having been caught out the once, behaved well for the rest of the evening. He managed to wolf down another half-pack of sausages, but thankfully, he showed no more inclination to become a master criminal. Instead, as night began to fall, he settled down in his box on Richard's windowsill, tucked his head under one wing, and dozed off. Richard also headed for bed and, for a few minutes, lay there watching the ceiling. He was getting a little concerned that Bobble wasn't showing any inclination to leave. On the contrary, he seemed rather to be making himself at home. Richard wasn't sure this was good for him. He had vague feelings that animals should be in the wild, in their natural habitat, living in trees and eating . . . natural things, not sitting in someone's kitchen eating sausages and sleeping in a shoebox.

On the other hand, he had heard about people keeping jackdaws as pets, so perhaps he wasn't doing Bobble any long-term harm. He decided not to worry about it until either Bobble started to become a nuisance—he mentally corrected that to 'more of a nuisance than he already was'—or decided for himself that he wanted to leave. He set the alarm, rolled over, and went to sleep.

It was half past eleven, and the white house was quiet. Outside in the gardens, accessible only by a long flight of stone steps from the terrace, huge ghost koi circled slowly in marble fountains. Occasionally one would give a wriggle and flip itself out of the water, flashing and scattering diamonds of water in the moonlight. The peacocks had finished strutting about the lawn and were roosting on the terrace railings, trailing their long tails like curtains over the side. In the conservatory, the white chrysanthemums, picked the day before, slowly dropped their first petals onto the tiled floor beneath. In the long gallery, strange night-breezes chased each other around and about the china figures and marble statues and in and out of rare porcelain vases, pausing only to giggle to each other at the stern expressions on the faces of the portraits. In the attic, a moth battered itself against a skylight, trying to get to the moon.

And in one of the upper bedrooms Helen Ng did not sleep. Not because she couldn't sleep, but because she didn't want to. She was sitting at a large mahogany desk by the window, the night air gently flapping at the lilac curtains. She could hear the soft sound of falling water from the fountains outside. It was peaceful. She was reading a slim volume, a much loved and much read copy of Tennyson's *The Princess*, still pristine despite much handling, and a Debussy record played on the old gramophone in the next room.

Everything was absolutely, precisely, and exactly the way she wanted it. So why did she feel uneasy? Helen was a creature of habit, of order, and somewhere in the back of her mind something had come out of place, and she didn't like it. She laid the book aside, tugged her white satin kimono round her a bit more comfortably, then got up and looked out the window. She could see the expanse of her estate, and all was as it should be, except . . . It was hard to see in the moonlight, but there was definitely a small, black shape in the sky flying straight towards her.

The magpie hopped sideways along the branch. The white of its feathers glared, stark in the moonlight.

'Here I thought you was daytime birds,' grumbled the old man, wandering along the path by the river. The magpie trilled shrilly and flashed its wings.

'It be no good you getting feisty with me,' muttered the man, staring out across the brackish water. 'I'm not one as understands you. I'm just out for a walk. I does my best thinking in the dark, like this.' As if to underline this statement, he took out a pipe and a pouch of tobacco from his battered jacket pocket and proceeded to stuff the sticky brown leaves into the bowl. Undeterred, the magpie waited in the starlight, fluffing its feathers. It watched, head on one side, as the man struck a match and carefully sucked on the pipe stem until the glowing embers caught.

'You can tell that Baron of yourn one thing,' he said, this ritual completed. 'I called the Lampton boy already on the telephone. Got the same result as Effie. He ain't listening to we Watchers, an' I don't think he understands who we be neither.'

The magpie ducked its head in acknowledgement, then took off rapidly into the night.

'Be seeing you . . .' muttered the old man.

The black shape was wheeling closer and closer. Helen opened the window and leaned out. It was a bird, a jack-daw, and once it saw the open window, it made a beeline for her. She held out a hand, and the bird gently settled on her wrist.

'Angel,' muttered Helen, bringing it inside, 'I thought it was you.' The bird shifted a little on her wrist, and Helen gently unclipped the capsule tied to her leg. She reached into a drawer of the desk and drew out a small wooden perch and a bag of sunflower seeds. She lowered her wrist, and delicately, Angel stepped onto the perch and began to eat.

'Long journey?' asked Helen. Angel shrugged. 'You're one of that strange girl's birds, aren't you? Very well. Let's see what she has to say.' Helen broke open the message capsule and pulled out the folded sheet of paper. 'It's from Kate,' she said after scanning the contents. 'She wants another valuation, as if I haven't got anything better to do with my time.' Helen sighed. She knew that when it came to identifying and valuing artefacts of a certain bent she was among the best in the country, and her word of honour was held in high enough regard that even an un-trustworthy pirate like Kate trusted her. But she resented being disturbed at all hours. Genius should not have to suf-fer such intrusions. Even from Kate, who was her oldest friend. Because she never did anything by halves, she sat down at the desk, pulled out a thin slip of paper and a smart fountain pen, and wrote her reply in a smooth, fluent hand. She folded the paper, slid it into the message capsule, and reattached it to the jackdaw's leg.

'I can't see her 'til later in the week,' she told her. Angel nodded, fluffed up her feathers, and began limbering up. Helen offered the bird her wrist. 'Thank you for the message,' she said and walked over to the window. Angel took off into the night sky, and Helen watched as she dwindled to a speck in the distance.

Well, the first shoe had dropped.

In bed, Richard rolled over, tying himself up in the duvet. He was too hot and just drifting in that state between awake and asleep. He couldn't quite tell which he was. His mind seemed to be awake, but his body wasn't responding; he felt detached from it and smothered. Odd things were flashing through his mind, things that he knew were dreams, knew were just pictures that he was watching. He didn't feel immersed in them the way one does when dreaming. He saw a flock of jackdaws, and for a minute, he thought they were there to take Bobble back, but they were all paying close attention to something else, someone else that he couldn't see. A forest clearing opened up, and he caught sight of a green clad figure disappearing behind a tree. He was running, and a dog was barking in the distance behind him. A petite Asian lady with a black elfin bob sat in a large house writing a letter. Kate Avery beckoned to him from the stern of a ship as it sailed away from him. A woman dressed in white robes stood by a tall stone pillar. Then a riverbank, and then darkness.

Richard tried to open his eyes, but in that horrible way

that dreams sometimes have, he found he couldn't. He knew he was still dreaming, and because he was only half asleep and he couldn't open his eyes in real life, he couldn't open them in the dream either. Still, he desperately tried because he knew there was something behind him that he had to turn around and face. He needed to know what it was, and he needed to know now, because the next time he faced it, it would be for real and he would be scared witless.

It was looking for him. Searching and gathering strength. There was no time. Once it had him in its sights there was no hiding, no running. He had to face it before he felt its eyes upon him and it was too late. It's just a dream, he told himself, just turn around and look at it. Look at it. Look at it. So he turned around . . . In his sleep, Richard rolled over, out of the bed, and hit the floor with a thump.

CHAPTER 5

FISH AND CHIPS

Dawlish woke when the bells in the church steeple above her head began to chime the hour. She sat up. The room around her was more like a nest than a bed. A double mattress, sagging in the middle and with at least one of the springs sharply poking through, had been thrown on the floor in the rough centre of the room. It was covered in heaped blankets, old clothes, and the occasional piece of newspaper, while all around it were piles of wooden pallets, stacked in such a way that they almost resembled furniture. Dawlish stretched and dislodged a flurry of feathers. The jackdaws roosting above her must have dropped them in the night. She let them lie where they landed, adding to the general debris. The pale light was slanting in through the cracks in the leads above her head. She felt its warmth on her skin without enthusiasm. It was another day.

Jenny woke at half past seven exactly as she always did, opened her eyes, and spent five whole minutes just staring at the ceiling. She had moved out of Ellie's spare room the day before and was now back in her own comparatively bare flat. She felt a little guilty about reneging on a friend, but once the funeral was over, various relatives had begun swarming in on all sides, and Jenny had felt uncomfortable. She really didn't like crowds. Ellie, distraught as she was, obviously didn't need her when the likes of Margot and the others were around, so Jenny made her excuses and left.

And now she was back home. And she was remembering why she had volunteered to stay over with Ellie in the first place. The flat was so empty. She hadn't re-decorated since she had moved in. Tacky posters of bands she had liked back in the eighties '90s were still stuck up on the on the walls. She had tried to diversify, but somehow she got as far as the art shop and couldn't find anything that she liked.

Jenny could never find new things that she liked. It was a problem she had, not being able to stray beyond her established tastes. She wished she could re-invent herself someday, but she knew it would be completely impossible. She had tried, but the little things that she picked up never stuck. If she bought a new vase, the next day she would knock it over, and it would smash. Her wardrobe was full of clothes that didn't fit or that she bought and found she hated the next day.

She wore grey all the time. The only colours she found

she could wear were faded blue jeans and a dark red T-shirt that she'd had since she was a teenager. They made her look like a kid, but she felt oddly comfortable in them. She could never get the hang of new hobbies. She played the violin, and had done so ever since she had been forced to at school, but she hated it. She never knew what to do with her time. She worried that perhaps she was a boring person.

She wanted to ring Richard. No. She couldn't. But she wanted to. It was more than a decade since she had last seen him, and she wasn't sure he remembered her. That was the worst thing. He hadn't even remembered her. But he'd said he hoped he'd see her around. She should ring him. No. She had to wait for him to ring her. She didn't want to seem totally pathetic.

But she had to see him. What if he went away, forgot all about her, and she didn't see him again for another ten years? Perhaps more? No, that was ridiculous. He had said he hoped he'd see her around sometime. But he could have just been saying that. They both lived in the same town anyway, so it wasn't like the situation was that desperate. This train of thought was making her sound desperate, though. She didn't want to sound desperate. It would be madness to ring him. But he had to remember her. She couldn't go on like this. Without him, nothing would change; nothing could. She was stuck. She should ring him; she had to ring him. No. She couldn't. She got up and flicked on the TV, but there was nothing on that she wanted to watch.

In the small white house on the cliff, Kate woke to the sound of the sea outside her window. A watery sun peered through the skylight of her crow's nest attic bedroom and slanted around the white room, lifting the colour like clouds on a breeze 'til the paint shone. She couldn't sleep with that kind of light on her face. Kate rolled out of bed and grabbed clumsily for her dressing gown. Dragging it on, she padded downstairs, over the sandy wood floors that creaked like a ship's timbers, to the kitchen where she set the kettle on the old black range to boil.

From the smell of the wind drifting through the open window, she could tell there had been a gale offshore in the night, and the coast was now being quietly washed by the storm's sheepish remnants—waves bearing their gifts of driftwood and bladder wrack as if seeking forgiveness.

Something was wrong. Something in the air that she could feel as instinctively as a gull feels the currents of the wind, or a sailor senses the barometer's rise and fall without needing to check the glass. She was ruffled and prickly; some intangible feeling was chaffing at her, like sand in her clothes or a stone in her shoe. It was a feeling born of long experience. There was going to be trouble, she knew it.

Passing the kitchen window, she caught sight of a magpie strutting on the back lawn. As she stopped and reached for the latch, it realised it had been observed and took wing in a clatter of black and white. Kate sniffed and shut the window. The kettle began to whistle. She poured herself some tea in a chipped blue-and-white striped mug and took it onto the lawn. The grass was still damp, and she could feel the wetness of it between her toes. The wind was coming in off the sea, a good strong breeze, and as she walked up to the fence that separated her garden from the cliff-top beyond, she could see the sails of early morning boats and windsurfers already out in the bay.

She stretched out her arms and felt the wind catch her full in the face.

'Good morning,' she whispered, as her dressing-gown fell open slightly at the front and fingertips of cold air slid over her shoulders and down her back. She tilted her head back and let the sea wind kiss her neck. On the edge of hearing, a voice like the rustle of sailcloth replied.

'You've been missed,' it said.

'It has been too long,' Kate agreed.

'You miss it too, don't you? Life with the winds and the waves. When will you come back to us?' asked the North Winds, tugging at her like a child.

Kate sighed and wrapped her dressing gown back around herself.

'When I can,' she replied, her voice tinged with regret. The wind replied with a sigh of its own. 'I have business to take care of. Lampton business.'

'Why do you get involved? Aren't you free? To come and go and choose as you please?'

'I am. And I choose to do this.'

'Then you don't love us any more.'

'No.' Kate smiled gently and took another sip of tea. 'I don't love you. I don't need to. You are part of me.'

The wind hummed and spun around her in a flurry, contented with her answer.

'I have this to take care of. Then, I promise I will be back.'

'Then you come now to ask our help? That we might speed you on your way and have you again all that sooner?'

'See? Part of me.'

'What do you need?'

Kate grinned wickedly.

'I need a . . . distraction. Not for myself, sadly. Robin—the Baron, I mean—he's sent his magpies out and about again, and I believe they're after something of mine.'

'Something of yours?'

'Well, something I currently have in my possession, shall we say? I don't want them finding it or finding out that I have it.'

'You want them led astray . . .' The wind trailed off into a laughing little gust by her ear.

'Exactly.'

'And your Baron . . .?'

Kate's expression froze.

'He's not mine,' she said firmly.

'Oh, but he is. We sense it. We know it.'

'I want nothing more to do with him.'

'You don't really mean that.'

'What would you know?' Kate brushed them aside irritably.

'Part of us, you said . . .'

'Did I say that?' She turned away.

'Going so soon?'

'Yes. Will you help me or not?'

'We will. Come back soon, Kate . . .'

'No promises.' Kate smiled and disappeared back into the house.

It didn't take long for Dawlish to dress, through the simple expedient of casting about in the piles on the floor 'til she found something still marginally clean. She ran a swift brush through her hair and reapplied the usual thick kohl around her eyes where the vestiges of yesterday's black smudges could still be seen. This done, she began hunting around in the piles again. A pair of jackdaws fluttered down onto one of the pallets. One of them cawed something that sounded like a question.

'Small bag,' Dawlish said. 'Black vinyl. Purse sized.'

The other jackdaw swooped to the opposite side of the room and landed on a bag very much like the one she had described.

'Thanks,' said Dawlish when she looked up. 'That's the one.' She opened the bag and pulled out a pink, sparkly lip gloss which she proceeded to apply. The first jackdaw made a sniggering sound.

'I'm going to see the Baron,' Dawlish explained. 'He got me this, so I might as well wear it. I'm hoping he'll get me an iPod. Doesn't hurt to show I'm the grateful sort.'

This toilette of a sorts complete, she grabbed her jacket and headed out, down the rickety ladder into the roof-space of Durham Cathedral.

f

Richard woke late. He hadn't slept well, and he missed the alarm. Not by much, because the alarm woke Bobble, and he seemed to see it as his duty to make sure that Richard wasn't late for work. His trick with the peanut hadn't gone down very well the day before, so this time Richard awoke to find Bobble tap-dancing on his face instead. His reaction, however, was predictably similar.

Breakfast was a fairly quiet affair. After his refusal of

the mealworms last night, Richard was anticipating Bobble would turn his beak up at anything but sausages, but nevertheless he offered the young bird a saucer of sunflower seeds and was gratified to watch him tuck in with gusto. He also deigned to eat a raw egg, which Richard felt a bit weird about at first, but then remembered that it wouldn't have been a fertilised egg, and therefore Bobble could be excused the accusation of cannibalism. And it was a hen's egg anyway, so that was probably all right.

He made sure that the little jackdaw seemed happy before he set out; he had found an old combination lock in the back of a kitchen drawer during his search for the tin opener on Sunday and, fascinated by Bobble's trick with his briefcase the night before, had given it to him to play with. It was just light enough that the bird could lift it, but not so light that he could fling it at something with enough force to cause any damage. Richard left him on the kitchen table, seeming delighted with this new toy.

As he was leaving the house, Richard caught sight of a magpie perched on the kitchen windowsill. He must have startled it with the sound of the door, because it flew off as he emerged.

'One for sorrow,' he muttered to himself, frowning, as the bird receded to a speck in the distance.

Richard forgot about the magpie on his way to work. He picked up a paper from the usual pile delivered to the front desk and read it with his morning coffee. The headline story was about some cabinet member being caught out in yet another affair, and there was an appeal on page two about a girl called Sarah Barnes who had gone missing over the weekend after a night out drinking. Mid-morning, Richard brought a coffee through to Maddy in the office, only to find her staring out the window.

'Dick? You want to come and see this?' she asked. Richard put the coffee down on the desk, then moved around to follow her gaze. Outside, a peculiar kind of confrontation was taking place. On the grass outside the window, a rough circle of birds had gathered. Jackdaws, at least ten of them. In the centre of the ring stood a magpie, facing down another jackdaw, this one slightly greyer than the others, with a ragged wing. For a minute, it almost looked as if they were having a conversation, snapping back and forth at each other like players in an argument, while the others looked on. Then the jackdaw lunged forwards, snapping at the magpie, which took off in a clatter of wings and storm of shrieking. The grey bird turned back to the rest of the assembled company, seeming to address them for a minute, before they, too, took to the skies, en masse, in the opposite direction.

'What was all that about?' Richard asked, half to Maddy, half to himself.

She shrugged and took a swig of coffee, then made a face. 'Did you put any sugar in this at all?' she asked.

'Damn, I forgot,' said Richard. 'You like three, don't you?'

'Normally, yes,' replied Maddy, getting up. 'No, it's alright, I'll do it. We're not going to have another distracted day like yesterday from you, are we? You're not sickening for something are you?'

'I don't know,' Richard replied, taking his own coffee back to the desk. All of a sudden he wasn't thirsty any more.

Dawlish slid through the Metro doors just as the warning tone sounded. The carriage was almost empty, but she stood anyway, hanging on to the central pole between the doors with one hand, leaning outwards, so her weight swung her around in time with the motion of the train. It was about twenty minutes out to the coast from the centre of town. She paced the carriage for a bit before flopping into a seat and gazing morosely out the window for the rest of the ride.

She jumped onto the platform at Tynemouth. A few market stalls had set up in the station itself, selling books and second-hand bric-a-brac. Small, gold-edged pillboxes and squashed faced china dogs. Royal memorabilia mugs and plates, brass pheasants, and a camera from the days before digital. Lamps without bulbs, lampshades without stands, and right at the back, a tiny figurine of Picasso's *Don Quixote*, standing guard. She briefly toyed with a couple of paperbacks so well-thumbed that their corners were curling up and with spines so lined she could barely read the titles. Catherine Cookson, Jackie Collins, half a box of Ray Bradburys that she hadn't expected and would have liked to have bought if she'd had the money. She cracked open the cases of a few Queen CDs, worn and battered as their paper neighbours, and found them missing inlays, slightly scratched.

'They're still playable,' said the bloke behind the stall. 'Though I guess you kids are all into your iPods these days.'

'I don't have one,' Dawlish replied.

'I can probably fix you up with one on the cheap?'

'Maybe some other time.'

She put down the CD and wandered into the street. It was shaping up to be a fine day. The sun was out, and the pavements bounced back the clear, white light that made her squint. A double line of cars was parked down the centre of the street, but there was practically no moving traffic, so Dawlish could hear the sea as she approached. The rushing roar of breaking waves, and the screaming of gulls. The wind carrying its fresh tang of salt. Her feet in their heavy boots clomped out a tattoo on the cobbled road as she made her way down the main street. Passing the open doors of the numerous chip shops, she kept catching the smell of vinegar and hot fat, then checking the change in her pocket to see if, magically, enough cash had appeared that she could get something, but she kept finding only a lone fifty pence piece and her Metro ticket.

The beach was a perfect *U* cut out of the coast. A natural cove in the shadow of the priory, the ruins of which stood on the hill to the south. Its uneven black spikes, like an iron coronet, perched on the brow of the cliff. Daytrippers crawled like ants up the hill towards it. Dawlish veered off to the left and headed instead to the sand-covered stone steps down to the beach. A man was leaning on the railings about half-way down, looking out to sea. He was dressed in a dark red linen suit, cut in a high-necked Eastern style. His black hair was thick and wavy but cut just too short for the curl to show, except at the nape of his neck. His skin was brown and weathered. He had a long, hooked nose which looked as if it might have been broken at least once, a wicked grin, and bright dark eyes which darted constantly. His fingers twinkled with rings.

Dawlish stopped at the top of the steps and leaned over the side. She was about to call down when the man threw a glance over his shoulder and beckoned for her to come to him.

'Yeah, like I would want to sneak up on you anyway . . .' she muttered to herself as she started to descend. The man watched her as she approached and, as she got closer, offered her a greasy paper packet.

'Eaten?' he asked.

'Thanks.' Dawlish grinned as she accepted the package and unwrapped the fish and chips inside. She began to bolt them down with indecent haste.

'Slow down, or you'll choke on that,' the man warned.

'What does it matter to you?' Dawlish mumbled between bites.

'I'm supposed to be drumming some manners into you. What will people think if they see you stuffing your face like a savage all the time?'

'That the Baron is an important person who has much better things to do than mind my table manners?'

Despite himself, the Baron smiled at her cheek.

'They'd be right at that,' he replied, turning to lean against the rails again. 'Especially now we have a new Lampton heir to worry about. And one who knows nothing of his fate.'

'Poor bastard.'

'It does pose something of an added dilemma. How exactly to make him aware without terrifying him into uselessness?'

'Don't look at me; I'm just the lackey. I don't have to deal with it.'

'I wouldn't be so sure about that.'

'Oh, come on,' Dawlish turned to him with a pleading look. 'Haven't I got enough trouble in my life?'

'Kate will want you to go and see him,' the Baron said, looking out across the foam, refusing to meet her gaze.

'I'm sure she will.'

'Will you go?'

'Thing about being owned—I don't really get much choice in the matter. Either of you says "jump" . . .' She sighed and stared down at the beach.

The Baron looked at her quizzically for a moment, but she didn't seem to want to make anything more of the statement, so he continued.

'I'd like you to go.'

'You would, would you?'

'I would rather like to find out how the latest of John's descendants is getting on.'

Dawlish rolled her eyes.

'Oh yeah, I'd forgotten how you were in on this whole mess from the beginning.'

'You make it sound like it's my fault.' The Baron almost sounded reproachful.

'You've had a thousand years to interfere, and you decide now is the time to do something about it? Well colour me suspicious.'

'If I told you my ulterior motives, then they wouldn't be ulterior any more. Rather defeats the object, don't you think?'

'Fine, keep your secrets. I'll draw my own conclusions. About you and a certain dark beauty who owns the other half of my time-share.'

'Wicked, suspicious child,' muttered the Baron with an arch grin. 'Think what you want; I shall tell you nothing.'

Dawlish merely speared another chip and ate it.

'Ulterior motives are so much fun,' continued the Baron. 'Without them, life would be terribly mundane.'

'No fear,' muttered Dawlish, eying her companion.

'For example, when you go to see Richard, you have the basic motive that Kate told you to do so. Dull, isn't it? However, with the addition of an ulterior motive, provided by myself, that trip should be made much more interesting.'

'Oh yeah? For your information, spying on Kate for you isn't as interesting as you think. Also, I don't do that any more.'

'I didn't mean that.'

'Oh? So what did you mean?'

'Richard Lampton has found your missing jackdaw chick.'

Dawlish suddenly perked up.

'Really?'

'And I thought you weren't interested in ulterior motives.'

'I'm interested in that. How did you find out?'

'A little bird told me.' As if on cue, a magpie glided down from the cliff-top to perch on the railings in front of them. The Baron greeted it by running a finger down the back of its head.

'Morning,' added Dawlish. 'I suppose that means the other six are around here somewhere?'

'Probably.'

'Lies. I happen to know that at least five of them are scouring the countryside out by Penshaw Hill.'

'And how might you know that?'

'A little bird told me.' Dawlish winked and took another bite of fish.

'Your little bird wouldn't happen to know exactly where they should be looking?'

'If they do, they haven't told me. Hell, I don't even know what it is you're all looking for.'

'Shame.'

'Not that I'd necessarily tell you if I did know,' she continued, finishing off the last chip and scrunching the paper into a ball.

'You would.'

'Probably. But I don't know, so I guess we'll never get to find out for certain.'

The Baron reached into his pocket and brought out a scrap of dried meat which he fed to the magpie.

'So you'll go talk to Richard?' he asked.

'I might. Think about it, at any rate. But even if I do, I'm certainly not reporting back on anything Kate might have to say about it.'

The Baron grinned, flashing a mouthful of gold teeth.

'Wouldn't dream of asking, my dear.'

CHAPTER 6

THE GIRL WHO TALKED TO BIRDS

I t was just after lunchtime when Richard's phone rang. He hadn't been expecting any calls, so he still had half a mouthful of ham sandwich. He answered the phone as coherently as he was able.

'Hello? Richard Lampton speaking, how can I help?'

'Dick? It's Kate here. We met at the funeral.'

'Kate?' For a moment Richard was confused, then memory suddenly kicked in. 'Oh, Katherine!' He nearly choked on his sandwich. 'How are you?'

'Why don't we skip the how do's? They're never the full picture,' came the voice on the other end of the line. It was still as sultry as ever, even down the phone line. Richard felt his hands sweating.

'From you,' he said, trying to sound suave, 'I'd be happy to hear the whole story.' Kate actually laughed a little at that.

'Oh no, no, no . . .' she said. 'That's sweet, but no.'

'All right. Did you just ring up for a chat, then? Because, much as I'd love to talk, I am at work right now.'

'No, I called to give you a heads-up,' continued Kate. 'I've sent a friend of mine around to yours this evening. She wants to meet you. Thought I'd better warn you. She's perfectly harmless. Just so you know. You should probably get some food in or something—she eats like a horse.'

'I'm sorry . . . what?'

'A friend of mine. Friend of your uncle. She didn't get to speak to you on Saturday. I said you'd be all right if she came around tonight. It is all right, isn't it?'

'Yes . . . yes, I suppose so . . . but—'

'Good. Expect her around about six.' And with that Kate hung up, leaving Richard sitting there with a phone in his hand, wondering what had just happened.

The shrieking of birds filled the treetops and, underfoot, dry bracken scrunched, but the woman picking her way through the spinney was making no attempt to approach silently. The Baron stepped out from behind the mossy tree he had been leaning on and watched as the white-clad figure drew nearer.

'You were looking for me?' he asked quietly. The woman brushed a stray twig from the hem of her skirts.

'Well met,' she replied, unconcerned by the edge in his voice.

'Well?' he scowled.

'You need to stay away from the Lampton issue.'

The Baron's amused look showed exactly what he thought of this suggestion.

'I'm not joking,' continued the woman.

'You had better be.' The Baron smiled, but there was no humour in it.

'I don't joke.'

'You know why what you're asking is impossible.'

'I am tied to this just as much as you are—'

'No!' he retorted. 'Even you must acknowledge the difference!'

'We are both tied to this,' she continued, as if he had never interrupted. 'I have stepped away this time, and so must you.'

'Must? Why must I?' The Baron shook his head fiercely. 'You may be able to forget, but I take my responsibilities seriously. Besides, I know you have that fledgling with Richard, spying on him. That's your idea of staying away?'

'He's there to help Richard, not to spy,' she replied, unconcerned. 'I'm not stealing your tricks.'

The Baron snorted in disbelief. 'Dawlish is going around to check on him tonight. She'll let me know if what you say is true. So for your sake I hope it is.'

The woman reached up and bent down the branch of a nearby sapling. She ran her fingers through its drying leaves.

'I can't force you to do anything,' she said blandly. 'Check on the jackdaw if you will. But if we're talking about birds now, I'd suggest you call your magpies off the hunt. They won't find what you're looking for.'

'Oh, so that's how it is,' the Baron snapped. 'You have it. How does that dovetail with staying away, exactly?'

'I don't have it, and I am keeping my distance.' For the

first time, her voice had developed a steely tone. 'And you should, too.'

'Why? Give me one good reason.'

'Kate.'

The Baron's incredulity, already souring, curdled. For a second, even the birds stopped singing.

'Are you threatening her?'

'No.' A little life returned to the spinney. 'Kate is taking the lead on this, and I intend to let her have her head.'

'Kate?' The Baron folded his arms across his chest. 'Why would she involve herself? She never has before.'

'Her reasons are her own. As ever.'

The Baron seemed to relax a little and leaned back against the tree with a sigh.

'All right,' he said, relenting. 'I've called off the Watchers already. Which I suppose you knew?' The woman nodded. 'The boy is more unaware than we suspected. This will have to be handled with more care.'

'Do you not trust Kate?'

'I don't trust you.' He smiled to himself. 'But if I know her . . . I won't get in her way. But that's as much as I'll promise, and don't for a second think I'm doing it for you.'

The woman bowed and faded away into the undergrowth.

By the time Richard got home, he had forgotten about Kate's phone call. He slipped his key in the lock and was surprised to find it wouldn't turn. He tried again, turning it back the other way, then pushed the door, only to find he had locked it. It must have been unlocked when he had first tried. That made no sense, he thought to himself. He was sure he'd locked the door on the way out. He paused on the doorstep, and as he did, he realised the kitchen light was on, and he heard voices from inside. Correction, a voice, and a cawing sound that could have been Bobble. He didn't sound panicked, as Richard would have imagined he would be with an intruder in the house. Silently berating the bird's ability as a watch-dog, he got out his mobile and had 999 ready-dialled as he entered, just in case.

He pushed open the door slowly and walked in. A girl was sitting at the kitchen table, leaning on one chair with her back to him and her Doc Marten boots up on the other chair. She didn't look very old—maybe fifteen? Her black hair was starting to show gingery at the roots, and she was wearing shabby black jeans with holes in them and a slightly fraying black T-shirt with a list of concert venues on the back. Bobble was standing on the table in front of her, to all appearances chatting away like old friends.

'Hello?' Richard ventured. The girl looked over her shoulder, then swung her legs down from the seat and stood up. From the front, she looked even younger. The smudged black make-up around her eyes made her look like a child playing with her mother's mascara for the first time.

'Hi,' she said. 'You must be Dick.'

'It's Richard, actually. Who are you?'

'Didn't Kate say? Dawlish.' She extended a hand.

'Sorry?'

'My name. Dawlish.'

'Oh.' Richard took her hand and shook it. Dawlish

looked at him sceptically.

'Kate did call you, right? You're looking at me like I'm a ghost or something.'

'What? No. Sorry. I mean, yes, Kate called. I forgot.'

'She told me to ask how you were holding up.' She sat down again without throwing her feet up on the furniture, Richard was pleased to see. 'You know, what with the funeral?'

'Well, I didn't know my uncle very well,' he said. 'We didn't talk much. He and my mother never got on.'

'I heard. Quite the bust up, and all over . . .' She paused and looked at Richard appraisingly. 'Well . . . you know. Families, huh?'

Richard crossed the room and picked up the kettle.

'Actually, Mum never mentioned why. I'm going to make some tea. Would you like one?'

'That would be great. Thanks.'

As Richard went to the sink, he noticed there were several more mugs than had been there when he left. It seemed as though Dawlish had already availed herself of his hospitality in his absence.

'These all yours?' he asked.

'Might be.'

'How long have you been here?'

'Dunno. How many cups?'

'Four.'

'Call it two hours?'

'Two hours?'

Dawlish shrugged but offered no explanation.

'How did you get in?'

'Your bird let me in.'

Richard put down the clean cups he had just got from

the cupboard.

'Look . . .' he said, turning round.

'Dawlish,' she supplied.

'Dawlish.' Richard fixed the girl with his best attempt at a steely glare. 'Are you taking the piss?'

'Who, me? Usually. Why? Does it bother you?' Dawlish seemed confused.

'A bit, yes. Really, how did you get in?'

'I said. Your bird let me in.'

'I wasn't kidding.'

'Neither was I . . .?'

'I'm not in the mood for games.'

'I'm not playing one!' She sounded genuine. Petulant, abrasive, but not sarcastic this time. Richard continued to fix her with a look.

'I don't appreciate people breaking into my house,' he said. 'Even if they're expected.'

Dawlish gave him a withering look. 'I talk to birds, okay? I asked him to open the door for me, and he did.'

Richard sat down in the chair opposite, and looked Dawlish full in the face. Either she was a very good liar, or she was telling him the truth. She reminded him of Kate. The same challenging stare, clipped manner. He could have taken them for mother and rebellious teenage daughter, if Dawlish hadn't been so paper-pale that there was no chance of their being directly related.

'Okay,' he said, at last. 'We'll let that one pass for the minute. So what are you doing here?'

'Sitting. Being interrogated.' She slouched down further in the chair. 'Look, I popped round to say hi. If you want me to go, just say so, all right?'

'I'm sorry. I didn't mean to be rude.' Richard deflated

somewhat. 'It's just . . . I don't know anything about you. And you appear like this, in my house . . . what am I supposed to think?'

Dawlish shrugged.

'I'm fifteen, I was born in London, but now I live in Durham. I work for Kate and a guy you don't know called the Baron—they like, literally saved my life this one time, so I owe them big. I talk to birds, which is something that the Baron does, too, by the way. I like pepperoni on my pizza, I don't drink Diet Coke, and your kettle's boiling. Anything else you need to know?'

'Why "Dawlish"?' asked Richard, getting up to make the tea.

'What do you mean?'

'Isn't it a place in Devon?' he ventured, searching for a clean teaspoon. 'I mean, not that I'm judging you or anything . . .'

'Maybe it is, maybe it isn't,' she replied, shrugging and catching up a hank of her long black hair to twine between her fingers. 'I've never been there or anything. It's the only name I've ever had.'

'What about your parents?'

'Gone.'

There was a finality to her tone that prompted Richard to ask, 'Dead?'

'Don't want to talk about it. Kate and the Baron make sure I'm looked after. Milk and two sugars, please.'

Richard brought the mugs over to the table.

'So how did you know my uncle?' he asked as he sat down.

'Everyone knew Tom,' replied Dawlish.

'So it seems,' replied Richard. 'Everyone but me.'

'Yeah, well . . .' muttered Dawlish, reaching for a mug. 'Life sucks that way sometimes. We lose people. Maybe it's better not knowing them first.'

'You don't really think that, do you?' Richard asked. It seemed such a bleak thing to say, even if she did seem to be going through the obligatory teenage Goth phase, but she merely shrugged and changed the subject.

'Nice ring, by the way.' Something about the way she said it made Richard pause. It was too casual, as if she was trying to catch him out. She was looking at him slantwise as she raised the mug to her lips, almost as if she was trying to judge his reaction to a question she hadn't asked.

'Apparently, it used to be Tom's,' he settled for saying.

'Yeah. Yeah, it did. Fits all right, does it?'

'Yes.'

'Good. That's good.' She looked as if she was about to say something else, but thought the better of it. Richard put his own mug down and held her gaze, but Dawlish refused to be drawn on the subject. 'Do you have anything to eat?' she asked.

'Eat?'

'Yeah. I haven't had dinner yet, and I'm starved. Even just some biscuits to go with the tea would do.'

She was a spiky kind of girl, Richard decided. But when he stopped to look, the teenage bluster she projected seemed to be a mask. She was thin. Very thin. She didn't look like she'd had a square meal in a long time.

'I could maybe do a frozen pizza,' he ventured.

'That'd be great.' She leaned back in the chair as Richard headed for the freezer, wondering exactly when he had become a restaurant.

'How are you getting on with the jackdaw?' Dawlish asked, eying up the bird on the table.

'Bobble?'

'You gave him a name?' Dawlish threw him a look of utter scorn. 'Well, that figures.'

'What's wrong with that?'

'Well, birds in the wild don't generally have them. Corvids—that's crows, jackdaws, ravens, magpies, and the like—they're brighter than the average bird. Kind of insulting really, calling him after a hat.'

'It's because of that little feather there . . .'

'Well yeah, but it's like calling your kid "Mackintosh" and expecting them to be normal. You'd better get used to having him around, because he's never going to be wild again with a name like that.' She shrugged. 'Name like that? He could be anything.'

'Maybe that's not such a bad thing.'

Dawlish acted as if she hadn't heard. 'Mind if I take a look at him?'

'Sure, if he'll let you.'

Dawlish gave him a brief but withering look, then turned to Bobble. 'C'mere, you . . .' she said, sticking a hand out. Obediently, Bobble fluttered up to her hand. She began to examine him, stretching out his wings to examine the growth of flight feathers, and dislodging handfuls of down all over the table.

'Just about fully fledged by now . . .' she muttered, and Richard, watching the two of them, could see the truth of her words. Bobble was looking less and less like a chick and more like an adult jackdaw, even if he still had that immature gawkiness to him that betrayed his youth. Dawlish caught hold of his beak. To Richard's surprise, Bobble didn't protest as she checked over his face, eyes, and feet. Eventually she let him go, and he hopped back down onto the table.

'Not bad,' she said. 'Healthy enough. And he seems to be getting enough to eat. You might want to give him something more than just sausages though. You'll spoil him.'

'How did you . . .'

'Do we have to do this again?' she said, sounding exasperated. 'You didn't believe me the first time.'

'Believe what?'

'I. Talk. To. Birds. He told me. But other than that, everything seems to be fine, and he's happy here, so I don't mind leaving him with you.'

'You're acting like he belongs to you or something.'

'He belongs to himself. But it's part of the deal. Birds don't talk to you unless there's something in it for them. They talk to me because I look out for them. That's what I'm doing. Looking out for him.'

'And he's happy here?'

'Yeah. He thinks you're funny. Personally, I can't see it.'

'He thinks I'm funny?'

'I know.' Dawlish shrugged. 'No accounting for taste.' The oven timer dinged. 'Shall I get that?'

'No, it's my house. I can do it.' Richard looked about for the oven gloves and, unable to find them, settled for using a knife to slide the pizza carefully onto a plate straight from the oven.

'They're on the microwave, by the way,' Dawlish said, as he brought the plate to the table and neatly divided the pizza into eighths.

'What are?'

'The oven gloves.'

Richard sighed and went to grab some side plates from the cupboard, but when he turned back, Dawlish was already nearly finished with her first slice.

'Help yourself . . .' he muttered.

'What? I was hungry.' She broke off a piece of the crust and held it out for Bobble. He gave it an experimental peck, then swallowed it with a jerk and a snap. Richard sat down and took his own slice of pizza, which he ate rather more slowly than Dawlish, who bolted her food almost as fast as Bobble. He quietly made sure he left her slightly more pizza than he took himself.

'For what it's worth, I reckon you'll be all right,' she said after a few minutes, during which only the sounds of chewing could be heard.

'What do you mean?' asked Richard.

'I mean with everything. I don't say this often, but you seem like an okay sort of guy.'

'Should I be flattered?'

'Can if you like.' She drained her mug and stood up. 'Listen, can I take a last slice to go? I hate to eat and run, but I've got places I need to be.'

'I suppose so.'

'Cheers.' Dawlish nodded, stacked up three slices, and took a bite out of them all at once. 'Take care, Dick,' she said, flipped her free hand at him in a half wave, half salute, and let herself out.

'Nice to meet you . . .' Richard sighed in the direction of the closing door.

CHAPTER 7

A MEETING AT THE SATION

Richard finished off the remaining slice of pizza, then cleared away the plates and flopped down on the sofa. He didn't quite know what to make of it all. It was as if the last hour or so belonged to some other Richard who inhabited a different world where birds could talk, telephone calls never made sense, and where Dawlish was a perfectly sensible name for a teenage girl. He had just been watching through that other Richard's eyes. His head felt like it was full of mashed potato. After a minute or so, Bobble hopped up and nudged Richard's foot.

'I'm sorry,' said Richard, 'I'm not sure if it's the world or me who's in a bad mood right now.' Bobble said nothing. Instead he flapped up onto the arm of the sofa and gently head-butted Richard's elbow.

'Aark,' he cawed softly. Richard wasn't sure, but it sounded like the bird was trying to be comforting.

'Thanks,' he said and stroked the little jackdaw's head.

He wasn't sure if he really believed what he had been told, but Bobble had always seemed to him an intelligent sort of creature. Whether he really could understand him, he didn't know.

And there was something else. Dawlish had been looking at him all evening in the same way that Kate had, as if they were trying to figure him out. As if they were waiting for him to do something and he had no idea what. He was too tired. He needed sleep. This would all make sense in the morning. It was too late to try and figure it out now. Still unsettled, he locked up and headed for bed.

The next morning, Richard woke up with a tension headache behind his left eye approximately the size of Glasgow. It felt as if he'd been crying—that kind of washed out achy feeling. Bobble, unusually enough, was still asleep when he woke. Richard lumbered slowly into the kitchen and put a pot of coffee on to brew. He flicked the telly on. It was the breakfast news, and the newsreader was in the middle of a story about some chief executive taking back-handers. Richard knocked back a couple of paracetamol and waited for the headache to subside.

'. . . the weather today is set to be grey and murky with patchy showers all across the North of England . . .'

Richard made a bowl of cornflakes and a mug of coffee. He was beginning to feel almost human, and the events of last night seemed far enough away to be a bad dream. As he stood up to take the dishes to the sink, he noticed a thin envelope poking through the letterbox. It wasn't postmarked or even stamped. It just had his name written in a scratchy, spidery hand. The paper was old and yellowed, and the edge that had been caught in the letterbox was slightly damp. He wondered if it had been there all night.

He slit open the envelope and into his hand fell a note, no more than a scrap of paper torn out of a notebook. It read, "Clock. Central Station. 9:30. For answers. Kate." Richard stared at the piece of paper, willing it to say something more. He felt tired and frustrated and slightly dislocated from reality, as if he were stuck in a nightmare that ought to have ended by now. And yet . . .

There was obviously something going on that he didn't know about. Something to do with his uncle's death, that much was clear, but more than that he couldn't guess. Richard had always been curious about his father's side of the family, but his mother had never got on with them, and after his father's death they had all but lost contact until, out of the blue, the call had come to let him know about the funeral. It had only ever been idle curiosity, but now he was beginning to wonder if there wasn't something important he had missed by not staying in touch, something more than just missed opportunities.

A treacherous voice in the back of his mind suggested that perhaps now was his chance to find out. The note did say that Kate would explain. If he did want answers . . . Only he couldn't possibly go. That was a given. He had work. What was she thinking? That he would come running the minute she called? And what was so important that she had to say in person like this? Not that the thought of seeing her again wasn't attractive—her arrogant half-smile, the way she moved like a ship in the breeze . . . He couldn't drop everything just for her. Even if he wanted to. Not that he did want to. He wasn't thinking of actually going; that would be madness. He had to go to work. He couldn't.

He ran his fingers through his hair and wandered back into the kitchen, still staring at the message in his hand. Didn't she understand that he had responsibilities? He couldn't. How had he managed to get involved with these strange people anyway?

It had started at Tom's funeral, hadn't it? That's where he'd met Kate . . . she'd come up to him, and given him the ring . . . The ring . . . Hadn't they been talking about the ring last night? How well it fitted? Dawlish had been right, it was like it had been made for him. The weight of it on his hand felt oddly natural. He still hadn't thought to take it off since he'd been given it. He looked at it again. The device that he had taken for a snake was actually an antiquated letter *L*. Well, it was supposed to be a family heirloom, after all. Still, the swirling script did look very serpentine.

Richard couldn't shake the feeling that the letter was a snake, a living creature, writhing on the gold. He felt a sudden revulsion towards the band around his finger. He grabbed at it and tugged. It wouldn't come off. He tried again. Still nothing. He headed to the sink and stuck his hand under the tap. Warm water and washing-up liquid failed to shift it. It wouldn't even move, just sat there like a golden eye, winking at him.

Richard was spooked. It had gone on fine, and it still twisted and moved around his finger normally, but when he tried to pull it off he came up against a sudden, forceful resistance as if the ring itself refused to be parted from his flesh. He felt trapped. Not just by the ring, but by something much bigger. The treacherous thoughts that kept him dozing off at work and making him wonder if there wasn't something else, something more that he should be doing.

That was the worst thing: that this seemed to be coming from within. He couldn't entirely blame Kate or his uncle or rings or birds. It was as if those things were just excuses. This was something he had to do. Only half aware of what he was doing, Richard poured out a bowl of sunflower seeds for Bobble and left it on the table, then got in the car and began to drive.

It was ten to nine by the time he drew up in the station car park, and he was already having second thoughts. He wasn't used to bunking off, and he was feeling guilty. He'd better go back, go to work, be responsible rather than go tearing off on a wild goose chase. He was just imagining things, like the ring not coming off and the distracted feelings. It was all nonsense, and he was being silly. What Kate had to say couldn't be that important, surely? He should buck up and go to work. He got out his phone and rang the office to tell them he'd be late.

'Dick!' Maddy exclaimed when she answered the phone. 'Good. I was just about to call.'

'I was just ringing to say that I'm going to be late this morning . . .'

'Oh, no, don't worry about it. I was about to say, all the electricity's out at the office. The road works on the corner only went and cut through a bloody cable, didn't they?'

'How did they manage that?'

'I don't know, but they've said they can't get someone out to fix it 'til later today, so there's really nothing to do but answer the phone, and since I've got to stay in anyway and wait for them to sort things out, I think I've got that covered.'

'You mean, I've got the day off?'

'Might be more than a day. The guy I spoke to said it didn't look too promising. I'm bloody furious, actually. It's going to make things a bit of a nightmare. But you know how workmen are. Can't rush them if they don't want to be rushed.'

'Oh. Right.'

'You sound about as happy about it as I am. It's a day off, make the most of it. Depending on how generous I'm feeling, I won't even take it off your annual leave.'

'All right,' replied Richard. 'Well, I'll see you tomorrow, then.'

'I'll let you know.'

'Are you sure you don't want me in to help?'

'That's sweet of you, but no. I have a lot of important clients to ring and apologise to, and I could do without you under my feet. Besides, Steve's coming in after lunch to help. Between the two of us we've got it covered. Take care.' And she rang off.

Richard stood underneath the clock in Central Station with his phone in one hand, looking a little lost. So. He didn't have to go to work. In theory he could stay here and not be shirking. It seemed too convenient. He checked his watch again. 9:05. The station was busy with the tail-end of the morning rush and the platform was awash with faces and bags and cardboard cups of coffee. A cool morning wind chased dropped newspapers around the ticket office. Pigeons limped and flapped and fought over abandoned croissants. A man in an orange vest and tattered jeans slumped on the floor by Burger King, selling the *Big Issue*. Directly in front of him, a tall woman stooped slightly to retrieve a few notes from one of the cash-machines, but a gaggle of youths with backpacks blocked his view for a moment, and when he next could see, the woman had gone.

Richard was at a loose end. If he wasn't going in to work, he didn't quite know what to do with himself. Should he wait around and see what Kate wanted or not? If not, what else should he do? Well, he didn't have to decide right now. He had plenty of time and could at least have a coffee first. There was a Costa on the platform in front of him, but it had a substantial queue, and on the other hand, he could see a cafe just past the Metro station on his left which looked fairly empty. He strolled over, keeping one eye on the spot underneath the clock, just in case.

The cafe was called the Centurion. It was quite chic. Long and narrow as it ran parallel to a platform, with faux-topiary and fairy-lights fencing off an outdoor seating area. Richard walked through, past the specials blackboard out-side, and into the main cafe. Inside, the style was minimal-ist. Dark red walls, wooden floors, and wooden chairs. It was empty. No, not quite empty. As Richard stepped up to the till to order a drink, he noticed the table tucked in im-mediately behind the counter was occupied. More than that, he recognised who it was.

Richard stepped into the body of the cafe and sat down opposite Kate.

'You're early,' she said, tearing open a sugar packet and pouring the thin trickle of white grains into her cup.

'As are you.'

Kate shrugged, stirring her coffee.

'Drink?'

Now that Kate was actually in front of him, Richard couldn't think straight. All the questions, everything he'd wanted to say to her this morning was evaporating off his tongue in the face of her plum-coloured smile. She was looking less immaculate this morning than when he'd seen her at the funeral. Her hair, escaping from a loose ponytail, looked ready to ensnare the wind, her draped white blouse was open at the neck, and the sleeves had been rolled up past her elbows, but her eyes were still dark with enough promise to give Richard shivers when she flicked them in his direction.

'I got your message,' he settled for saying.

'You wouldn't be here otherwise.' She raised the coffee to her lips. 'So. Freaked out yet?'

'No.'

'Liar. If the strange woman giving you a ring at a funeral wasn't enough, then meeting Dawlish last night ought to have done it.'

'She seemed like a perfectly normal teenager to me.'

'I'm impressed. Two massive lies in under a minute. That's almost up to my standards. Let's go for a third— have you been getting the phone calls yet?'

Richard started.

'How do you know about those?'

'Oh, and you were doing so well . . .' Kate made a faux-disappointed face. 'Coffee?' She gestured to a second cup and a cafetière on the table in front of her. Richard poured himself a large cup of coffee, noticing as he sipped that it seemed to have had a little whiskey added to it.

'So . . .' he said after the first few mouthfuls had started to warm him through, 'you promised me answers.'

'I? I promised nothing,' smiled Kate. 'But I am here to help.'

'Help me?' asked Richard, bemused. 'Why would I need help? And who are you to be offering it?'

'Katherine Avery. You know that.'

'Should the name mean something to me?'

Kate sighed in a disappointed fashion.

'Evidently it doesn't,' she replied. 'It's enough that you know I was a friend of your uncle and of your father. They trusted me, and I hope you will come to trust me as well.'

'You're not exactly making that easy for me.'

'I'm not, am I?' Kate grinned. 'I was hoping you'd think it was part of my charm.'

'It is. Sort of,' Richard muttered.

'Glad to know I still have some charm left.' She poured herself another cup of coffee, still smiling. 'But this isn't supposed to be about me. We came here to talk about you.'

'Did we?'

'You, your family. Things you should have been told a long time ago.' She reached down underneath the table and withdrew a small silver hip-flask, presumably from a hand-bag, and surreptitiously topped up her coffee from it.

'What's my family got to do with it?' Richard asked.

'Everything.'

'I thought they might,' Richard sighed. 'This all started with Tom, didn't it?'

'Actually, it started a long time before that, but your part in it, I suppose, started where Tom's ended. The two of you weren't close, were you?'

'No. He and Mum never got on, and I don't think I

even saw him since Dad died.'

'That might have been a problem, in hindsight.'

'I always assumed she had her reasons.'

'Reasons?' Kate scoffed. 'Oh, we all have our reasons. Doesn't change the fact that hers were bloody stupid. Not wishing to speak ill of your mother or anything, but it was a damn fool thing of her to do, cutting herself off like that, and you with her.'

'Now hang on a second!'

Kate held her hands up.

'I'm not flinging blame around here, I'm just saying. This would be an awful lot easier if Tom had been able to clue you in on a few things rather than me having to do it now. I am not good at this, you may discover.'

'Good at what, exactly?'

'Exposition. The Big Reveal. I prefer a fait accompli.'

'Well, who doesn't?' added Richard glibly. Kate treated him to a raised eyebrow, then continued.

'I tend to blurt things out. Like, I could say to you right now, "Dick, your uncle didn't die of a heart attack like we told everyone." And . . . well, I guess I just did. Sorry about that, by the way.'

'What?' Richard blinked hard, his brain trying to make sense of what his ears had just heard.

'Sorry. About him dying. He was a good friend to a lot of people, and we're sorry he's gone.' She said it very matter-of-factly, but Kate's voice was devoid of her usual half-mocking tones. It was the first time Richard could believe she was being entirely sincere.

'Thank you,' he said.

'It's true,' Kate said, after a moment. 'It wasn't a heart attack. We lied.'

'We? But the doctors . . .'

'Were lying too. I was the first person on the scene after the accident. I saw his injuries. I know what really happened. So I saw him brought in to the hospital and taken to a doctor who owes me a favour, and then I phoned Ellie, and then I paid the ambulance drivers a lot of money to forget about what they'd seen.'

'Why would you do that?'

'Because it was a lot easier than the alternative.'

'Which was . . .?'

'Explaining to the hospital, and most likely the police, what I'm going to explain to you now. The reason why your uncle really died.'

Richard shook his head, as if to dislodge the troubling thoughts that were filling it.

'Real reason? Are you trying to tell me someone killed him? That this was murder?'

'No. Nothing like as simple. And I'm afraid I'm going to have to go back rather a long way before this is going to make any sense to you.'

'How far back?'

Kate hesitated for a moment. Richard couldn't tell if the look she shot him was more worried or appraising.

'Have you ever heard the story of the Lampton Wyrm?' As she mentioned the name, Richard had a feeling of foreboding, a feeling in his stomach like the sudden drop going over the edge of a rollercoaster. For half a moment, he felt a cold wind on the back of his neck that brought with it the smell of fish, cold sweat, and the tinny taste of blood.

'It's a children's story, isn't it?' he said. 'I think . . . I think my dad used to tell me it . . . before he died.'

'That sounds like Harry,' Kate nodded. 'How much of it can you remember?'

'Not a lot. It was a long time ago.'

'Then I'd best start from the beginning.' Kate took her hip flask out again and topped up both her own and Richard's mugs from it.

'Steady on . . .' muttered Richard.

'Trust me, you'll need it. Because I'm about to tell you a lot of things that you probably aren't going to believe.' She put the hip flask back, then looked pointedly at Richard. 'All I ask is that you keep an open mind and that you let me finish before you tell me to piss off.'

'I wouldn't tell you to piss off.'

'I may have to hold you to that.'

This time it was Richard who shot an appraising look across the table. Kate seemed as much in earnest as she ever was, and there was something in her gaze that Richard couldn't be sure of. It almost looked like fear.

'Go on,' he said quietly, 'I'm listening.'

CHAPTER 8

THE STORY THAT KATE TOLD

Autumn, long ago, and the leaves turned to mulch underfoot. Trees, like many fingered hands, made signs in the air, scratching messages in the clouds. The River Wear sluggishly wound its way through pale countryside, reflecting a dark grey sky, thick with clouds bearing the promise of snow. The wind was already bringing the taste of winter to the North, scattering the seeds of cold over the dark fields. Fires were kept stoked, log piles kept high. The mornings were shrouded in mists that clung and seeped through clothing. Animals took shelter wherever they could. People kept indoors for the most part, telling stories around the fires.

The Wear was black. Like the fabled Niger, dark with silt. But no soil of this earth is that dark. The water was thick, heavy, as if laden with viscous night. It devoured light, like a hole in the world or a gateway to the voids of hell. No movement could be seen beyond its surface; not the flicker of a fin, or the flutter of weeds in the current.

The water was still and dark and empty. That was how John Lampton found it one Sunday morning when he should have been in church.

John sat on the bank in the wet grass, waiting, too concerned for the rod and line he held to notice the way the water seemed not quite real any more. The mists grew up around him, and still he played his line idly, waiting for a bite, while the water ran cold and black and deep below him. The world was still, as if listening. The church bell tolled, an eerie sound in the half-light. Then, with a jolt, the wire snapped taut, and John found himself jerking something up onto the ground beside him, where it flopped and writhed uncontrollably.

It was not a fish. It most resembled a snake, six inches long, legless and black. Its head was pointed and fox-like, with two papery ears of skin, taut as a bat's wing. Its mouth was filled with tiny, sharp teeth like broken glass, and nine small spots or holes ran down the side of its jaw. Even out of the water it looked wet and slimy, as if covered in oil, and it gave off a stench like the bottom of a drained pond left out in the sun of a hot day.

Repulsed, he would have thrown the creature back, but a voice drifting across the river through the mists stopped him.

'No,' it said. 'You can't do that.'

'Why not?' called John, straining to see the voice.

'You caught it,' the voice continued, and John began to make out the crumpled figure of an old man on the other side of the river. 'You brought it into this world, and for every action, you know, there must be consequences. Keep the Wyrm. It will be easier on you that way.' And then a sudden, empty feeling from across the water told John the old man was gone.

Hellfire rose in John's mind. As the evil, squirming thing lay at his feet, making little snaps with its tiny jaws, John thought of devils, demons, and the marks of sin. He needed to be free of it. The church bell was clanging in unison with the blood rushing in his ears. There was a dry well on the edge of the Lampton estates. The Wyrm banged against the sides on the way down with little wet thumps, and John fancied he heard a splash as it hit the bottom, then nothing but its eerie hissing echoing up the sides of the well.

A year passed. King Richard took his knights and marched off to drive the Saracens out of Jerusalem, and John Lampton went with them. The family of swallows that roosted in the eaves of the Hall never came back after the winter. Cows that had recently been good milkers suddenly produced nothing. An entire field of corn withered overnight. It was a good year for mushrooms, but few edible ones were found. Instead, poisonous fungi began sending their spores out on the wind, and children who didn't know any better were sick from eating them. Sickness stalked the villages, and not just the old and the young suffered. One little girl began complaining that there was something wrong with the mill pond. Sometimes it would develop an oily patina or a matt blackness in which nothing would be reflected, and sometimes something would be seen to stir in the depths. Fishermen reported the same disturbances along the Wear and even the Tyne. It was a bad year for fish.

One night, a boy, late out on the roads, passing by the dry well near Lampton Hall, saw something which made him take fright and run hell-for-leather back to the village. What he'd first taken to be a shadow, slipping across the fields in the moonlight, had transformed into a huge beast, fanged and with a pointed face and nine holes down the side of its jaw. It was black, he said, and stank like the pits of hell. It had glided up to a sheep, cowering against the hedgerow, thrown its massive coils around it, and sunk its fangs deep into the animal's throat, sucking it bloodless as veal. The next morning when the shepherds went to check on the flock, three sheep were missing, and the carcases of two more lay in the field, drained of blood with gaping wounds at their necks.

The Wyrm came in the night. It stole livestock, children even, leaving mothers scared, panicked, bereft. It set up home on a small island in the middle of the Wear, where it would spend its days curled round the rock, sleeping, sluggish, and remote. As night fell, it uncoiled itself, swam the river, and made its way up towards Lampton Hall. There it would call, three times, as if in challenge, hiss, swell its throat up, and screech a harsh, piercing shriek like tortured metal. When no answer came, it set about its nightly wanderings, killing, destroying. Then, when it had its fill, ooze its way back to the middle of the Wear, and lash itself to the rock until darkness came again.

Already, the toll on the surrounding area was too great to be brooked. Taking what measures he could, Lord Lampton ordered that a stone trough be set out by his gates and filled to the brim with milk in order to placate the Wyrm. For a while, it worked. When the creature came to the hall to deliver its nightly challenge, it found the offering and drank its fill of that, abandoning its usual rampage in favour of the easy meal. And so things continued.

Whispers spread. It was a plague which everyone spoke of, but they were too scared to mention it by name.

Then quietly one evening, a man arrived at the Hall. A heavy-set, swarthy man, wearing thick, travel-stained leathers. His name was Bollbrook. He dined that night with Lord Lampton, ate well, but spoke seldom. He asked about payment for dispatch of the monster, heard there was no official reward offered, and nodded. He looked long and lingering on Mary, the eldest daughter of the Hall, but said nothing but gruff civilities to her. Later, Mary would wonder to herself what he might have said, had things been different.

Dusk, and the Wyrm came to the Hall, uttering its challenge. Bollbrook was there to meet it. His measured eye ran over the size of the beast, and he seemed undaunted by the stench and the green snake-eyes. He hefted his sword, ready. The Wyrm turned, hissing and hungry, striking out viciously, fangs ready. Bollbrook jumped sideways, avoiding the first lunge, and brought his sword down on the beast's neck. There was a crunch, and metal bit deep. The knight yelled in triumph, brought the sword through, the Wyrm screamed in pain and anger, and the severed head fell from its carcass to the turf below, spraying black blood. Bollbrook waited, then stepped back. The Wyrm's eye lay open. As he watched, the head writhed in its death throes, lurching backwards towards the body of the serpent. It rested against the neck, the two halves lying alongside each other. The cut was so clean, it was as if they had joined up again. Then the Wyrm heaved and raised its head. Bollbrook stepped back, but it was too late. The Wyrm flung its coils around the knight, pinning his sword to his side, and squeezed. Mary, watching from the Hall, could not look, but she would always remember the screams of that dying man, so abruptly silenced.

Others came. Others met with the same fate. It seemed no blade could sever the Wyrm for good, even if the challenger got the chance to deal such a blow before he was wrapped in a fatal embrace. Even those who evaded its coils to begin with tired eventually. The Wyrm never tired. It crushed plate armour, was stronger than the toughest steel. The hideous scraping and ringing of the metal as it gave under the creature's fangs was painful to the ear, sometimes drowning out even the screams of the man inside. The blood stained the grass next morning red.

Blood. Blood and steel, and the screams of dying men and horses almost indistinguishable. John had never heard a horse screaming before. It is a horrible sound, weirdly human but wilder, keener. And the heat, and the black biting flies which suck what blood flows from gaping wounds, lay eggs in dead flesh, and the stench of putrefying man-meat and horse-meat. The Holy Land, for John, had become a hell. Constantinople was a world away from the green hills he knew. He had taken an arrow wound to the left shoulder, and in his fever, he imagined the earth teeming with black and white devils riding burning steeds, faces disfigured, wielding whips of flame and burning irons. He bit down on the wood between his teeth, smelled burning flesh as the hot irons cauterised the wound.

In England, spring was coming round again, but the land that should have been re-born still reeked of death. Winter's forces never really withdrew, and the ice and snows whitened the land 'til March. April brought the rains, and the damp and the rot began to spread. Fields were washed away, corn never getting the chance to ripen before it began to mildew. And still the Wyrm came to take its toll from the starving countryside.

In his fever, John saw the land he loved and knew that the time had come. He had to get home. Home. Green fields, white cliffs, and the lifting of spirit that comes with once more having his feet planted firmly on native soil. The drifting smell of clover in the wind. Having shaken off the fever, John shook off the dust of the East and headed back through war-torn mud—back, back, back. Called, compelled, his feet took him north. Not just his feet. The road kept whispering to him, strange stories of monsters, demons, dragons in the North. Fear and guilt whipped John home like a slave, stung by his master's lash.

No one from the village recognised him. He was no longer the boy he had been. War had not made him a man, but it had changed him, and old friends could no longer see in him the features they once knew. His father looked at him, pale and dark-eyed, then drew him to his chest, both wondering how the other could be the same person. Only Mary looked on her brother and saw him for himself, not a battered knight in a red and white tunic, a man hiding behind the cross. That night by the fire, she told him what had happened, and they watched from the window as the Wyrm dragged its filthy form up to the gates. John felt sick at the sight of it, but at least he understood.

She wasn't a witch, just a lone woman who knew a little bit more than the rest. How to birth a child, how to mend bones and cure a fever, how to lay out the dead. John had to stoop to clear the doorframe of her cottage.

'How do I kill the Wyrm?'

'Only you can do it.' The smoke from the fire obscured her face as she replied.

'I know,' he said. 'Tell me how.'

'Fight it on the rock,' came the answer. 'In the middle

of the river. Why let evil choose your battle ground? Wear mail, and weld it with spines. Pray to God, and you may succeed.' He understood and turned to go.

'You should not have to do this,' said the woman as he was leaving. 'But sacrifice must be made. Appease the Wyrm's spirit, and on your return, kill the first living thing that greets you. Else for nine generations, no son of Lampton shall die peacefully in his bed.'

John gave his orders to the house.

'As you love me,' he said, 'stay indoors. Do not come out to meet me on my return. Send my dog first,' and he knelt to pet the creature. 'Goodbye, lass,' he whispered to her. 'I'm sorry.' And he took up his sword and went to the chapel.

Holy Father, sweet Jesus Christ preserve me. Hold me in your hand, give me strength to do your will . . .

. . . *Kyrie eleison, Christe eleison, Kyrie eleison* . . .

. . . Dear God, I'm sorry. I never meant for this . . . *forgive us our trespasses as we forgive those* . . . please God forgive me. All those lives on my head . . . please God, please God forgive me my sins . . . forgive me my trespasses, dear God please . . .

. . . *Absolve, Domine, animas omnium fidelium defunctorum . . . et lucis æterne beatitudine perfrui* . . .

. . . I have seen your wars, I have fought, believing I fought for you . . . I cannot believe that hell was your work. I can't . . . Men create hells, not God. Like I created this one . . . I'm sorry, I'm so sorry . . . God help me, sweet Jesus Christ save me . . . Holy Mary, mother of God, watch over me, intercede for me . . . Jesus Christ help me . . .

The Lord is my shepherd, I shall not want:
He makes me lie down in green pastures

He leads me beside still waters,
    He restores my soul,
He leads me in paths of righteousness
    For His name's sake . . .
. . . Even though I walk through the valley of the shadow of death,
    I fear no evil,
For thou art with me—please God, be with me—
    And thy rod and thy staff
They comfort me—please God, comfort me—
Oh God.

If I die today, I die doing what is right . . . and if I die, then what? Dear God, please protect my family. Please, God, watch over my people. Oh God, what if I die, what about them? Holy Mary, look after my sister. Look after my father. Watch over the village . . . please God preserve me to look after them . . . *forgive us our trespasses . . .*

. . . God give me strength. Jesus give me strength. God give me strength. Help me kill this Wyrm. Help me purge my sin. God grant me victory, Jesus guide my sword . . .

. . . Please, God, don't let me fail . . .

Pater noster, qui es in caelis, Sanctificetur nomen tuum.

Adveniat regnum tuum, Fiat voluntas tua . . .

Six inch spikes had been welded to his shoulders, his back, arms, and shins. He wore only half-plate, and chainmail for the rest, but it weighed heavy on him as he dragged himself down to the river. He wore the surcoat, the red cross he had worn in the Holy Lands, for the sake of what it was supposed to represent. The Wyrm lay coiled round the rock, asleep. John reached the bank, his iron-shod feet sinking and sliding in the mud. It was as if a mist filled his mind. He was tired, terrified, he could barely see through the river's morning fogs. The Wyrm reared its head. Its harsh cry filled John's ears. Blind and deaf, John fell to his knees in the mud. It was going to kill him, he knew it. He deserved death, and as its eyes fixed on him, he almost wanted it. With an effort of will, he dragged himself to his feet and staggered into the water.

He was free. The icy touch of the water released him and filled him with the courage he was lacking. He felt a sudden rush of energy, wiping away the blindness, the fear, the sin. He could do this. And the Wyrm lashed out, its coils tightened around John, and then it screamed. The spines welded to his armour bit deep into the Wyrm's flesh. It couldn't hold him. John swung his sword. He said later that God guided the blade, that he remembered nothing of the fight, but as he hacked at the body of the Wyrm, the river washed away the pieces, and they could not join together again. Finally, there was nothing left. John stepped out of the water. The energy he had been given left him, and he staggered. He fumbled, nearly dropped the blade in his hand. Only the thought of what he had to do now to finish it all made him hold on to it.

The house was upon him, almost before he knew it. His hand reached out to touch the gatepost when he remembered the horn he was supposed to sound. That was the signal to release the dog. He had hardly brought the instrument to his lips, when to his horror and confusion, he saw the door open, and before John could say a word to stop him, his father flung himself into his arms. The dog was at his heels. John raised the blade . . . He could not. There had been enough killing. He struck, and the dog fell. His father looked up at him with enquiring eyes.

'It is done?' he asked, 'The Wyrm is dead?' John looked at the dog at his feet. It wasn't what he had been told, but surely this was sacrifice enough. He hugged his father and Mary, who had rushed up, concern all too evident on her face.

'It is done,' he told them, praying he spoke the truth. 'It is done.'

CHAPTER 9

MUSEUM OF THE ANTIQUITIES

And there Kate finished.

'I'm not sure I understand,' said Richard, who was by now on his fifth cup of coffee. 'You brought me out here to tell me a fairy-tale?'

'Not a fairy-tale.'

'Myth, legend, whatever it is.'

'Neither. It's the truth.'

'Oh, come on,' Richard raised an eyebrow. 'It's just a story. My dad used to tell me it when I was a kid.'

'I said you'd have to keep an open mind,' said Kate flatly. 'That story your dad told you—it's real. It really happened. Back in the twelfth century, there was a John Lampton. You're descended from him.'

'All right, I can perhaps accept that. But all the rest of it? The Wyrm, the curse? That's just a story made up to explain a family's run of bad luck.'

'Awfully long run of bad luck,' said Kate under her breath.

'What, nine generations?'

'No.' Kate shook her head. 'That's the only bit they got wrong. It's still going. Have you ever had a look at your family history? I'm willing to bet you haven't.'

'What about my family history?' Richard was starting to get annoyed.

'How there seem to be an awful lot of accidents happening to them. Your uncle, your dad. Neither of them saw fifty. Nor did your grandparents. In fact, can you name a single Lampton relative of yours still alive?'

'So?' Richard looked over at Kate, brows pinched in anger. 'People die. Accidents happen. I don't like it, but there you go.'

'So many of them? Really? You don't think that at some point a heart-attack is just starting to sound like a convenient excuse?'

'It sounds more likely than what you're suggesting. Congenital heart disease is hereditary. I don't remember anyone ever saying anything about them being cursed by a giant snake.'

'Well they wouldn't, would they? No one would believe them.'

'But you're asking me to?'

'You don't have a choice.'

'What do you mean, I don't have a choice?'

'Well . . .' Kate gestured at Richard. 'Isn't it obvious?'

'Isn't what obvious?'

Kate gave him a look of what might have been pity.

'Dick, you're next.'

'Next?'

'The next in the Lampton line. You see, John Lampton never really killed the Wyrm all those years ago. He simply banished it to another place for a time, and since then it's been trying to return. Your family has been trying to stop that from happening. And it's been killing them. Now you've turned up, and you haven't got a clue, and you're going to need to shape up or else you're going to die.'

This was too much.

'I don't believe you,' Richard replied. 'I can't believe you. You look so serious, and I can believe that you really think what you're saying is true, but . . .' He ran both hands over his face, grinding the heels of his hands into his eyes for a second. 'I just can't believe it. I'm all believed out. I don't have the capacity for any more, I'm sorry.'

'Well, I suggest you try, because the damn thing's got your scent now, and there's nothing else for it.'

'All right, I'm trying. But I'm having some real difficulty even getting my head around the concept of what this Wyrm is, if it's real. I mean, what's it supposed to be? A dinosaur? A dragon? A really big earthworm?'

'Well, that at least I can help you with,' said Kate, draining her coffee cup. 'There's somewhere I can take you that might answer some of your questions.'

'Where?'

'The Museum of Antiquities.'

'What, that place in the university? I've been there before. I don't remember anything there about any Wyrm. And didn't it close recently?'

'Close?' Kate sniffed and stood up. Richard watched her long legs unfold from under the table with a certain degree of longing. 'That place couldn't close if it wanted to. Come on, I'm sure there's a way in near here. Let's see if we can find it.'

Dawlish and Jenny sat around the table in Jenny's apartment, slowly watching their cups of tea go cold.

'She'll be talking to him now, I suspect,' said Jenny, twirling a spoon in the drink.

Dawlish looked at her watch. 'She's probably filled him in on the basics by now.'

'Do you think she's mentioned me yet?'

'Why would she mention you? Is it really the best time?'

Jenny sighed. 'I suppose not. I know this is about more than just me, but he needs to remember. Otherwise . . .'

Dawlish softened slightly and put a comforting hand on her arm. 'Buck up. She'll get to it. She said she would, didn't she?'

Jenny nodded. 'She said so, but can you ever tell with Kate?'

'She usually keeps her promises.'

'Usually. That being the operative word here.'

'Yeah, and if she doesn't there'll be a good reason for it.' Dawlish stood up to re-fill the kettle. 'Trust her,' she said, flicking the switch to boil. 'I do.'

It was a door. Kate hadn't even led him out of the station, just along the platform to a blue door that clearly led to some sort of employees-only area. Except at the moment it didn't because it was locked. It was one of those with a little grey keypad over the door handle, and it looked like it might be alarmed as well. Kate, however, was paying this fact no attention and was instead staring at the door as if she had decided where it ought to lead and was waiting for the universe to re-arrange itself to her convenience.

'Kate . . .' said Richard. 'What are we doing?'

'I'm taking you to the museum.'

'Then I think we're in the wrong place.'

'What makes you say that?'

'Well, for starters, this is a station, not a museum, that door's locked, and we clearly don't belong here. We could get into all sorts of trouble.'

'Don't be silly,' Kate replied, studying the keypad. 'You don't get into trouble for looking at things.'

'We look like we're breaking and entering.'

'Entering, maybe. Breaking, no. Unless you intend to trash the place when we get there—I'm assuming you don't?'

'Well . . . no, but . . .'

'Good. Then shut up.' Kate reached out and gave the door handle a firm pull. To Richard's surprise, it offered very little resistance and immediately swung open. There was nothing on the other side. Not even the offices Richard had been expecting. Just a blank wall of dirty red brick.

'Kate—'

'You're wearing your ring, right?' she interrupted.

Richard frowned.

'Yes. It won't come off. I discovered that this morning.'

'Really?' Kate didn't seem perturbed. She had stepped forward and was closely examining the brickwork inside the frame. 'It's been a long time since I used this . . .'

'I mean, really, won't come off. Physically won't. I've tried running it under the tap, soap. Just about everything short of bolt cutters.'

'They wouldn't work either. It's meant to stay on. Come over here a minute.' She seemed to have found something. Richard walked over to where she was standing in front of the doorway.

'What?'

'Put your hand on the bricks. The hand with the ring.'

Feeling a bit of an idiot and still rather scared that someone would see them, Richard obediently put his hand up to the wall.

'No . . .' Kate immediately re-positioned him, twisting the ring so that the signet was towards the inside, and pushing his hand down so it was flat. 'The gold needs to be in contact with the bricks.'

'This is mental . . .' muttered Richard.

For a moment, they just stood there in silence. Kate seemed to be waiting for something. Richard felt her breath on the back of his neck, making the hairs stand on end. Her hand was still pushing his against the wall, the warmth of her skin more urgent and immediate on the back of his hand than the rough grit of the bricks and mortar beneath his palm.

She stepped in closer. The world around him stilled, and all he could hear was her breathing and the sound of his own heartbeat quietly speeding up. He felt her other hand move up to rest, gently, in the small of his back. He wanted to kiss her. She was so close. He could just turn around and kiss her. He shifted position slightly, and as he did so, he felt her suddenly shove him, hard. Caught off balance, he fell forwards into the wall beyond the doorframe.

'I take it this morning's mission went well, then,' said Jenny, for want of anything else to say. Dawlish reached up to get some more teabags down from the box in the cupboard.

'Not a problem,' she said, dropping them into mugs with studied nonchalance. 'The only tricky part was timing it so that there was enough light to see the cables by, but not so much light that people would see what I was doing.'

'No one noticed you? You're sure?'

'There was a hairy moment when I thought I'd been spotted,' continued Dawlish, kettle in hand, 'but that's the thing when there's road works. If you're wearing the right kind of hat and a high-vis vest you can get away with anything you like. Even at five a.m.'

'Even cutting the power to an entire street?'

'They won't be fixing it in a hurry either,' Dawlish smiled as she passed Jenny her mug. 'I trashed it good and proper.'

'Isn't that a bit unethical?' asked Jenny.

'Not really. Means to an end and all that. If Dick Lampton doesn't get his act together soon, the Wyrm will be back properly, and then no one's safe. I think outing the power to one street is a small price to pay to save who knows how many lives, don't you?'

Richard had expected to hit the bricks full in the face, but instead, as they rose up to meet him, he felt a cool, prickly sensation run down his arms, and he found himself falling forwards through the wall which was suddenly as insubstantial as mist. He staggered, righted himself, and found he was somewhere else altogether. It looked, to all intents and purposes, like the great hall of some stately home or castle. Wood-panelled walls arched upwards into a high vaulted ceiling where massive crystal chandeliers hung, dripping with light.

Richard's second thought was that this was some sort of library. He was surrounded by books; it was like some sort of temple to the printed word. Shelves stretched from skirting to ceiling, each heavily stacked. Large bookcases lined up back to back across the room, packed full to bursting with volumes. On benches and tables, slim hardbound publications nestled up to vast leathery tomes and weighty folios. Pamphlets and manuscripts papered every available surface.

He swung around to see if there was any way back. Behind him was an empty door-frame. It stood there, a blank arch in mid-air. Richard could look straight through it to the bookcases on the other side. There was no sign of Kate, Central Station, or the brick wall he had just walked through. As he stared in incomprehension, the air in the centre of the arch rippled, and Kate stepped out of nowhere through the doorway. For a second, he could see a flash of the station visible through the frame behind her, then it was gone.

'Good, you got here all right,' she said, dusting herself off.

'I'm not sure I did,' he replied, still casting about for a

glimpse of something familiar. 'What the hell happened there? Where are we?'

'Weren't you listening?' Kate asked. Then she sighed. 'I suppose it is all a bit new to you. Welcome to the Museum of Antiquities,' she said with an expansive gesture. 'It's amazing the places you can find just behind a locked door.'

'Just behind a locked door?'

'Every locked door. That's where this place is. Behind every locked door. There are hundreds of places like it, just tucked away in odd corners where no one usually looks: behind locked doors, inside a reflection, under an archway. All waiting just a step away for someone with the right key or the right set of circumstances. They're called Brigadoons.'

'Brigadoons . . .'

'This, however, is called the book room. No prizes for guessing why.'

'So, is this what we're here for, a book?' asked Richard.

'No.' Kate was thumbing idly through a small red monograph she had picked up off a table. 'This is a museum, not a library.' She dropped the book back on top of the pile. 'It's quite extensive. Luckily, the room we're after is close by.'

'Where?'

'Just over there, in the corner.' She pointed to where a small, white door was half-hidden behind a bookcase. 'You go ahead. I'll meet you in there.'

'What? Why?'

'Do you need me to hold your hand or something?' Kate frowned at him and picked up another book. 'I won't be a minute.'

Richard headed across the room in the direction which Kate had indicated. As he approached, he noticed the door wasn't entirely white, but covered in a delicate silver tracery that could only be seen from a slight angle. He could tell there must be some sort of pattern in them, but it was difficult to make out exactly what the pale loops and coils portrayed. There was also no obvious way of opening it.

'There's no handle,' he called back, but either Kate didn't hear him or wasn't listening, because she gave no reply. Richard looked more closely at the silvery design. Its curves seemed somehow familiar, but he couldn't quite place them. He froze with realisation. The faint central lines formed the outline of a giant snake, exactly like the one on his signet ring. Without really knowing why, he reached out and pressed the back of his signet ring against the eye of the creature. Beneath his hand, he felt a shifting and a slight click, and the little white door swung inwards on silky hinges.

The room beyond was filled with a pale, greenish light, as if it was at the centre of a block of ice floating in the sea. Dotted around the room stood glass-fronted cabinets and flat display cases the height of tables, and for the first time since stepping through the wall, Richard felt like he was in a museum. Straight in front of him and slightly to the right was a tall, glass box inside of which stood a suit of armour. It was smaller and stockier than Richard would have expected. He was not tall himself, but the metal shell in front of him was shorter by a head. Six inch steel spikes protruded from the shoulders, upper arms, legs, breastplate, and back. One spike, welded to the left side of the breast-plate, had been snapped off, but from the remaining stump of metal it was clear that, prior to that, some trauma had bent it back against the arm. A corresponding hole in the chain covering the left lower arm was just visible, and the torso had a slightly bent, squashed look. To all appearances it was as if some huge hand had grabbed it around the middle and squeezed, jamming that left arm into the damaged spike with such force it had punched straight through the arm and snapped off, still embedded in the flesh. Richard shuddered.

'Rust or blood stains?' said Kate behind him. She had appeared and was now leaning casually on the doorframe, a book in one hand, looking on.

'What?'

'The brown spots. What would you say they were?'

'I don't want to know.' He turned away.

To his left was a glass-topped box, such as is seen in museums, positioned at the right height for viewing the objects within, neatly arranged on a sloped cushion of black velvet. The box was full of teeth. They were all of a similar shape—long and pointed—but of varying sizes. Each had a neat little white card pinned next to them. The first tooth was proclaimed to be that of a timber wolf, the second an Indian wild dog. Next to those lay a set of three teeth purporting to be a tiger shark's, then a tooth from a Bengal tiger. There seemed to be all manner of predatory creatures represented: the killer whale, brown bear, Nile crocodile, ferret, but all were represented the same way—with one canine tooth.

'Next case,' said Kate, her voice low and gentle, as one might talk to a nervous horse. 'These ones are only for comparison.'

It was a small elephant's tusk. Except it wasn't. The small type-written card bore only one word: Wyrm. It was

another canine, and it was almost a foot long. The case beyond that was full of snake skulls, again presumably for
comparison, their jaws prised open, fangs displayed promi-
nently. Hooded cobra, puff adder, coral snake, Indian py-
thon. It was only too easy to imagine the kind of skull that
would have held that other tooth when faced here with its
miniature counterparts.

The rest of the cases on that side of the room contained
books held open with strings of cloth-covered beads, showing illustrations of mediaeval dragons and sea-serpents. On
the wall above them were a series of framed photographs,
some of which looked rather familiar.

'Is that Nessie?' asked Richard, staring at an image labelled 'The Surgeon's Photo.'

'Those are probably hoaxes,' Kate assured him. 'Some
of this stuff needs clearing out. It's just here for the tour-
ists.'

Richard took a step closer to peer at a greenish-black
photo of a diamond-shaped flipper. 'Yeah, well it's not doing much to convince me.'

'You need convincing?' asked Kate

'Isn't that why you brought me here?'

'Turn around.'

Richard turned to look at the left-hand side of the room
and almost fell backwards into the case of snake skulls.
Tucked inside a large glass-fronted alcove in the wall directly opposite was a skull. It was similar to the snakes',
but the snout was longer and more pointed, the brow ridge
less flattened. There was something fox-like about it, something of the crocodile. But it was the size of the thing that
caught the attention more than the subtler details. The foot
long fangs fitted easily into that gaping mouth. Too easily.

'Holy shit . . .' Richard breathed.

'It's real,' said Kate. 'Real bone at least. The teeth are fakes. We had to remove them for safety. Don't ask me why, I don't know the technical details. That fang in the case behind you is one of the originals though.'

'What is it?' Richard asked. 'Some kind of dinosaur?'

'No,' Kate replied. 'It's not a dinosaur. It's a skull that was unearthed in Durham a few years ago when they were doing excavations of the Iron Age settlement round Penshaw Hill. In the case below are the first three vertebrae of the same skeleton.'

'But that doesn't make sense,' said Richard. 'How did it come to be found in the remains of an Iron Age settlement when you said that John Lampton lived around the time of the Crusades?'

'I never said it was found in the remains of the settlement, just that it was found on the same dig. The archaeological layer it was discovered in does date back to the late twelfth century, so it's the right period.'

Richard hesitantly approached the case and stared at the skull.

'But these are bones,' he said.

'So?'

'So that must mean it's dead?'

Kate shook her head sadly.

'I'm afraid it's not that simple. Remember the story of John Lampton? The Wyrm can re-form itself. And if it can't do that, then it just grows another body. Takes it a while, but eventually it comes back.'

'This is too much . . .' Richard shook his head. 'I don't understand why you're doing this, going to so much trouble. What do you even want me to do?'

'Fight the Wyrm. Kill it. Try not to die.'

Richard looked at her, and the last of his patience evaporated. Kate could see the pain and disbelief in his face.

'You're insane,' he said. 'I've had enough. This isn't real. Just . . . leave me alone.' He turned to go.

'Goodbye, then,' called Kate behind him.

'What, just like that?'

'What else should I say? You obviously think I'm crazy, and you don't want my help.'

'Help?' Richard retorted, but his foot had stopped in the doorway before he could cross the threshold.

'Yes, help. Because you're going to need it. You're the last Lampton we have. A lot of lives are riding on this, and if you can't be bothered . . .'

'I'm not listening,' said Richard, half to himself.

'You won't have a choice,' said Kate matter-of-factly. 'If you don't stop it, it will come for you. And you will die.'

Richard walked away.

CHAPTER 10

THE UMBRELLA AND
THE PHOTOGRAPHS

T he house was in darkness when Richard arrived at his mother's. It wasn't late; she must be out, he reasoned. He had hoped for a dose of clarity, for someone to tell him this nonsense wasn't true. Even if it meant having to admit that she was right, that he should never have let himself get caught up in these new friendships, he wanted an end to it. For a few hours he had been caught up in some madness, but now he wanted to walk away.

Even if she wasn't in, perhaps if he looked around the house he could find something—perhaps something of his father's?—anything his mother had kept that would prove that he had been a normal person who couldn't possibly have had anything to do with monsters from the Dark Ages. He let himself in with the spare key.

His mother was sitting at the kitchen table. Where usually she would have a half-finished jigsaw, spread out on the cloth was a thin layer of photographs. An empty shoe-box sat on a chair nearby, proclaiming their origin. The light shed by the standing lamp in the corner was just enough to see by, just enough to be kind on the memory and the old features before her, but it didn't seem to matter, as she wasn't really looking at them anyway.

'No, don't do that,' she said, as Richard moved towards the light switch.

'Mum? What are you doing?'

'Indulging in ridiculous sentimentality,' she muttered, brushing something from her cheek. Richard stepped into the room and took a closer look at the photographs. The same few faces stared back at him from every little rectangle. His father. Tall and gangly, his ginger hair starting to thin on top and his eyes bright behind chunky eighties glasses. His shorter and stockier brother, Uncle Tom. Richard had never really noticed how alike they had been. That slightly crooked smile, the way they both ran their hands through their hair, making it stand all at odds with each other. In his mind, Richard could hear laughter, and he didn't know which of them he was remembering. They looked happy.

He reached for a photograph. A banner on the wall of the flat proclaimed "Happy 25th Harry!", and his father stood among a group of friends, a bottle in one hand, pushing a party hat out of his face with the other. It looked almost ordinary. But the way the light was falling showed up a glint from a ring on the back of his hand, the same ring which Richard now wore. And surrounding him, those faces. Tom, happy and laughing, one arm around Ellie who was pulling the string of a party popper. A red-haired child who might have been Dawlish, before her slightly gothic phase, curled up on the sofa, knees to her chest, face sticky with cake. And Kate, her dark curls tumbling around her jawline, a fizzing glass raised high in the air. There was joy in that room. It spilled to the edges and Richard felt a strange kind of pain thinking of those times, the fringes of his own life that he had never known, never touched— gone, never to be again.

He reached for another: his father again, at the same birthday. Only this time Richard could see a shadow over him that hadn't been there before. Something in his eyes and in the eyes of the people around him. They were faces that knew loss and expected more. Richard felt he was looking in a mirror, except if he looked up now, he would see his father's expression in his own reflection.

'Mum,' he said, putting down the glossy rectangles, 'tell me it's not true. All this, the Wyrm, the curse. Tell me it's not true.' And he looked across the table in the thin light and saw his mother was crying. 'Mum . . .?'

'I tried to keep you away from it,' she said. 'When your father . . . I don't want you dealing with that. I didn't want to lose you, too. But apparently that's not how it works. I hoped . . . but it doesn't matter now. I'm sorry.'

Richard felt like the floor had fallen away beneath him, and there was nothing, nothing left he could turn to. He started to back away out of the room. He couldn't stay. Couldn't stand there, looking at those dead men's faces on the table, knowing he could be soon to join them.

'Richard . . .?'

He turned and fled outside to where his mother's appeals couldn't reach him.

He stopped when he reached the river. His breath started coming back to him in fits and starts. It couldn't be true. He couldn't let it be true. In the growing dusk, he followed the gravel path down the side of the burn to a spot where the long grass was growing tall, and a bench stood in the shade of a lone tree. Some unknown had left an umbrella propped up against it. Absently, Richard picked it up and began swinging it at the long grass, despondently at first, but within a few strokes he was thrashing it through the undergrowth like a madman, tearing the stalks, flattening the rushes and reeds by the water in pure frustration, hot, angry tears stinging the corners of his eyes.

Perhaps because he was looking for it, dreading it almost, Richard's eye caught sight of something stirring in the water. As he watched, the surface of the river began to grow thick and black and oily and give off a smell like a quayside on a hot day. Rotten fish, decaying river-flesh, and a streak of something dark and acrid, like petrol. Richard felt as if all his insides had seized up, paralysing him, as the darkness began to swirl, and something huge started emerging from the depths. He made a sudden lurch away from the edge as the thing broke the surface of the water.

A head, shaped somewhere between a snake's and a fox's, slime-covered, scaled, and the colour of tar. Tendrils of weed hung from its ears and its jaw in dripping curtains, and along its jaw were nine large black cavities that looked as if they had been hollowed out with a giant melon-baller. It hoisted itself out of the water on a long serpentine neck until its features were level with Richard's own. It opened its mouth, baring its fangs, which Richard noticed were almost exactly a foot long, and made a tortured metallic noise somewhere between the hiss of a snake and the screech of a train whistle.

Richard did the only thing he could do. He hit it. With the umbrella. There was a satisfying *whap* sound as the blow connected, and the Wyrm drew back, surprised. Richard looked around for assistance, but no one was in sight. He contemplated yelling for help, but his natural embarrassment took over. Instead he whacked the creature again on the snout. It hissed and lunged for him, but Richard was waiting and took a two-handed swing at it as if he were wielding a baseball bat. The Wyrm recoiled in surprise and pain.

'Go on, clear off out of it!' yelled Richard at the creature, and to his astonishment, it did so, retreating back under the water, leaving no trace of its presence.

About half a minute passed in stunned silence before the rest of the world caught up with Richard, and he stumbled backwards to sit down heavily on the bench behind him. He put his head in his hands and attempted to breathe. Everything had clicked into place. There was something unavoidably horrible about the whole thing, but at the same time it felt right. Not right as in good, but in the sense of correct. Nothing would ever be the same again, but it was like the moment in a film when the villain is unmasked. Nothing had actually changed because it had been like that all along, but suddenly it was a whole new ballgame.

He was interrupted in his train of thought by the sound of someone clearing their throat.

'Excuse me, but you appear to have my umbrella.' Richard looked at the implement in his hand. It was now irreparably bent, and the impact with the Wyrm's nose had torn a large hole in the material. It was looking rather forlorn. Richard glanced up at the man standing over him with a concerned expression and a mouth full of gold teeth.

'I'm sorry,' he said. 'It appears to have got a little damaged.'

'What did you do?'

Several yards downstream, just out of earshot of the bench, the Baron, having retrieved his umbrella, was accosted by Kate. Her tone was level, but the chill and fury bleeding through her words would have curdled milk at twenty paces. He met her gaze without flinching.

'I am tasked with watching over John Lampton's kin. You know that. It is my word and my blood that keeps the creature leashed for now. My responsibility.'

'And letting it out to play with the one remaining Lampton heir, that's protecting him?'

'Yes.'

'I fail to see it,' she hissed, 'or what you hoped to achieve with this little stunt.'

'He needed to face up to his responsibilities. To decide, then and there, what kind of a hero he's going to be. And it worked. Did you see him take a swing at it like that?' He tried to keep his tone as level as Kate's but couldn't quite stop a note of pride from creeping in at the last.

'Do you have any idea the kind of risk you were taking? If he hadn't—'

'But he faced it. He didn't flinch. And now he's ready for you to talk to him.'

'I . . .?' Kate's eyes widened. 'What makes you think—'

'That is why you followed him here, isn't it? Besides, he hasn't met me yet—that business with the umbrella doesn't count—something I intend to remedy as soon as possible.' He smiled and reached out as if to brush a loose strand of hair away from Kate's face. She slapped it away, and his face fell.

'He needs someone to be kind to him,' he continued, as if nothing had happened. 'You used to know how to do that.' And he picked up his umbrella and walked off.

Richard was sitting on the bench, elbows on his knees, staring without seeing at the gravel path in front of him. Kate sat down beside him.

'Don't say anything,' he said. 'Not one word. I've been an idiot.'

'Not really,' said Kate grudgingly. 'You're doing better than most.'

'What do you mean?'

'Most people don't even notice.'

'Notice what?'

She made an expansive gesture.

'It's called the Weirding. The Other Place. The Overlay. Many names. It's right there all around us for everyone to see, but so few people ever stop and find it. Have you ever thought how hardly anyone looks above the shop fronts of a city? An entire world of Georgian columns and stained glass and gilt clocks, crumbling brick and signs of unknown provenance all papered and plastered over with history, and all they see is the Starbucks below. They miss so much just staring around at ground level. The Weirding is like that. There's a whole world that coexists a shadow's breadth away from the one you've been living in up 'til now. It's been there all the time, but you never noticed it until, one day, you looked up.'

'I'm sorry I didn't believe you.'

Kate shrugged.

'Doesn't matter.'

'I ruined someone's umbrella,' said Richard, sounding quite despondent.

'He'll get a new one. I wouldn't worry about it. In the grand scheme of things it's really not what you should be concentrating on right now.'

Richard ran his hands through his hair.

'I can't think straight,' he said. 'There's too much to ask, too much I don't know.'

'There's no easy way into this. It's like jumping into the sea on a cold morning—you just have to let it hit you all at once. Then flounder around for a bit until you get used to it and try not to go under in the meantime.'

'There's no life raft?'

'It's a metaphor. Of course not.' Kate leaned back on the bench and began fitting a cigarette into her long, black holder. Richard watched her, trying to find something, some clue to how he was to proceed. Eventually Kate sighed and took pity on him.

'Start with small movements. Little questions, little answers. They'll lead to bigger questions, but you have to start somewhere.'

'Where?'

'That's cheating.' Kate grinned and blew out a lungful of smoke. 'I don't know what's bothering you, do I?'

'What did you want to know when you first found out about this world?'

Kate looked thoughtful for a minute. 'That's a clever thought,' she smiled. 'I wanted to know about the rings.'

'The rings?'

'So that flash of cleverness was just a fluke, then? Pity.'

Richard scowled. 'No need for that. I meant, "rings" plural? I only know of my own.' He held his hand up to display the Lampton signet. 'I presume you mean this one?'

'And this one.' She held her right hand up, mirroring Richard. Another signet ring glistened on her ring finger. It was decorated with the symbol of an anchor over crossed keys. 'And all the others.'

'There's more?'

'Everyone in the Weirding wears one. To recognise one another, and they're also keys to get into the secret places, the Brigadoons. Places like the museum, behind locked doors and in lost cupboards, where no one remembers to look. They all have stories woven into the gold: the symbols on them signify the wearer. Heraldic nonsense, but useful sometimes.'

'What does yours say?'

Kate shook her head.

'You have to learn to read them yourself.'

'It'll pass the time 'til the Wyrm comes and kills me.'

'Another time, perhaps.' Kate stood up and wandered

over to the water's edge. 'Have you had any thoughts about that, by the way?'

'Thoughts about what? Dying?'

'No, what you're going to do about the Wyrm. I imagine you're not just going to roll over and let it kill you, are you?'

'I suppose not.' He got to his feet and stood next to her, keeping a wary eye on the river burbling past, just in case. 'You don't have any hints about that?'

'You don't ask much, do you?' tutted Kate. 'Next thing you'll be asking me for world peace and next week's lottery numbers.'

'Floundering, remember?'

'Not really my speciality, I'm afraid. I tend to avoid fights when I can, and it's going to be a bit tough to avoid this one. You won't be able to do it forever.' She tapped the end of her cigarette out of the holder and scrunched the glowing butt under her foot. 'Good luck, by the way.'

'I've got another question,' said Richard with a half-smile. 'How do I get in touch with you? You know, if I need more questions answered?'

'You don't need me for that,' Kate brushed him off. 'There's plenty of us around, and you need to get to know other people as well.'

'But what if I just wanted to talk to you?'

'Richard Lampton, are you trying to ask me for my phone number?' She sounded more amused than shocked.

'I'm not doing a very good job of it, am I?'

'No. You're not.'

'Come on, I was nearly eaten just now . . .'

Kate looked at him askance.

'Tell you what, I'll give you a phone number. It might

be mine. It might not.' She took a little pocket book out of her jacket. It was black and had a small pencil tucked into the spine.

'You can't be more specific about that?' asked Richard as she jotted down a number, tore out the page, and handed it to him.

'Can, but won't,' she said. 'It's part of my charm.'

'So many things seem to be.'

'You're learning.'

Kate didn't stay much longer. Richard, too, headed home; he needed to sleep on this. His car, parked where he left it in his mother's driveway, looked, somehow, too familiar, but by the time he got back home, he felt almost normal. It was quite comforting to just do normal things like put the keys in the lock and walk in the front door. Bobble was already dozing off on top of the fridge. A half-eaten pack of sausages on the floor, plastic unsubtly slashed open with a sharp beak, suggested that he had made his own tea, though how he had managed to get the sausages out of the fridge on his own and close the door behind him was a mystery. Richard sleepwalked through the house, turning off lights, and dead-bolted the door, just in case. Bobble woke up enough to jet down from the top of the fridge and land on his shoulder. Richard absent-mindedly scratched the top of the bird's head.

'You would not believe the day I've just had,' he said as he collapsed fully clothed onto his bed and slept like a log.

Thursday morning, Richard was woken by the telephone. It was Maddy from the office. Someone had really done a number on the cables. The power was still down and did not look like it was going to be fixed for at least another day. Maddy told Richard he may as well not come in 'til Monday. Once she had hung up, Richard rolled over, intent on making up some more sleep, but the phone had woken Bobble as well, and he was clamouring for food.

Richard dragged himself out of bed and set about fixing breakfast. Bobble was in his usual high spirits and attacked his plate of sausages with relish. Richard was more pensive. Even though he hadn't consciously been thinking about the events of the previous day, overnight his brain had been turning them over and had presented him with some ideas.

'I'm going out today,' he told Bobble.

'Aak?'

'I want to see if I can look over Uncle Tom's papers, see if I can find anything.'

Bobble seemed to think this was a good plan, and he showed his approval by flinging a piece of sausage at Richard.

'I'm going to have to leave you here,' Richard continued, removing the sausage from his hair and returning it to Bobble's saucer. 'I hope you don't mind, but Aunt Ellie doesn't like birds very much.' Bobble shrugged his wings in a gesture of disapproval but appeared to acquiesce without too much trouble. 'Don't worry,' said Richard, who was feeling oddly guilty for leaving the bird on his own all day every day, 'I'll take you out for a walk when I get back.'

'Aark,' replied Bobble, which Richard took to mean 'I'll believe it when I see it.'

Richard was just clearing away the plates when the doorbell rang. He went to answer it. A dark man with a bright smile and flashing gold teeth was standing on the doorstep.

'Good morning!' he said. 'Richard Lampton?'

'I broke your umbrella,' Richard said, with a sudden look of horror and recognition. 'You . . . I can buy you another one . . .'

'What?' the man laughed. 'That's terribly kind of you, old boy, but really, there's no need. I'm here on business.' And he held out a hand, palm downwards, like a woman might if she wanted it kissed. Richard was about to take it when he saw the ring on his middle finger. It was a signet ring with the device of an arrow in flight, and Richard knew without having to ask that it was one of those rings.

'Still,' he said, shaking the proffered hand, 'I'm sorry for breaking it.'

'Not at all, not at all. May I come in?'

'Of course,' Richard replied, adding under his breath, 'Most people these days don't bother to ask.'

The man inclined his head and wandered past Richard into the kitchen. As he passed, Richard caught the smell of cloves and pine and a wet forest morning.

'I hope you don't mind the intrusion,' continued the

man, 'but you must be aware that you have become some-thing of a curiosity within our circle. I just had to come and see you for myself.' He stood back and with a comically exaggerated gesture examined Richard for a moment, then relaxed and smiled. 'And there, I'm done. Now we can set-tle down and get to know one another, if you like. No pres-sure.'

Richard smiled. 'No pressure?'

'None at all.'

'Can I get you a cup of tea?'

The man slipped into one of the chairs around the ta-ble.

'Marvellous. Tea is an excellent first step. A much more civilised social lubricant than beer.'

'So,' said Richard as he filled the kettle, 'if you don't mind me asking, who exactly are you?'

'They call me the Baron,' his guest replied. 'But that's not what you're really asking, is it? You want to know whereabouts I fit within this strange new world you've found. What magics I can wield, what powers I command?' He struck a pose, like a conjuror producing a rabbit from a hat.

'Would you tell me if I asked?' replied Richard, his scepticism showing through.

The Baron laughed at that.

'Let's wait 'til the kettle's boiled and see, shall we? You don't happen to have any digestives, do you?'

Richard examined the contents of a cupboard and dis-covered half a pack of rather ancient HobNobs.

'Will these do?'

'Admirably.' He took the packet and settled himself down at the table while Richard made the tea.

'How do you like it?' asked Richard, fishing the tea-bags from the mugs.

'Black as night and sweet as sin. With a dash of lemon, if possible.'

'Black with two, then. I don't think I have any lemon.'

'No matter.'

'All right,' said Richard, bringing the mugs over to the table and sitting down. 'Tell me a little about yourself.'

The Baron smiled. 'I'm Folklore,' he replied, taking a drink from the proffered mug. 'Much like your Wyrm and about as old.'

'Please.' Richard winced. 'It's not my Wyrm.'

'The Lampton Wyrm, then, if you prefer. I have been walking this earth for about as long as it has. I actually knew John Lampton. The original one.'

'But that would make you over a thousand years old.'

'And I don't look a day over thirty? True, but then legends don't age. This is good tea, by the way.'

'Thank you,' said Richard. 'Legend? What, like a character from a story?'

'Aren't we all? Characters in someone's story? Are we not the stuff that dreams are made on, and our little life surrounded by a sleep?'

'You're not Shakespeare, are you?'

'Ha!' The Baron laughed at that. 'If only I were. No, no. My story began centuries before, when I met John Lampton in the Holy Land, back when the Lionheart's men first landed in Acre.'

'During the Crusade?'

'Indeed.'

'Kate didn't mention you in the story she told.'

'She wouldn't. Because that's not the way I told it to

137

her. How else do you think we could have such a detailed knowledge of things? I was there. I came back to England with John Lampton, and I've never left.'

'Why not?'

'At first I had business to attend to. Then, I found I was enjoying myself too much. And then I fell in love.'

'In love?'

'With this country. Every forest, every moor, every fen and lake and hill and standing stone. The coldness of her moods and the warmth of her people. Their eccentricities. The freshness of the air after rain. Her palette of grey and green and brown, so fluid and vibrant and ubiquitous. There's nowhere else like it.' He took another biscuit, snapped it in half, and dunked one half in his tea. 'Don't you think?'

Honestly, Richard had never thought about it very much at all. 'I suppose so?'

'But I am rhapsodising, yes? And this is not the British way. Unless we talk about sports.' He sighed. 'Sometimes it takes foreign eyes to see the beauty and the extraordinary in those places we see every day. Eyes like yours, I think?' He looked slyly at Richard over the rim of his mug. 'Tell me, what do you see, now that you know of our world? How does it seem to you?'

'Dangerous?' Richard ventured. 'I don't know, I think it's too soon to tell.'

The Baron smiled then continued. 'Enough then to say that, by the time I thought of leaving England, I found that I couldn't drag myself away. This land had seeped into my soul, and I was as much a part of it as it was of me. I had been claimed forever; something, again, I think we share. They wrote songs about me. Even elevated me to the nobility, after a fashion. The strange and wonderful things the English will do, making thieves into lords. I forgot my birthplace after a while, all but a few parlour tricks here and there. England is home to me. And now here I am, one of her undying heroes, though doubtless I don't deserve it.'

'Sounds like you were rather famous.' Richard dunked a biscuit of his own.

'Yes. I am rather.' Something of a self-satisfied smirk played around the corners of his lips.

'How come I've never heard of you?'

'Oh, you probably have. But I don't go by that name anymore. It wasn't the one I was born with, anyway.'

'So who are you?'

The Baron steepled his fingers in front of him.

'It is the way of it in our world that you have to see things for yourself. I am, however, a friend.' The Baron took another slurp of tea, and Richard took his chance to examine the gold band round his finger. Kate had said that you could read them if you knew the trick of it. The device was an arrow. And the time-period would be about right . . . It was obvious, now he came to think of it, though he found he couldn't quite wrap his head around the notion.

Richard shrugged and drained his mug. As he took it over to the sink, he looked back at the man—the legend—sitting at his table.

'So what is it you're doing mixed up with the Lampton Wyrm? That's not what you're about in the legends.'

'What makes you think I'm involved?' The Baron's nonchalance could have stripped paint. Richard raised his eyebrows.

'You wouldn't be here if you weren't. Or left your umbrella by the river yesterday. And I'm sure Dawlish said that the magpies I've been falling over since Saturday are your handiwork as well. I could believe you were just here for a good gawk, but I'm pretty sure you're getting enough reports that it wouldn't be necessary. Did I miss anything?'

'Some telephone calls perhaps?'

Richard sighed.

'I wondered when those were going to become clear. Go on, then.'

The Baron gave a paternal nod.

'I was a great friend of John Lampton,' he said, 'and I made a vow, many years ago, to look after his descendants. One part of that Guardianship involved recruiting the Watchers—those people who know the signs, who are primed to watch for the Wyrm's return. Those people who have been calling to warn you until it became clear to them that you didn't know what they were talking about.'

'Ah . . . yes . . .' Richard gave him a sheepish look. 'Not entirely my fault, that.'

'Not at all, dear boy. Though I hope this is something you intend to remedy?'

'It is indeed.' Richard reached for the biscuits. 'For starters, you said "one part" of your guardianship, just now. What else is there to it?'

'I helped to create the cage that keeps the Wyrm in that other place. The place between the worlds where it slinks off to wait and lick its wounds between Lamptons. Your blood and mine keeps it tethered—somewhat. As yesterday proved, the system isn't perfect.'

'How does it work?'

'Magic.'

Richard gave a small, tired groan and popped the remainder of the biscuit in his mouth.

'Another time I shall try and explain,' the Baron continued. 'It is a pity Tom could not have told you all of this.'

'Would he have known any more than you?'

'I cannot say. But quite possibly. After Harry—your father—died, he became terribly studious about the whole business.' He stood up and took his empty cup to the sink.

'You know, it's funny you should say that,' said Richard. 'Do you think he kept any notes? Because I had something of an idea of trying to find them.'

'You can but ask . . .' smiled the Baron, gold teeth glittering.

CHAPTER 11

THE WIDOW AND THE
WRITING DESK

On the corner of the cul-de-sac where Richard's aunt lived was a large spruce tree. As Richard drove up, he noticed a solitary jackdaw perched in the branches lower down. He stopped the car and got out.

'Good morning,' he said, casually approaching the bird. It didn't fly off as a normal bird might, merely shifted its weight from foot to foot for a minute as if it wasn't sure it should be staying. 'I hope you're well? I'm all right. I'm just going to visit Aunt Ellie, see if Uncle Tom left anything that might help me.' The jackdaw cocked its head to one side, but didn't make as if to answer.

'You can tell Kate that. Or Dawlish. Or whomever it is that you report to.'

At that the jackdaw gave a shivery sort of flutter, as if to assert its independence from that sort of business.

'Well, anyway,' Richard continued, 'it was nice to

have met you. And I promise I'm taking care of Bobble for you. Um. Goodbye, then.' He gave a little wave and headed across the street to his aunt's. The jackdaw watched him go.

Aunt Ellie appeared not to have changed clothes since the funeral on Saturday. Her voice, too, was curiously flat and expressionless.

'Richard,' she said, opening the door. 'Yes, come in.'

'I'm sorry if I'm intruding,' said Richard, following her inside, 'but it is quite important.'

Ellie led the way into the living room. It was full of flowers. Every surface was crowded with bouquets. Lilies, mostly, their waxy white blossoms dripping with cloying perfume. Here and there white roses poked through, or sprays of tiny, white-blossomed gypsophilia. It looked as if it had been snowing. And like snow, after five days they were beginning to deteriorate. All around, petals were dropping to the floor, flower heads wilted and drooped. White faded to cream faded to sepia, and the scent was starting to develop tones of decay.

'Please, sit down,' Ellie said with a listless flap of her hand. 'I suppose you'd like some tea?'

'Um, no thanks, I'm all right,'

'Everyone wants tea. I've had to go out for more. And milk. Twice this week.'

'Really, I'm fine.'

'Oh. All right.' She sat down and fumbled with her hands in her lap. Richard wanted to say something, but there wasn't much he could say that wouldn't make things unbearable.

'So what is it you wanted?' Ellie asked, before he could think of something. 'Or are you just here to make sure I'm not wallowing in grief like all the rest of them?'

'Well . . . no, actually,' Richard replied. 'Though I hope you're not wallowing and all that.'

'Oh, shut up.' She brushed a strand of hair out of her eye. She wore no rings, Richard noted, only a thin band of pale skin around the fourth finger of her left hand. For whatever reason, she wasn't involved in this world. He couldn't ask her outright.

'I was wondering if you'd had a chance to go through Tom's papers yet, and if you hadn't, could I have a look, please?'

'His papers?' Ellie looked confused. 'What, like bills and things?'

'No, I mean personal papers, research,' replied Richard, embarrassed to be asking. 'I know it's a long shot, but I was hoping to find something that might help me.'

'With what, exactly?'

'Just something,' mumbled Richard, growing ever more uncomfortable. 'A problem that seems to have been passed on to me. Look, if it's an issue, or not my place . . .'

'Well,' Ellie softened a little. 'I suppose you could have a look in his study. I haven't had time to go through anything. I can't even set foot in there, so I've no idea what kind of chaos it's likely to be in. But you can have a poke around if you think it'll help.'

Richard escaped to the calm of the study, glad to get away from the oppressive air his aunt was generating. It was a pokey kind of room. Its large windows looked out over the garden and let in plenty of light, but the room itself was little bigger than a garden shed and about as full. The desk took up much of the far wall, with barely any space left around it. The walls, where you could see the paper, were green, but mostly they were obscured by shelves full of books, and above the desk to the left was a large-scale map of the Tyne and Wear area. It was not, Richard was disappointed to note, covered in coloured drawing pins.

In fact, the whole room was a lot neater than Richard had expected. His heart began to sink. He had anticipated piles of paper to be sorted through. There barely seemed to be a spare sheet lying around anywhere. He scanned the book titles on the wall. Most of them seemed nothing out of the ordinary: a lot of volumes from the Reader's Digest, as well as hard-backed copies of the classics. One or two looked to have some promise—books of local legends, myths, and fairy-tales, English history, and the history of the Crusades, but nothing Richard couldn't have found in any decent bookshop or library.

Disheartened, he sat down at the pristine desk. It was far and away neater than any desk Richard had ever seen. Too neat. It was a beautiful desk, old, dark wood, rich brown, with a green leather panel set into the top with brass studs. The draw handles were brass lion heads, each holding a ring in its mouth to form the handle itself. Richard supposed that was the next step.

Three drawers ran down the side of the desk, each of them as neat as the rest of the room. The top drawer was filled with stationary: a tray of pens and pencils, a sheaf of blank notepaper, a stack of envelopes, and three small, clear plastic boxes, one of paperclips, one of drawing pins, and one of elastic bands. A small, metal tin with an art deco flower pattern contained several books of stamps, and a slightly larger one held what Richard first took for oddly shaped candles but then realised were actually sticks of sealing wax. One of them was half burned down, but the others were pristine. In the same tin was a cigarette lighter and half a book of matches.

The next drawer down was even less helpful. It contained a blue cash box, a stapler, a hole-punch, and three thin, black books. The cash box, which Richard had expected to yield results, wasn't even locked and contained nothing more helpful than a smattering of loose change, two cheque-book stubs, and a pair of cufflinks. Of the books, two of them were appointment-book diaries in the academic style which began in August. One was almost entirely full, the other had just been begun, but neither of them detailed anything more interesting than haircuts and meetings with the bank. The third was an address book. Richard flicked quickly through it but saw nothing out of the ordinary and was about to put it back when an envelope fell out from between the back pages. It was a letter, and it was addressed to him.

All at once, the bottom fell out of Richard's stomach. He had never before received a letter from a dead man. It felt strange and unreal, the kind of thing to happen in a story, not real life. But then, so many things had changed now, who knew what was normal any more? He held the envelope for a moment, not wishing to open it. Then slowly it dawned on him—it had been addressed and stamped. It didn't look like it had been left in a drawer in order to be found, but in order to be posted. This wasn't some final request from beyond the grave. This was something Tom had meant to get around to before he died. He wasn't sure how comforting that ought to be. Richard slit open the envelope. It was a short note, only a few lines long. As Richard read it, it was hard to remember that the hand that wrote it was less than a week dead. It read, in its entirety:

> *Dear Richard,*
> *I apologise if this letter comes a little out of the blue. My only excuse can be that it is long overdue, and better late than never. I need to see you. I'm working on a project that I'm sure you'll find of the greatest interest. Give me a ring sometime, and we'll talk.*
> *All the best, Tom*

The words floored him. Richard read and re-read the note several times. Nothing in it suggested that his uncle had been expecting the worst. If anything, quite the opposite. What had Tom wanted to talk to him about? It had to be the Wyrm. If only he'd had even a week more . . . but there was no use in wishing. If he had meant the Wyrm, then perhaps there was more to be found. He opened the bottom drawer of the desk.

It contained two things: another black book, similar to the diary and address books, and a slightly battered box folder. Richard reached for the book, and as he opened it his heart skipped a beat. "*Autumn, long ago,*" he read, "*and the River Wear sluggishly wound its way through pale countryside, reflecting a dark grey sky, thick with clouds bearing the promise of snow . . .*" It was the story of the Lampton Wyrm, almost word for word how Kate had told it. The text was heavily annotated, parts were highlighted, parts scribbled over or underlined. The whole book was a mess. Dense, tiny writing covered the margins, pages had been added and notes crossed through, and Post-its were liberally sprinkled throughout the volume. Richard flicked onwards through the book. Every leaf was filled with descriptions of the Wyrm, of the Lampton family, drawings, or family trees with ominous black marks next to names. It looked like Tom had been trying to compile a complete history of the creature. Everything was annotated and cross-referenced in what looked like Tom's personal, slightly archaic system. Richard had hit pay dirt. This was exactly what he had been hoping to find without really knowing it.

He opened the box file to find it was full of plastic freezer-bags. It reminded Richard of all the crime dramas he'd seen on TV, all the forensic evidence, bagged and tagged, except instead of DNA samples or fingerprints or a bloody knife, these bags contained fragments of bone, letters, and a worn and dog-eared diary. There was a locket with a piece of sandy hair carefully preserved in it, half a snapped rosary, and five spent cartridges from a rifle. The bags were all numbered, and looking back at the book, they seemed to correspond with small numbers written in the margin when the main text was referring to a physical item. Each was carefully noted, labelled, and referenced, both in Tom's notebook and on a sheet of paper taped to the inside of the box lid. His uncle had been thorough.

He was about to shut the book, gather his things, and go, when he caught sight of a name on the last page: Cimron. It had been written in a large felt-tip pen and underlined. On impulse, Richard turned to Tom's address book and flipped to the Cs. The name was listed alongside a number. Richard copied it down in the notebook. Then he replaced everything in the box file and stuck his head out the door.

'Aunty Ellie?' he called. 'I think I'm done here.' Ellie appeared from another room.

'Are you?'

'I'd like to take this with me, if I may?' he indicated the box file and book. Ellie shrugged.

'What is it?' she asked

'Just some notes and bits of paper.'

'All right.'

'I really appreciate this,' said Richard apologetically, 'and I'm really sorry to be intruding at a time like this.' Ellie shrugged and said nothing. Richard left with as much swiftness as decorum allowed.

Getting back home, Bobble greeted Richard at the door by dive-bombing his head.

'Hello, you,' said Richard, as the bird rode on top of his head into the kitchen where he dropped the box and book on the table with a thump. Buoyed up with success, Richard felt in the mood to share his news with someone and confident enough that he could even consider asking Kate if she might have a drink with him sometime. If he was lucky, she might even be nice about turning him down. He did have the number she'd left with him—and why would she do that if she didn't want him to call? He picked up the phone and began to dial.

Jenny was sitting at home lounging on the sofa watching a bad film and not enjoying it. After sitting around the day before with Dawlish, she had been living on her nerves and endless cups of coffee. Kate had promised that she would mention her to Richard, but Jenny was still worried. So much was hinging on this. She wanted to call him. She couldn't settle. She had been wandering from room to room, picking up the phone every time she passed it, beginning to dial, and then hanging up and determining to do something else. She had settled down to watch a film but kept getting up to go to the loo or get another drink, invariably coffee, which made her more jittery. So when, at about one o'clock, the phone actually rang, she almost fell off her chair. She made a wild grab for the receiver.

'Hello?'

'Erm . . .'

'Richard?' came an agitated female voice. It wasn't Kate. Richard suddenly panicked.

'Yes?' he ventured.

'Oh, hi!' the voice continued in calmer tones. 'Hi. It's Jenny. Of course, you know that: you called me. How are things going?'

'Not too bad, not too bad. Kate gave me your number.' Flustered, Richard was racking his brains. He wouldn't have put it past Kate to give him a complete stranger's number, but in a way this was almost worse. The woman on the phone obviously knew who he was, but he didn't know anyone called Jenny, and while it was familiar, he couldn't place her voice at all.

'Oh, yes . . . well, it's great to hear from you.'

'You too.'

'So what have you been doing with yourself?'

'Not much. A bit of research, you know.'

'Research? Turn up anything good?'

'Yeah, I hope so.' And then something clicked in the back of Richard's mind. 'Jenny! You're Jennifer from the funeral!'

There was a slight pause. 'Oh.' Jenny sounded disappointed. 'I thought you would have remembered me.'

Richard hastily tried to repair the damage.

'Sorry, yes—of course I remember you,' he said. 'You gave me a lift in the car with all the flowers.'

'Yes, yes I did.'

'And you caught me sneaking out during the wake, and you called me Richard instead of Dick.'

'Yes.' Jenny sounded awfully quiet.

'Are you all right?' Richard asked.

'I'm fine.'

'You don't sound fine.'

'It's nothing. Hay-fever.'

'But it's September.'

'Grass pollen.'

'Oh.' Richard wasn't sure, but he guessed that Jenny was trying not to sound like she was crying. The worst of it was that he had no idea what he had done. 'Have you taken something for it?'

He heard a sniff on the other end of the phone. She sounded worried. Disappointed? He couldn't quite understand why. 'I'm sorry,' she said, and there was a catch in her voice. 'Look, I've got to go.'

'All right,' said Richard. 'I won't keep you, then. But listen, give me a ring sometime, won't you?' Again, there was a pause on the line.

'Kate didn't tell you to say that, did she?' asked Jenny.

'No,' Richard lied. 'You sound like a nice person, and I'd like to get to know you a bit better. If that's all right with you.'

'Okay,' said Jenny, and there was a rustling sound, as if she was wiping her nose on her sleeve.

'Well, bye then.'

'Bye.'

Richard put the phone down with a sigh of relief. Bobble was looking at him, head cocked to one side, as if to say 'how did it go?'

'That was awful,' Richard told him, flopping back into a chair. 'I mean, you heard me. Blundering around with no clue who she was. I felt like a right idiot. And then I told her to call me! What was I thinking? I don't even know if she's got my number.'

'Aark?'

'Don't get me wrong,' Richard continued, 'it's not that I don't like her. I just don't know her. I'm sure she's great, and it would be nice to hang out with someone normal for a change. But that's the problem. I don't want to end up dragging her into all of this. It's not fair of me. But then why would Kate want me to phone her?' Richard sunk his head into one hand. Bobble came up and rubbed the top of his head against Richard's bare arm. 'Hey! That tickles!' he spluttered. Bobble backed off.

'Aark?'

'All right, all right, I'm moping, I know.' He sighed and got up. 'Cup of tea?'

CHAPTER 12

THE BOOK, THE BRACELET AND MEETINGS AT MIDNIGHT

up of tea made, Richard settled down on the sofa and opened Tom's book. The handwriting was small but neat, and he had little difficulty in figuring out what was written. What was meant by it, however, was a little more complex. Tom had his own system, it seemed, but it wasn't until Richard had gone past the original Wyrm story that began the book that things started to unravel. On the next leaf was a list. It had been added to and crossed over so much that eventually another piece of paper had to be stuck over the top. It was only because the glue was peeling slightly and the paper was coming away from the page that Richard could make out that there was any underlying text, but from what was written on the insert, it seemed this information superseded it anyway. Entitled "The Rules," the piece of paper comprised a list.

✓ You are not alone
✓ It can be caged
✓ Every jail has a key
✓ Water is thin
✓ It can be killed
✓ It cannot be avoided forever
✓ It always comes for you sooner than you expect

Each bullet point was followed by a string of numbers which seemed to refer to either one of the evidence bags or a later section of the book where Tom had transcribed several other documents, the originals of which were nowhere to be found. Richard read on and found himself delving into a complete history of the Wyrm and its dealings with the Lampton family. The story was full of yawning gaps, peppered with fragments and guesswork, but it seemed like Tom had been trying, not just to compile an account of events, but also some sort of framework for dealing with them.

Some of the information Richard knew already, or could have guessed, but most of it was completely new to him. Like an account in Tom's own handwriting of a young girl living in Lancashire during the eighteenth century. She had not been intimately connected with the Lamptons; her grandmother on her mother's side had been one but had married away, and their connections with the main family branch had dwindled. At age sixteen, the girl had begun to see 'visions' in pools of water and kept suffering nightmares in which she said she saw a hill which opened and a monster inside it.

Otherwise quite sane, her parents decided to send her away to see a doctor in Bath, who specialised in 'female hysteria.' She never made it to the doctor's. While taking the waters in Bath, she began shrieking that there was a devil in the water and it was coming for her. Onlookers saw nothing, only the girl, arms pinioned to her sides, struggling with empty air, before she collapsed, lifeless to the ground. The point of many of these stories was to illustrate the 'thinness' of water. The bonds of its cage seemed to be weakest there, but even before it was trapped, it seemed to display a preference.

Much of Tom's second rule was old ground to Richard, having heard some of it previously from the Baron. Penshaw Monument, the Victorian folly on top of Penshaw Hill, had always been a fixture of the Gateshead landscape, but reading through the collated evidence, it seemed this was the gate in their world to the Wyrm's prison in that other place where it was trapped. While a Lampton lived, it found it difficult to break through, though evidence suggested that in later years the gate was weakening. The Watchers were reporting shorter times where the creature lay dormant, and more and more it seemed to be testing its limits. A few times it had even broken through, as it once had—such as yesterday's incident by the river—though not for long and always through the water, where the worlds brushed up against each other and the walls were at their thinnest.

There was, however, a price to pay for trapping the Wyrm like this. Unable to seek them out, instead, the Wyrm had begun to call the Lamptons to it. They could resist, but only for so long. Eventually the call of the Wyrm would drag them to the hill to face it and either slay it or be slain themselves. The most recent of Tom's research spoke of a key to the cage, tied to the blood of the Guardian. The

Baron had hinted as much, but that part of the book was incomplete and offered Richard no further clues.

That the Wyrm could be killed was not as surprising as all that. After all, John Lampton had managed it once, hadn't he? But from what Tom had gathered, he hadn't been the only one. The spent cartridges in the box, Richard discovered, were relics from the turn of the century, saved by one Colonel George Lampton, who had the dubious honour of being the only person to have killed the Wyrm, not just once, but five times during his life.

Unusually for Tom, he had referenced a diary, but the plastic bag which should have contained it was empty, so Richard had no way of knowing what had driven the colonel to do it. Family pride? A desire to survive? Sport? He had lived for some time in India and parts of Africa as a young man, and like many ex-pats of the time, had been a keen big-game hunter. Perhaps on his return to England, with nothing to shoot but deer and pheasants, a Wyrm was just a bigger challenge.

Whatever the reason, whenever the Wyrm reappeared, the colonel would head up to Penshaw Monument with his old elephant gun and do battle. He had been determined to die in his sleep, believing that if he could manage it, that he would have broken the curse.

Tom's fifth rule was chilling. Richard had never expected that he would be able to avoid the Wyrm altogether, but apparently several of his family had tried. One of them had even kept a diary, a slim, stained, and worn little volume included in the bottom of the box. His name had been Jonathan Burgess Lampton, and he had been born in 1896. At eighteen, knowing himself next in line to the curse, he emulated his namesake, the first John Lampton, and ran away to war.

He, like so many others, left for the trenches believing, naively, that he couldn't be in any more danger in the fields of France than he would be at home with the Wyrm on his trail. He survived but watched his brothers at Ypres, the Somme, and Passchendaele get caught in the hail of bullets. Three days after he returned, Jonathan, too, was dead. Too exhausted and defeated to care, he was found, dead from exposure, on the steps of Penshaw Monument.

This last was added as an addendum to the diary. The writing wasn't Tom's, and Richard wondered whose it was. Even just flicking through the diary, Richard felt very sobered. He disliked war stories at the best of times, but this one was more vivid than most. That eighteen-year-old boy, Richard realised, was his great-uncle. That, more than most, made it real. It spoke to him too clearly for comfort.

But in the end it was the first of Tom's rules that finally provided a slight shred of comfort. Those four words: you are not alone. The main reference for this seemed to be a letter written in the sixteenth century by Lady Mary Lampton to her son, counselling that he make a trip to the Continent for the sake of his health. She made allusion to 'the family trouble,' and the way it was worded, she could easily have been talking about some hereditary illness. From a first reading it was hard to see what it had to do with the Wyrm at all. And then Richard realised—she knew. Lady Lampton knew. About the Wyrm, about the curse; she was trying to protect her son.

'Til now, Richard had been thinking about the creature as his problem alone. He'd even given Jenny the brush-off, thinking he would have to isolate himself from everyone to protect them, like some comic book superhero. In light of this letter, the thought just seemed absurd. Evidently Tom had thought so, too. He'd certainly thought it important enough that he made it the first rule, and he had been about to contact Richard before he died. Things might have been so different if he'd be able to do so. It was chilling evidence in itself for rule number six: it always comes for you sooner than you expect. Richard went to bed with a lot to think about.

Even the peacocks were quiet in the gardens of the white house. In the stillness around half-past one, Helen woke, slipped out of bed, and wrapped herself in a white silk kimono she had left out. She padded quietly along the long gallery and down the elegant sweep of stairs in slippered feet. She opened the back door at exactly 1:37 as Kate's hand was halfway to the bell.

'You're good,' she said as Helen opened the door.

'You're late,' Helen replied and ushered her inside.

'Am I still late if you know exactly when I'm going to get here?'

'You make an interesting philosophical point. Which is based on a technicality and therefore irrelevant.' She turned away and Kate rolled her eyes at the petite woman's back.

Helen led the way down the corridors to a small room where she had set out a table with a white tablecloth and neat rows of paper, tweezers, and a set of jeweller's lenses.

'All right, what have you got for me?' she asked. Kate removed the small black box from her handbag and opened it.

'A few gems I need to off-load,' she said, passing over the small twist of paper from within. 'And three blanks.' She placed three blank signet rings on the table. Helen took the small paper packet first and emptied it onto the table. Four stones fell out onto the surface with an expensive rattle: three pale diamonds and one so white it seemed almost blue. With each of them, Helen took a piece of stiff, white paper, made a crease in it, placed the stone in the crease, and held it up to the light.

'A north light would be best,' she muttered, 'but if you will see me at this time of night. . .'

'I thought you had a blue light bulb fitted.'

'No substitute.' She took a moment then to hold each stone in a pair of tweezers and scrutinize it through her loupe before finally weighing it on a delicate set of balances in a corner of the room.

'Badly cut,' she said. 'And it looks like they've been prised from their settings. See how they've been cut to a certain shape? They are, however, a good colour. Especially the blue.'

'How many carats are we talking about?' Kate asked.

'1.33, 0.52, 1.0, and 1.90 for the blue. But they're going to lose some of that when they've been cut properly.' Helen opened a desk drawer.

'No cheques, please,' Kate interjected. Helen sighed and opened a different drawer. She took out a wedge of notes and began to count them out on the table. She paused occasionally, to gauge Kate's expression, then continued adding notes until she nodded, and both women seemed satisfied. Then she tucked the remainder of the notes back in the drawer and turned to the three rings.

'Our usual price for the blanks, yes?' she asked, examining the gold. 'Unless you've someone in mind who needs one?'

'No one that I know of.'

'History?'

'Spanish. You know I don't deal in much else.'

'All right.' Helen added a few more notes to the pile. 'That should do it, yes?'

'Admirably.'

Helen began tidying up her equipment.

'One final thing,' said Kate, dipping into the box once more. 'What do you make of this?' Kate handed over the snake bracelet. In the artificial light and with the darkness closing in outside the windows, for a moment it looked as if a real snake lay coiled in her palm.

'Now where did you get that?' breathed Helen. 'I've never seen anything like it.'

'Really? That's disappointing. I was hoping you could tell me a little more about it.'

'May I?' Helen reached out to take it. For a second, Kate seemed reluctant to hand it over, but she relinquished it when Helen picked it up. She took it back to the light.

'Silver and jade bracelet,' she said. 'Shape of a snake. That much is obvious. Very fine detailing in a style I've never seen before. The jades are good ones but not large. It's solid silver, not plated, but I can't see a hallmark. That's about all I could tell you without some more idea of its provenance.'

'I was hoping you'd be able to tell me a bit more.'

'Tell me where you got it.'

'I'm not sure I can say.'

'Then I can't help you.' Helen held out the bracelet as

if to hand it back.

'Tom Lampton gave it to me.'

'Gave?' Helen raised an eyebrow.

'Left. In his will.'

'And you don't know where he got it from? No, I don't suppose you would.'

'Helen,' Kate was firm, 'you know more about this than anyone. There's something odd about that bracelet, and I want to know what.'

Helen nodded. Nothing more need be said. She left the bracelet on the table and continued tidying away her things.

'Wait, what's that?' Helen put her hand out to stop Kate closing the box.

'What's what?'

'That's a soul gem, isn't it?' She pointed to the little silver ring nestling in the red velvet. Kate snapped the box lid shut.

'It's just a ring,' she said quickly.

'Fine, lie to me if you wish.' Helen gave a dainty half shrug. 'I suppose you'll lie to me again if I ask you whose it is? Not your own, I think.'

'I've told you it's just a ring. And I came by it legally, if that's what you're thinking.'

'I wasn't thinking anything.'

'Oh, stop it.'

'It's none of my business, I know.' Helen held her hands up in surrender. 'I just hope you know what you're getting into with those. It's not a nice trade to be involved with.'

'It's a one-off. I don't deal in them. But thanks for your concern.'

'Even having one is a danger.'

'Unless it was freely given.'

'No such thing.'

Kate said nothing and returned the small box to her handbag.

'I'm much obliged to you for this,' she said, turning away. 'Do please let me know as soon as you find anything out about the bracelet.'

'That is what you're paying me for, isn't it?'

Kate eventually emerged from the old house into the shadowy walkways of the grounds. It was the darkest hour of the night. Soon the eastern sky would start to brighten, but not yet. Her shoes crunched over the gravel. One of the peacocks on the terrace took flight at her approach and clattered awkwardly to the ground. She stopped for a moment to scan the sky. No long-tailed birds flew across the light of the moon, and for half a second she was disappointed.

However much it irritated her when the Baron sent his spies after her, it was somehow worse when he didn't. How else was she to know that she was still one step ahead? She at least wanted to know that she was worth watching. She made her way down Helen's drive, hugging the hedge, and was just about to turn left onto the road when she saw the flare of a cigarette end in the darkness of a shadow. She sighed and stopped, secretly relieved.

'What do you want?'

The Baron breathed out that last mouthful of smoke, then crushed the butt underfoot.

'To see you,' he replied. 'You don't call, you don't

write . . . so here I am, in person. It has been too long.'

'It's been less than a day.'

'Each day is like a thousand years to a heart that beats alone,' he smiled, gold teeth glittering in the dark.

'Stop it.' Kate turned away.

'Stop what?' He took a step closer, slipped an arm round her waist. She stepped out of his hold.

'That. You're not going to get any information out of me that way.'

'Information?' The Baron pressed a hand to his chest in mock-horror. 'That hurt, Kate, right here.'

'That's what you want, isn't it? That's always what you want.'

'Kate.' The Baron was suddenly serious. 'That's not what I'm here for. You know that.'

'This isn't one of your games?'

'No games, no information, no spying. I promise.'

'Then what's left?'

'Us.'

'Memories.' Kate shook her head. 'Long gone.'

'Gone?' He stretched out a hand and brushed a strand of hair back behind her ear. 'Forgotten?'

'I wish.'

'Don't say that. We had our good times, too, didn't we? Don't you remember? Those nights under branches and stars, listening to the heart of the trees, lying on beds of feathers and moss.'

'Days of running, with the wolves at our heels.'

'We were always a step ahead. You used to enjoy the chase.' He moved in closer, and this time she didn't pull away from his embrace. 'That necklace I made you from an acorn and a gold chain, do you remember that? You told me that jewels didn't matter to you as much as I did. I had to press that necklace on you.'

'You always thought a gift was enough to make things right.'

'Kate . . .' He cupped her face in one hand. She let him kiss her, but there was little warmth in it. He held her longingly for a moment, then sighed and stepped away. They began to walk along the verge together in the direction of the sea.

'Come back to me.'

'I'm not interested.'

'You've spent five years not being interested.'

'What makes you think anything's changed?'

'Everything changes. And you're as changeable as they come. A woman of winds and waters.'

'Not in this.'

'If you ever do . . .'

'Don't wait for me.'

The Baron gave a knowing smile.

'I won't even say goodbye,' he said, and disappeared into the dark. Kate saw his eyes vanishing backwards and watched him until they had gone.

CHAPTER 13

THE CAVE AND THE CREVICE

That night, Richard did not dream, nor did he sleep exactly soundly. He kept waking at odd hours, seeing Bobble's silhouette on the wardrobe. Drifting off and not remembering. He knew he must have slept by the changing numbers on his clock face, but if it were possible to have spent the whole night awake and feel moderately refreshed in the morning, Richard might have been convinced he had done so.

It was just gone six when he finally gave up on sleep and went through to get some breakfast. He liked the sensation of being up early. The sun was just beginning to stretch sleepy fingers of light over the horizon, and the birds were still tuning up before the dawn chorus. It had rained in the night, and the streetlamps outside were dabbling their light in the puddles. It was as if he were the only person in the world. He flicked on the radio and listened to the shipping forecast as the kettle boiled for a cup of tea.

'. . . Viking North Utsire South Utsire Forties, variable

3 or 4 becoming northwest 5 to 7. Slight or moderate, occasionally rough later. Showers. Good . . . Cromarty Forth Tyne, Northeast backing southwest 4 or 5, occasionally 6 in Tyne. Slight or moderate. Showers. Moderate or good . . .'

The kettle clicked off, and Richard poured a cup of tea. Bobble glided through the open doorway and landed on the edge of the table. He seemed still sleepy and surprised Richard was up but ready to take advantage of any sausages that were going.

'. . . Dogger Fisher, Northeast 4 or 5, becoming cyclonic then northwest 5 to 7, occasionally gale 8. Moderate or rough. Rain or showers. Moderate or good. German Bight Humber Thames, East becoming cyclonic then northwest, 6 to gale 8. Rain or showers. moderate or good . . .'

It was relaxing. A slow sense of anticipation filled the air, some gathering potentiality. He felt like he was part of something; he had a purpose. He decided that he ought to start changing his lifestyle to accommodate this kind of early rising. He knew it would never last, but he still thought it. He wanted to live life. Not least because behind it all was the deep underlying feeling of an hourglass running out. He even began to whistle a few bars of some song by The Who as he poured the tea. Bobble croaked at him, so he blew a raspberry back and rummaged through the cupboard to find a packet of cereal.

'. . . Biscay, Southwest veering northwest 7 to severe gale 9, decreasing 4 or 5, occasionally 6 later. Rough or very rough, occasionally high. Squally showers. Good. Fastnet, North 7 to severe gale 9, backing southwest 5 or 6. Moderate or rough, occasionally very rough. Rain or showers. Moderate or good . . .'

Trying to give the little bird some variety in his diet, Richard decided to cut up some bacon for Bobble instead. Thankfully, the jackdaw wolfed down half a pack of it quite happily. He made a mental note to pick up more at some point.

Last night, in between the cycles of sleep and waking, he had decided to try and find out more about the name at the back of Tom's Wyrm book. Cimron couldn't be a very common name; he must be able to find some way of tracking them down.

Bobble finished off the last of the bacon scraps and jumped onto his shoulder. It felt oddly right having him there. Comfortable. He even allowed Richard to quickly ruffle the feathers on his head and repaid the favour by running his beak through his hair.

Yes. It felt like it was going to be a good day.

Dawlish tumbled out of her nest in the cathedral roofspace at a slightly later hour. From below she could hear the vague sounds of distant religion, like being upstairs at a party she hadn't been invited to. She paid it no heed and went about her own business.

As she stomped down the stairs, she trailed a finger against the wall possessively. Here, she felt safe. The cathedral had stood for centuries and would stand for centuries more. The old pale stones still echoed with the hallowed thoughts of ages past, even the bit of plaster-board disguising a dry-riser inlet, left there by a film crew some years ago. It all felt solid and dependable.

Outside, a troupe of jackdaws wheeled and dived around the tower, calling their good-mornings. She hung out the slit window for a moment, enjoying the wind and their cries on her face, then continued down to the body of the church and into the south transept. A clock stood there, elaborately gilded and four times as tall as a man, with the number four represented as IIII instead of IV on the face. The time it showed was three minutes to eight. She walked round to one side of it where there was a door into the clock mechanism. She looked around to make sure that no one was watching, then quietly opened the door and slipped inside.

In a park just around the corner from Richard's house, in the centre of a bed of geraniums, a large clock which looked a little bit like Big Ben finished striking eight. Like all clocks of its kind, it had a door in the side of it. At precisely eight o'clock and fourteen seconds, Dawlish stepped out of the door in the clock into the flowerbed.

The phone line was dead. Richard had waited until a more reasonable hour before calling, taking the time to do the Guardian crossword and re-read some of Tom's book. He didn't read the rest of the newspaper. The mundane world just didn't seem important any more. Having run out of things to do, he felt that enough time had elapsed and dialled Cimron's number, only to be met with a dead line. Disheartened but not yet willing to give up, Richard poured himself another cup of tea and took it outside while he contemplated what to try next. Bobble came with him and seemed to be glad of the chance to stretch his wings a little. It was somehow cheering to watch him swoop round the rooftops, rolling and tumbling effortlessly in the clear sky.

After a while, he fluttered back down to Richard's shoulder, then tried to stick his beak in his mug of tea.

'It's empty,' Richard countered, turning the mug over to demonstrate. Bobble gave a disappointed croak, then sped off into the distance. For a moment, Richard thought that the bird had finally decided he'd had enough, but he only flew as far as the end of the road before he returned with Dawlish tagging along behind.

'Are you not dressed yet?' she asked when she came in earshot. Richard glanced down at his blue striped dressing gown.

'I'm comfortable,' he said weakly. Dawlish just shrugged and flopped down on the lawn.

'Any tea left?' she asked.

'There's hot water and teabags inside.'

'Fine, I'll wait 'til you get some clothes on.' She lay back on the grass with her hands under her head, while Richard sighed and went indoors to change.

When he came back out again, laden with two mugs of tea, Dawlish was still lounging there, apparently deep in conversation with Bobble. She looked up as he approached.

'He says you're trying to find Cimron,' she said, accepting the mug.

'You know him?'

'Her. And more "know of" than know.'

'Do you know where she lives?

'Vaguely.'

'Vaguely?' Richard raised an eyebrow.

'Well, I know roughly where, but she may take a bit of finding.'

'Would you care to help me look?'

'If you buy me lunch.' Dawlish drained her mug. Richard, deciding this was an acceptable forfeiture, took the empty mugs inside and fetched his keys.

'All right then,' he said, returning and unlocking the car. 'Where to?'

'Belsay.' Dawlish clambered into the passenger seat as Richard settled himself behind the wheel.

'The town?'

'No, the castle.'

Richard smiled.

'I haven't been there in years. Not since I was a kid.' He slipped the key in the ignition, then paused, looking at Dawlish.

'Aren't you going to put a seatbelt on?' he asked.

'Why, do you plan on crashing?'

'I've stopped making plans,' Richard replied, starting the engine. 'They inevitably go wrong.'

It was a pleasant enough drive. Dawlish refused to wear her seatbelt and kept turning round in her seat, much to Richard's consternation.

'You should really get a convertible,' she said at one point.

'If I could afford a convertible on my salary—'

'Talk to Kate. I'm sure she could get you one.' Richard gave this suggestion pause, then decided he didn't really want to know how Kate could get hold of a car for him and changed the subject. He wasn't quite as put off by Dawlish's brusque manner now that he was used to it and knew what to expect. On her part, she appeared to soften a little and not snap at everything he said. Before they knew it, they were driving up to the gates of Belsay Hall.

'I suppose it's too much to ask if you have a membership card, is it?' asked Richard under his breath as they pulled up to the ticket office.

'Do I look like the kind of person who has a membership card?'

'A simple "no" would have sufficed.'

'Where's the fun in that?' she said, and Richard heard echoes of Kate in her voice.

'It's all right,' he said, as Bobble ducked down into the footwell. 'I'll pay. It can't be that extortionate.'

The green jacketed attendant bent down to the window.

'How many?' he asked.

'One adult and one child please.'

'Taking your daughter out for the day, sir?' he asked, taking Richard's money. It was somewhat more than he had remembered.

'Yes, that's it,' he replied. Next to him in the passenger seat, Dawlish made a noise that could have been a sneeze but sounded like a snigger.

'Thought about getting a family membership?'

'We don't really come here that often.'

'Well, I can give you an application form, if you like. You can always fill it out later.'

'All right,' said Richard with reluctance and was handed a sheaf of papers. He passed them to Dawlish, who casually tossed them onto the back seat.

'Enjoy your day,' smiled the attendant and waved them through into the car park.

The quarry gardens were quiet. Excavated in order to furnish the Victorian Belsay Hall with stone during its construction, they had since been planted out with ferns, shrubs, and exotic flora. Great walls of rock, sculpted into shapely arches and crags, curved gently skywards, covered in flourishing greenery. Walking under the huge stone arches was like walking into another world, one of echoes and whispers, the rustle of birds in the trees, and the trickle of water over stone. Branches hung, heavy with the morning light, and every turn seemed to hold an entrance-way to a land less ordinary. Expecting the fantastic around every corner, Richard was almost disappointed that everything looked so much like he remembered.

Dawlish tramped through the gardens like a world-weary cop trudging the streets of big-city America. Richard and Bobble followed in her wake.

'Where are we heading?' he asked.

'Cimron's.'

'Ask a stupid question . . .' Richard murmured to Bobble, who was again perched on his shoulder.

Eventually though, Dawlish turned off the main path where a tall crack in the rock walls led into a circular cavern filled with moss and lichen. The walls stretched up, high above their heads, thick and damp with vivid green flora, but it was open to the sky, which, disappointingly, was beginning to grow quite overcast. Dawlish started hunting round the verdant sandstone, looking intently at the cracks in the rock.

'What are we looking for?' Richard asked.

'I'm looking for Cimron's house,' Dawlish replied, not breaking off her search. 'I'm not sure what you're looking for.'

'Can I help?'

'Do you know what you're looking for?'

'Do you?'

Dawlish paused for a moment.

'Well, not in so many words,' she admitted. 'But I know it's here somewhere.' Richard had opened his mouth and was about to say something rash, when Bobble hopped off his shoulder and flew up to a ledge in the wall about chest height.

'Bobble, come back,' called Dawlish, attempting to coax him down, but the bird did not respond. Instead, he started poking at the dangling moss at the back of the crevice.

'Come off it, bird, this is an English Heritage site,' muttered Richard half-heartedly, but Bobble was not to be deterred. He kept poking further and further back into the crack in the rock. Suddenly, with a croak, he disappeared altogether. Richard frowned.

'Stop messing about, you,' he said and stepped forward to peer into the hole. It was pitch black, and he couldn't see the jackdaw. 'Bobble?' he called cautiously. There was no reply. 'If I have to come in there after you . . .' A very faint call echoed out from the hole. It sounded far away and echoing, further away than the hole looked like it extended. Richard glanced at Dawlish, who shrugged, then sighing, plunged his arm into the hole to retrieve the bird. His arm disappeared easily into the stone up to the elbow, and yet all he felt was empty space. He pressed his cheek up against the moss covered wall, his arm shoulder-deep in the crevice.

'Come off it, you blasted bird,' he muttered, but he could still feel no feathers, and instead, a strange prickling warmth from within the rock began to tickle at his fingers. He stretched just a little further—the fissure couldn't extend that far, surely—and the wall in front of him suddenly gave way. He stumbled forwards, through what he thought had been solid stone and almost fell headlong into a small cavern.

It was warm, much warmer than the mossy quarry he had just left. The sudden step into hot air made Richard feel like he had just opened an oven, a feeling that was compounded by the flickering orange light which suffused the room. And it was a room; someone had taken great pains to make the cavern Richard now found himself in as homey as possible. The walls, where they were visible, were an attractive peachy-coloured sandstone, but for the most part, they were covered in large, red-and-gold bordered tapestries depicting an odd mix of Celtic knot-work and mediaeval hunting scenes. The floor was the same peachy colour as the walls—stone, but sprinkled over with a fine layer of soft sand.

To his left was a large walnut desk buried beneath scattered papers and a tall bookshelf stacked with so many leather-bound volumes that they were two layers deep, and half of them were piled on their sides. To his right, two small and rather faded red sofas stood on either side of a coffee table, one leg of which had been entirely replaced with a stack of yet more books. Behind those, on the far side of the cavern, a deep stone sink was set into the wall. A table next to it stood host to an old copper kettle and a mug tree. Opposite him, on the far wall, a curtain had been tied back to expose an archway, beyond which Richard could see a large, sandy courtyard. A hot, sweet smell of cloves and oranges drifted on the air.

Standing in the middle of the room was a woman. Her hair was a vivid red, darker than flames but just as vibrant. She wore it pulled back into a thick plait, but still hanks of chestnut strands had managed to escape to frame her rather sharp, angular face. She was wearing a burgundy-coloured boiler suit and a long, leather apron, along with high-topped boots which looked as if they'd seen better days. She was holding a raggedy cloth bundle under one arm, and strangely, she didn't seem all that surprised to see him.

'Hello!' she said with a bright smile. 'I'd almost given up on you! Here about the dragon?'

CHAPTER 14

HERE BE DRAGONS

ragon?'

'I was a tad worried about her,' the woman continued, in rich, well-rounded tones. 'She's been off her feed for a few days, and she was looking a bit peaky, but I've just been dosing her with that apricot brandy stuff, and she's perking up already. I think it must have been a touch of colic. Do sit down, will you? Cup of tea?'

'Yes, please,' said Richard automatically.

'If you'll just take her while I put the kettle on, then.' She thrust the bundle into Richard's arms and turned to the sink behind her. Richard accepted the cloth parcel awkwardly, without thinking, and then nearly dropped it as it gave a sudden wriggle.

'Um . . . what am I holding?' he asked.

'That's the Crested Green we were talking about on the phone. Why?'

'I'm fairly sure I've never spoken to you on the phone,' said Richard, the nervousness starting to show in his voice. 'Your line was out when I tried to ring.' The woman turned round, kettle in one hand, a glass jar of tea-bags in the other, and a surprised expression on her face.

'You mean you're not the breeder from Ipswich?' she asked, slowly putting the kettle and teabags down on the side board, still keeping her eyes on Richard.

'Sorry?' He winced.

'So you're not here to buy a dragon?' she continued, her tone now tentative, and in that instance, both her and Richard's gaze travelled down to the bundle in Richard's arms that was now smoking gently.

'Um . . . no.'

She reached for it.

'Shall I . . .?' she gestured. 'I'd better just take that then, shall I?'

Richard nodded gingerly and allowed himself to be swiftly relieved of the wriggling creature. The cloth wrapping fell open as the woman took hold of it, and a small scaled head popped out on a long neck.

'There we go now,' crooned the woman, joggling the little dragon carefully, 'That's better.' The creature looked up at her and made a hoarse blarting noise, like a sick sheep. Richard caught sight of sharp looking fangs in its pale green horse-shaped face.

'Is that really a dragon?' he asked.

'Of course it is.' She frowned. 'The only question here is who exactly are you?'

'Oh, I'm sorry.' Richard was jolted back into reality by the question. 'I'm Richard Lampton.' He stuck out a hand, but the woman still had an armful of dragon and couldn't take it, so he let it drift awkwardly back down to his side. 'I assume you must be Cimron?'

Her face softened. 'Oh, how stupid of me! I should have recognised you from the funeral. I was so sorry to hear about your uncle. You have my condolences, truly.'

'I barely knew him,' Richard shrugged. 'I'm starting to wish that weren't the case.'

'I can imagine. Who's your friend?' she asked, as Bobble had by now fluttered down from the top of the bookcase where he had been perched and took up his usual position on Richard's shoulder.

'Oh, this?' he said. 'This is Bobble.'

'Aark.'

The little dragon, hearing the noise, cocked its head in Bobble's direction and hissed noisily. Cimron's mouth turned up at one corner in a wry smile.

'He's sweet.'

'Oh, and there's someone else outside. Dawlish. Um, can we let her in as well?'

'No need,' said Dawlish, appearing suddenly behind them, stumbling forwards as if she'd been pushed. 'I worked it out myself.'

'Dawlish . . .' muttered Cimron. 'Kate's ward?'

'That's me.'

'Very pleased to meet you, my dear. I would shake hands, but you see . . . Oh, dammit . . . look, do you mind? It looks like my breeder is a no-show, and if that's the case, I need to put this thing back in her cage, and all the others need their noon feed.' She frowned, casting her gaze about the cavern. 'Look, there's cups and tea by the sink, and I think there's a cake in the blue tin on the shelf—the one with Roses on the side. Feel free to help yourself, and I'll try not to be long.'

'Is there anything I could do to help?' Richard asked,

polite to a fault.

'All right, then,' Cimron smiled, surprised. 'It'll just be lugging buckets for me, but I suppose I could give you the tour, if you liked?'

'That sounds . . . interesting.'

'Jolly good.' She turned to Dawlish. 'What about you? Would you like to see?'

'I think I'll stay with the cake, if that's all the same to you,' she replied, flopping onto the sofa and rolling her eyes at Richard when Cimron turned away.

'Suit yourself.'

Evidently Bobble had the same idea and fluttered over to perch on the back of the sofa next to Dawlish.

'Come on, then,' called Cimron and led the way out through the hanging curtain and into the courtyard behind the cavern.

It was warmer outside, with no sign of the clouds which had been threatening rain back in the quarry gardens. They had emerged into a large round bowl of burnt orange cliffs, bathed in blazing sunlight and dotted about with large black shadows that looked like the mouths of other caves. One of them, about half way up the cliff face, seemed to be emitting small irregular blasts of flames.

'So, dragons . . .' Richard began.

'I breed them.' Cimron led the way into one of the caverns on the left where a small pen stood open. She un-ceremoniously dumped the small dragon she was carrying into the pen and swung the door shut behind it. It blarted again and shook off the blanket before retreating into a corner and curling up like a cat.

'Aren't they dangerous?' Richard asked, peering through the bars at the huddled green creature, which admittedly didn't look particularly malevolent.

'Well, they're not poodles,' replied Cimron, looking at him with an amused expression. 'It's all right, you'll be safe enough with me.'

'I wasn't worried,' muttered Richard without much conviction as he followed Cimron back out of the cave.

'I don't think we've really got time for the full tour,' she continued, disappearing into another of the openings. 'I'll just show you round the ones that need feeding today. They're like big cats, dragons. They only eat once every couple of days or so.' Richard was about to follow her, when she returned, hefting a large metal bucket.

'Do you need a hand with that?' he asked.

'If you wouldn't mind.' Cimron dumped it at his feet, then headed back into the cave. Richard examined the bucket. It was full of large haunches of meat, many of them with skin and bone still attached. A moment later Cimron re-emerged with a second and led the way across the court-yard.

It was smaller than Richard had anticipated. About four feet tall at the shoulder, with an elegant swan-like neck, wings that curled over its head like furled umbrellas, and vermillion glowing eyes with slotted pupils. When it blinked, Richard noticed that the eyelids slid up from beneath the eye instead of dropping down from above. It curved its neck down to their level and stared at him with its head slightly to one side.

'It's beautiful,' he said and found that he actually

meant it. Cimron dipped into the bucket, brought out one of the smaller haunches of meat, and passed it through to the creature which started to pick at it daintily.

'This is Didi,' she said. 'She's a Falchion Blue.'

'But she's green.'

'No. Blue.' Cimron bent down and reached through the bars. She brought out a shed scale and handed it to Richard. 'See?' Richard studied the thing in his hands. It was light, surprisingly flexible, slightly translucent, and indeed, blue.

'They have yellowish skin, so it looks green from a distance,' Cimron explained. Richard turned his attention back to the creature.

'I was expecting bigger,' he said.

'Oh, this one's only an adolescent,' Cimron replied nonchalantly.

'Ah.'

'These usually get to about six feet at the shoulder. That's the females. They're always slightly bigger than the males.'

'That's not too bad.'

'But then, Falchions aren't that big, as a breed.'

'How big do they get?' asked Richard.

'Dragons in general? Nobody knows for certain. The largest ever in captivity was about twenty-four feet at the shoulder.' Richard blanched. Cimron saw his expression and laughed. 'Oh, don't worry; I haven't got any that size here. Place isn't really big enough. The largest I've got at the moment is only nine and a half, and he isn't going to need feeding for another day or so.'

Cimron led the way to the next cavern. Inside was a smaller dragon, about the size of a large house cat, vivid orange and spouting gusts of flame. When the beast saw Cimron, or rather the bucket she was carrying, it flung itself against the bars, screeching like a parakeet. Richard jumped hastily backwards. Cimron flung a haunch of meat through the bars with a quick flick of the wrist. It dived on the food with enthusiasm and proceeded to shred it with little harsh whistling shrieks of enjoyment.

'I think I preferred the other one,' Richard said, watching the creature tear into its dinner.

'The fire breathers are always a bit bad-tempered.'

'Don't all dragons breathe fire?'

'No, not all of them. And they don't breathe fire as such.'

'It sure looks like it to me,' muttered Richard as, on cue, the little dragon belched a small ball of flame.

'No. Actually, they spit out flammable stomach gasses, and ignite it by striking a spark on two plates in their mouth.'

'How do they not melt straight through the bars?' Richard asked, still wary.

'Small animals like these can't produce a flame hot enough. And I check the bars regularly for warping.' She stopped, one hand on the bars, looking at Richard. 'I'm not boring you am I?' she asked, tucking a strand of hair behind her ear. 'I know I can get a bit carried away with my dragons.'

'No, not at all. They're fascinating.' At that moment the dragon flamed again, and Richard jumped sideways. 'Woah!'

'Well, you'll like the next ones.' Cimron smiled and led the way through a side passage and up a short flight of steps to the next level. The cave they entered next was set further back in the rock, and instead of being a straightforward hollow with bars across, this one was accessible through a short tunnel that bent round at the end. It was darker and looked much more like the mossy cave outside rather than the hot, dry red rock of the rest of the caverns. It was also damp and humid and seemed quite empty. Richard couldn't see any bars.

'Cimron . . .'

'Shh . . .' She laid out a piece of meat in front of them and, squatting down in the entrance way, waited quietly. Through the wavering heat haze, Richard could make out the outlines of boulders dotted here and there on the floor of the cave. None of the caverns they had visited so far had been exactly rough, but the floor here was smooth stone, not sand, except for the boulders, most of which were grouped around a pool in the centre. He heard a splash but didn't see what caused it. He was scanning the water's surface for further signs of life when Cimron nudged him gently, and his gaze returned to the piece of meat. A dragon had landed on it, no bigger than his hand. It took off briefly and hovered for a moment before landing again with the fluttering wing-beats of a carnivorous hummingbird. In a moment, it was joined by another. They snapped a bit at each other before taking off together, flying round each other as mating butterflies do, before settling again. Meanwhile a third and a fourth, and then more and more little dragons were flocking to the leg of lamb on the floor, tearing strips off it, taking off, fluttering in the air and over the meat, and dancing and spiralling and chittering to one another. They seemed to Richard like a swarm of huge insects or a shoal of piranha, but far more beautiful, because each of the dragons was a different colour, vibrant and metallic, with an oil-slick sheen to their scales.

'Wow . . .' Richard breathed. 'I mean, really . . . wow .
. .'

'Amazing, aren't they?' Cimron whispered, not taking her eyes off the creatures, an enraptured smile playing across her face. 'They were your uncle's favourites, too.'

'My uncle?'

Cimron sighed. 'Shall we go back outside? Quietly, they're very timid.' Cimron began to back very slowly towards the exit. Richard did likewise. Once outside the cavern, Richard voiced the question again.

'Your uncle came to see me,' Cimron replied. 'Because I'm a leading expert in my field. He wanted to know a bit more about dragons. More specifically, this Wyrm that's been bothering you.'

Hope flared in Richard's chest.

'What did you tell him?'

'Shall we go have some tea, and we can talk?'

'For starters,' Cimron said, once they were both sat down in her living cave with Dawlish and a large pot of spicy tea, 'it's not a dragon.'

'I'm sorry?'

'Well, not technically speaking.' Cimron got up and retrieved a large encyclopaedic book and a pair of reading glasses from above her desk. 'See, there are two major families that draconids fall into—true dragons and wyrms. Or *Draconae* and *Serpentae*, if you want the proper Latin.' She laid the book out on the coffee table, and flicked it open. '*Serpentae* can then be further divided into the land wyrms and the sea-serpents. What you have seems to me to be a classic example of the latter.' She tapped the book in front of her. 'This is a *Pelagipentis vulgaris*, or common sea-serpent to you and me.'

Richard scrutinised the drawing. It showed a long, legless creature with a pointed snout, fangs, and a frill round the back of its head. It looked very much like the creature he had come face to face with in the river a few days ago. He nodded.

'That looks about right.'

Cimron looked back at him over the top of her glasses.

'That's pretty much the conclusion that your uncle and I came to,' she said. 'Do you know about the colonel? George Lampton?'

Something flickered in Richard's memory.

'Yes, I think Tom mentioned him in his notes.'

'Genius. Utter lunatic, but a genius nonetheless. He fought the Wyrm. Killed it five times, and not only that, but he provided the most comprehensive accounts of it all. Detailed notes, anatomical detail. The man was a born naturalist. He even dissected one of them once he'd killed it. Had only a vague knowledge of what he was looking at, mind, and got so much wrong, but if he hadn't tried, we'd have less than no information about this thing.'

'What information do we have?'

'Well, it's definitely a sea-serpent.' Cimron topped up her tea. 'It can't really be anything else. But it's like no sea-serpent on record.'

'Why's that?'

'Because it keeps coming back. And it's the same creature every time. I can't explain it.'

'How do you know it's always the same Wyrm?'

'Because of the holes down its jaw,' replied Cimron. 'They're the same size and in the same place in every incarnation. You don't get that kind of similarity, even in two different animals of the same species. Every zebra has a different pattern of stripes, every leopard a different distribution of spots. This is identical.'

'So it really is the same creature?' asked Richard. 'Every time? Isn't that impossible?'

Dawlish let out a snort of derision. 'There's no such thing as impossible. Don't you get that yet?'

'I'm beginning to. What else do we know about it?'

Cimron took off her glasses. 'Well, the good news is that sea-serpents don't breathe fire. And their scales are like snake skin: not built for protection and fairly easy to penetrate.'

'And the bad news?'

'It's highly venomous. It hasn't been killed in over fifty years, and it seems to grow continually, so we don't know how huge it must be by now. It's fast; it's deadly. And worst, it can re-form itself. So the only way to kill it is to pretty much mince it. Or at least the head. A single blow won't do.'

Richard gulped.

'That's fairly bad news.'

'The biggest problem, though,' continued Cimron, 'is that though we've got a fair amount of data on it, biologically speaking, we still have no idea how it keeps coming back. So even if you kill it the once, we can't be sure you've killed it for good. If I could get a good look at it, close up, perhaps I might be able to make more progress, spot something that others missed,' fumed Cimron. 'No one who's ever seen it ever had any experience in dragons or in the occult. But it would be impossible to get that close to it.'

'No, it's not,' said Richard, his voice quiet but firm. 'You need to see a specimen first hand; I can get you one.' He noticed Dawlish rolling her eyes.

'What are you suggesting?' asked Cimron.

'I'm going to have to kill it for you.'

Cimron's eyebrows shot up like they were on strings.

'You're not serious?'

'Deadly serious.'

'Oh, deadly's the word all right,' muttered Dawlish darkly.

'Look, you said you needed to see one for yourself. . .'

'Yes, and I also said that it's bloody dangerous!' Cimron looked as if she were about to strangle Richard herself.

'Well, what else am I going to do?' he said, more violently than he had intended. 'I can't just sit here waiting for it! I'm going to have to kill it at some point anyway, why not now?'

'Because you don't know the first thing about what you're doing?' chipped in Dawlish from across the sofa. 'And even if you do kill it, it'll still come back again?'

'I have to do something!' exclaimed Richard in plaintive tones.

'You're dead set on this aren't you?' Cimron sighed.

'I'm afraid so.'

'All right, then.' She got up and took the book back to her desk, then beckoned for Richard to follow her. As he approached, she pressed a piece of paper into his hand.

'This is the address of some friends of mine,' she said, lowering her voice. 'Among other things, they supply me with tranquiliser darts for the dragons. They might be able to help you. They keep late hours though, so don't call on them before the evening. Oh, and don't take her.' She inclined her head in Dawlish's direction. 'You should take someone, though. And don't you dare tell Kate I sent you there.'

Richard glanced down at the scrap of paper. It was an address in Gosforth. He nodded and pocketed it.

'Thanks,' he said, turning to go. 'I'll probably drop in there tonight. I might as well; I've got nothing else to do.'

'Nothing to do on a Friday night?' asked Cimron with a glint in her eye, 'What an exciting life you lead . . .!'

CHAPTER 15

LOST CHILDREN

They left Cimron's house the same way they had come in—through the wall, and back out into the cave of moss. As they were leaving, they crossed paths with a mother chatting to her young daughter. Richard happened to catch a snippet of what they were saying.

'You know, I heard there's a dragon lives in this cave!'

'Really?'

The mother smiled indulgently. 'Really, really. And if you're very quiet, he might come out and play!'

Richard smiled. He didn't need to check for rings; it was just an attempt to liven up a family outing. The small child turned round and looked at him briefly before running after her mother. Richard strolled down the path after Dawlish in the direction of the car park.

'Do you want to go out for some lunch somewhere?' Richard asked, fishing in his pocket for his keys. 'We can head into town, grab a bite to eat if you want.'

'You're not asking me for a date, are you?' asked Dawlish with a raised eyebrow. 'Because you know you're way too old for me.'

'No! No, I mean, it's about lunchtime and I just wanted to say thanks for your help today, and . . . you're pulling my leg, aren't you?'

'Maybe.' Dawlish gave him a wry smile.

Richard drove them back to his flat where they left Bobble and the car, then caught the bus into town. Unsure of where to take someone Dawlish's age, he eventually settled on TGI Friday's, a restaurant in The Gate complex, as being suitably youthful. Dawlish cast a critical eye around the assorted memorabilia on the walls, sniffed, shrugged, and settled herself in a booth with a menu.

They ordered, then waited quietly for their food, Dawlish swinging her legs against the seats and playing with the napkins. She took one and folded it into the shape of a bird, then tucked it behind the salt and pepper. The waitress returned with their starters, and when she had gone, Richard turned to Dawlish, determined to start some sort of conversation.

'So tell me a little about yourself?' he asked, dropping his napkin into his lap.

'What?'

'I mean, I know you say you can talk to birds, but you seem like a normal kid to me. Mostly.'

'I am just a normal kid. Talking to birds is something I do, not something I am.'

'I'm sorry, I didn't mean to offend. I'm just trying to understand it all.'

Dawlish shrugged and shoved half a potato skin into her mouth.

'Well, we're not all like you,' she mumbled, still chewing. 'We don't all have some grand purpose or destiny or super-secret crap. Some of us choose it, and some of us . . . well, for some of us it's an accident.'

'An accident?'

She scowled.

'They do happen, you know.'

Richard gave a half shrug.

'I just can't imagine the kind of accident that would land you as, say, a dragon breeder, for example.'

'What, Cimron?' Dawlish took another bite. 'Nah, that's been in her family for years. She's a Pendragon, isn't she?'

'What's one of those?' Richard asked, taking a sip of his drink. Dawlish's mouth fell open. Thankfully it wasn't full.

'You mean you haven't . . . Arthur? Arthur Pendragon? The Once and Future King? You've never heard of him?'

'King Arthur? Like Camelot?' Richard scoffed. 'That's just . . .' He stopped. 'I was going to say that's just a legend, wasn't I? You'd think I'd learn. So he was real, too, then?'

'Absolutely! He was a great king in the Weirding a long time ago, before he disappeared.'

'Some say he'll return, right? In England's time of need?'

'Who knows.' Dawlish shrugged. 'I certainly don't.

Are you going to eat that?' She gestured at the remainder of Richard's bruschetta. He wordlessly pushed the plate over to her.

'So Cimron's descended from King Arthur?'

'Well, not directly. The genealogy's a bit muddled. But yeah, something like that.'

Richard sat back and let the waitress take the empty plates, then continued when she was out of earshot.

'That's pretty impressive, I suppose. I mean, doesn't that technically make her a princess?'

'You get used to it,' Dawlish replied, leaning back in her seat. 'And it's not like she makes a big fuss over it. Look, show us your ring.' Obligingly Richard held out his hand. 'See that circle round the sigil? That means it's a hereditary title. Double circles means it's a distaff title— passed down through the female line only.'

'How do you know all this stuff?'

'Because I asked people? Learned stuff?' Dawlish scowled. 'You think you're the first person to fall into this world without a clue?'

'Yes, you mentioned accidents.' Richard gave her a knowing look.

'We're not all born to this life.' Dawlish sullenly crossed her arms across her chest. 'Sometimes normal people get caught up in stuff that they shouldn't, and then they have a choice to become part of this world or shut their eyes and go back. Only sometimes that choice gets made for you. Because you can't go back, even if you wanted to.'

'That's what happened to you, isn't it?' Richard guessed. Dawlish wouldn't meet his eyes.

'I was stupid,' she said after a long pause. 'I ran away. I was only a kid, a stupid kid. But when I realised . . . when

I tried . . . There wasn't a home for me to go back to, okay?' She sat back in the booth and pulled her knees up to her chin.

'I'm sorry,' said Richard gently.

'What for? You didn't do anything.'

'Is that why you owe Kate and the Baron so much? Because they took you in?'

Dawlish gave a shocked little laugh.

'God, no! I said I owe them my life, not just a bed for the night. That actually means something in this world, you know.'

'So tell me, then, what happened?'

The waitress returned at that point with their meals. Dawlish watched her warily until she had retreated and pointedly ignored the tutting noise she made when she saw Dawlish's feet up on the booth's seat. She made a face at the woman's back then turned to her food. She took a giant bite out of her burger and examined Richard as she chewed.

'All right,' she said as she swallowed. 'If you must know. The Weirding isn't all sweetness and light and dragons and unicorns.'

'I hardly think dragons count as sweetness and light.'

Dawlish flashed him a dark glare.

'Compared to some of the things that are out there, they are. There's some real evil shit out there, and if you're not careful—well, there aren't any second chances. When I ran away, I tried to go back home but one of those evil things got there first. It was there, in my home, wearing my face.'

'Wearing . . .?'

'I don't mean all Hannibal Lecter or anything, just, it

looked like me. A changeling. It was this horrible, freaky thing, and it was in my home, with my parents, pretending to be me.' Dawlish's expression was like a wounded dog, the hurt stinging in her face.

'That sounds . . .' Richard couldn't find the word.

'What? Awful? Sad? What a terrible thing to do to a kid? Please, spare me.'

'I'm sorry,' Richard said. 'I lost my parents young, too. Well, my dad. But at least I could grieve. You didn't even have that, and worse, it must have been hell knowing they couldn't tell the difference. That's worse than losing them, in a way.'

Dawlish gave him another appraising look. 'You're not quite as clueless as you look, are you?'

'Coming from you, I'll take that as a compliment.'

Dawlish sniffed, but didn't contradict him.

'So what happened?'

'I did something very stupid,' she said, taking another bite out of her burger. 'I tried to cut a deal to get my life back.' She swallowed. 'You remember those evil things I mentioned? Well, I gave one of them something. Something very important. To make the thing go away. And it did, but . . .' she sighed and looked away. 'It wasn't the same. I couldn't forget what had happened, how easily I'd been, you know . . .' She pushed her plate away despondently.

'I think I know what you mean,' Richard said.

'I tried to call it off. The deal, I mean. Because it wasn't worth it. What I traded . . . What I got wasn't worth a fraction of it. But he wouldn't give it back.'

'What was it?' Richard asked. Dawlish stretched out a hand. Like all the others, she wore a signet ring, but the disk that adorned it was blank.

'That,' she said. 'My essence. What makes me who I am.'

'Your soul?'

'If you like. That's how much I owe Kate and the Baron. They got it back for me. And they still have it, 'til I can repay the debt. That's why my ring is blank. No soul. Nothing to see here.' She sighed and picked at the chips still on her plate. 'Look, can we skip pudding? I'm not really hungry any more.'

The jackdaws circled the hill—black specks in a grey sky, wheeling through the clouds like tea leaves floating in a cup. They could feel the pressure in the air. The grey stone of Penshaw Monument squatted, looming over the landscape, a slate-coloured crow perching haggard on a fencepost, waiting for the slaughter.

Echoing through the mind's ear came a dull thump, a distant crack of drums and grating ancient screams. The boundary between the worlds shook like a speaker with each impact, as again and again, the Wyrm battered itself against the walls of its cage. Somewhere out there was the prey that would slake its thirst, but it was wary now, and the bars were holding. Coils lashing in pain and unfulfilled need, it curled around itself, a hunched spring of deadly energy. It could not reach the prey, but the prey could reach it. It began to hum. A deep, gentle buzz, lilting and soaring discordantly. Eerie, inhuman, and compelling as an itch. The jackdaws scattered as the sound grew, throbbing through the ground. The Wyrm settled down to wait—after all, every cage has a key . . .

'How are you getting back home?' Richard asked Dawlish as they wandered back down Grainger Street towards Grey's Monument.

'I have my ways.'

'Why do I get the impression that you're not talking about the Metro?'

'Because I'm not.'

'Oh?'

Dawlish sighed and looked at Richard askance. 'You want me to show you? I could drop you off at your place before I head back to Durham.'

'Won't that be rather out of your way?' Richard frowned.

'Yes, but it'll only take five minutes or so.'

'All right,' he smiled. 'Colour me intrigued.'

'You know, I think that's the same Earl Grey that the tea's named for,' she said, gazing up at the distant figure atop the column. 'Helped abolish slavery as well. If it's the person I'm thinking of.'

'I really couldn't say,' said Richard. 'Local history's not my strong point.'

'Doesn't really matter.' Dawlish turned away. 'I was just wondering.' She circled the column to the right and stopped in front of what Richard could now see was a small blue door, set low into the base of the plinth. He didn't think he'd noticed such a thing before. Dawlish leant nonchalantly against the monument, next to the door, and slipped a hand into her trouser pocket.

'Keep an eye out for anyone watching us, will you?' she asked. 'And just act casual.'

'Why? What are you going to do?'

'Just do it,' she hissed, and before he could protest further, she crouched down and started fiddling with the door.

'Dawlish?'

'That's got it, come on.' He looked down and saw that she'd managed to get the door open somehow.

'Should we really be—'

'Talk later, come on,' she cut him off and ducked quickly through the doorway. Richard cast a quick glance around, but no one seemed to have noticed, so he followed Dawlish as she disappeared inside the statue.

CHAPTER 16

KEYS AND CLOCKS

I t's a key,' said Helen when Kate picked up the phone. 'That bracelet you wanted looked at. It's a key.'

'A key?' asked Kate.

'Very much like the signet rings. I had no idea you could make them from silver.'

If Kate was surprised, her voice didn't show it.

'What does it open?' she asked.

'A single lock.'

'Which one?'

Helen paused.

'You say Tom Lampton gave you this?' she said, looking sidelong at Kate.

'Yes.'

'Tell me . . . was he wearing it when he died?'

'How would I know that?' Kate answered a little too quickly.

'All right, don't tell me. But if he was, then I think you

have your answer.'

Kate considered this for a moment. 'You'd better forward it to Richard,' she said at last.

'Any note?'

'No. He's the Lampton heir; he'll figure it out.'

Richard didn't know what he was expecting as he stepped through the doorway, but what he found on the other side wasn't it.

'It's like a TARDIS,' he said. 'Bigger on the inside.'

It was a round room, much bigger than the plinth could have contained but still quite small. The walls, where you could see them, were smooth grey stone, but mostly they were covered with doors. Each door was, itself, covered with pieces of paper, criss-crossed with spidery black lines and webs of ink. One of them looked almost like a map of the London Underground, another like a timetable of the tides and phases of the moon, a third like an astrological chart.

'What is all this?' he asked, attempting to figure out what any of it meant.

'It's a control centre,' replied Dawlish, who was studying one wall of paper, her nose almost pressed up against it.

'Control centre? What do you control here?'

'The world. No, really. I have a white cat and a shark pool around here somewhere.' Dawlish rolled her eyes.

'I'm just asking.'

'I control the clock-roads,' she replied. 'And if you don't let me concentrate for a minute or two, I won't be able to find out how to get you back home, and we could end up in outer Mongolia by accident.'

'Outer Mongolia? Really?'

'Probably not. But the wrong end of the country, certainly. Now will you shush?'

'Will you tell me what you mean by a clock-road if I do?'

Dawlish gave him a withering look. 'Sheesh, you're like a child. All right, all right, I'll explain once we get there. Now zippit.' She turned back to the charts and started muttering to herself.

After a few more minutes, while Richard waited as quietly as he could, trying to make sense of some of the papers on the opposite wall, Dawlish straightened. She licked a finger and held it up, as if testing to see which way the wind was blowing; then, seeming satisfied, turned to the door nearest her on the right and counted round three doors clockwise.

'All right,' she said, moving to that door. 'It's this way.'

'Are you sure?' asked Richard in a mock-serious tone. 'I don't like the sound of outer Mongolia this time of year.'

'Jokes don't suit you,' Dawlish said, shifting a few of the papers out of the way so she could see the door-handle. 'You're enough of one already.'

'Thanks,' muttered Richard, scowling.

'No problem.' She reached into her pocket and pulled out a thin silver chain, like a rope of rainwater. On it hung two old-fashioned looking keys, each about five inches long, one a bright silver, the other, slightly smaller, deep black. The haft of each key fanned out into lacy circles of intricate metalwork. The detailed twists seemed to have a pattern in them, but at that distance, Richard couldn't see what it was. Dawlish reached for the silver key, slipped it into the lock of the door, then turned it three times in the lock. The door opened with a soft click.

'Coming, then?' she asked as she walked through. Richard followed her and was startled to find himself stepping out into a flowerbed. He turned around and saw that the door they had just emerged from was set in the side of a large ornamental clock.

'This is the park near my house!' he said, looking round him as if to check that what he was seeing was true.

'Don't look so surprised,' said Dawlish, clumping over the petunias and onto the lawn. 'People will think you're an idiot.'

'But how is that possible?' Richard asked, following her with somewhat more care for the plants.

'I don't know; it just is.'

'You said you'd explain how it works,' Richard reminded her.

'Did I?' Dawlish sighed. 'Oh all right, then. But can we walk and talk? I could do with a cup of tea.'

Richard nodded, and they fell into step next to each other.

'The clock-roads are my discovery,' Dawlish began. 'Most people in the Weirding have some way of getting about quickly, and this is mine. It's tricky, but it's still faster and cheaper than the bus.'

'So I can see.'

'You know clocks, like the one in the park? The big town clocks that you find in squares, looking like little Big Bens? They're everywhere in this country. So are monuments and statues. And most of them have doors in them.

All the clocks do, so you can get to the mechanism. And inside they're all the same.'

Richard shook his head slightly.

'I can't say I've been inside enough clocks to compare.'

'No, I don't mean they're similar; I mean they're all the same inside. The same space. You step inside one clock, you end up in the same room as you would if you stepped into a different clock half a mile away. It's the same place. Of course, it's only the same place in our world—the Weirding one—and you need a special key to get to it, but I've got the key.'

By this time they had reached Richard's front door, and he took out his own key to let them in. Bobble, with his usual affection, dive-bombed their heads as they entered, then snuggled up to Dawlish to be petted.

'I've actually got two keys,' she said, tickling Bobble's chest, fluffing up the feathers. 'I've just not figured out what one of them does yet.'

'How do you mean?' Richard automatically began filling the kettle for a cup of tea.

'I mean, I haven't figured out how to work it. With the silver key it's difficult enough. You don't just have to pick the right door, you have to open it the right way. And it all depends on so many different things. It's taken me ages to map out the safe routes, and that's just the major ones and the ones immediately round here.'

'Safe routes?'

'I wasn't kidding about outer Mongolia, you know.'

'Can I see these keys?' Richard asked as he brought the mugs of tea to the table. Dawlish looked wary for a moment then drew the silver chain out of her pocket again.

As she passed it over, Richard was struck by how heavy the keys were. They felt solid and reliable in his hands, and he understood why Dawlish was drawn to them.

'I like the patterns on the handles,' he said, examining the intricate metalwork. 'Is there any significance to the pictures?'

'What pictures?' asked Dawlish, frowning.

'In the metalwork. The clock and the door.'

'What clock?' Dawlish sat forwards, snatching at the keys. Richard shifted round to show her.

'Here, see?' he pointed at the silver one. 'The handle and frame? That's a door, isn't it? And the black one, doesn't that look like a clock to you?'

'Only if you squint,' replied Dawlish acerbically. 'If you turn it upside down it looks like a wine glass.'

'Do you think it's important?'

'Could be. Might be just decoration. I can't really say. Especially when I don't know what the black key actually does.' She sighed and took a draught of her tea as she slipped the keys back into her pocket. 'Look, it's getting late.'

'Do you want me to walk you back?'

'What am I, six?' Dawlish drained her mug and stood up. 'Thanks, but I think I can manage.'

Richard saw Dawlish to the door, then stood, watching her disappear down the road. She was right; it was getting late. The gorgeous autumn evening, all greens and ochre light in the trees, was just beginning to work up a lustre.

Richard would have loved, just at this moment, to relax in the burnished glow of the day's last sunshine, but inwardly he was steeling himself to make a phone call. He took the piece of paper with the name and address Cimron had given him out of his back pocket and stared at it.

"Take someone with you," she had said. Well, once you had ruled out Kate and Dawlish, there wasn't really that much choice. He only had a phone number for one other person who might not think he was completely insane. Richard sighed and typed Jenny's number into his mobile. He only had half an idea of what to say to her; he was still conscious of having called her before, thinking it would be Kate answering, and messing it up quite badly. Oh well. Time to bite the bullet.

The phone didn't ring enough times for him to second guess himself before she picked up.

'Hello?'

'Hi, Jenny?'

'Yes?' She sounded tentative.

'It's Richard.'

'Oh.'

Her silence was worrying.

'I'm sorry for whatever it was that I said wrong last time we spoke. For everything I said wrong. Probably just for everything. I'm sorry.'

'Okay.' She still sounded sad more than anything. Richard decided to get to the point.

'Listen, I'm sorry for this as well, and you're probably going to think I'm insane for even asking, but . . . well, I need a favour.'

'Yes?'

'I need to go and see some people in Gosforth tonight,

and I wondered if you'd like to come with me? Not, like, to hold my hand or anything. Just . . . yeah. We could go out for a meal or some drinks afterwards?'

He heard a whispering on the other end of the line, like someone was covering the mouthpiece, then Jenny sighed.

'All right,' she said.

'Great!' Richard began to breathe again. 'Shall I head round to yours, then, and pick you up?'

'Sure. I'm just off Osbourne Road. If you park in the Pizza Express car park, I'll meet you there?'

'Okay, sure,' Richard glanced at his watch. 'I'll see you in about an hour, then?'

'Sure.'

And Richard found himself holding a dead receiver.

'Well played,' said Kate as Jenny put down the phone.

'What do you mean?' Jenny folded her legs up underneath herself, making a little ball on the sofa.

'Terse, calm, you didn't cry once! No, really, hard to get is probably the best way to go at the moment. Keep him guessing.'

'Don't,' said Jenny, snuffling into a tissue. 'I just didn't expect him to call. And I didn't want him to think I'd been crying.'

'But you have been crying. Almost non-stop since I got here. It's getting very wearing.' Kate started tapping her unlit cigarette on the table in an impatient way.

'He doesn't have to know that.'

'No, he doesn't. But I do.'

'Kate . . .'

'I'm insensitive, so shoot me.' Kate sat back in exasperation and drained her mug of tea.

'How could he just forget about me like that?' Jenny started sniffing again.

'Oh, for God's sake Jen, you've had ten years to get over this! Grow up!'

'I can't!' Jenny sobbed.

'Yes, I suppose that is the point, really.' Kate got up and took the empty mugs back into the kitchen. 'But you've got to pull yourself together. For my sake, if not your own.'

'But what if—'

'Enough!' Kate slammed the kettle down onto its baseplate. 'I've had enough of this! Now,' she pulled Jenny off the sofa, 'you are going to go into your bedroom, and you are going to wipe your eyes, and you are going to get out of those pyjamas, put on something absolutely stunning, with a pair of heels, and then you are going to go out there and see what he wants.'

'But—'

'Go!'

Jenny nodded and meekly slipped off into the next room.

'Where is he taking you?' asked Kate through the door.

'Somewhere in Gosforth,' replied Jenny. 'Why?'

'What's he doing in Gosforth?' muttered Kate, almost to herself. 'There's no one lives there I can see Dick wanting to see.'

Richard pulled up in the car park Jenny had described. Osbourne Road, a strip of restaurants and bars, was heaving with people dressed up for a night out, but no one that he recognised. A week ago, he might have been one of them. Here, just off the main road, he could hear the bustle of life without being part of it. He wondered if this was how it would always be from now on: only ever looking in on normal life, not participating any more. This world he had found himself part of would preclude the kind of existence he had been used to.

He hadn't been waiting long before he heard the click of heels on the pavement coming towards him, and a mousey-haired woman in a flattering black halter-neck dress appeared in his rear-view mirror. It took him a second glance to realise that it was Jenny. He hadn't recognised her for a moment. He got out of the car to meet her and suddenly realised that, in her heels, she was actually taller than he was. It was almost more disconcerting than the rest of the ensemble put together.

'Hi,' he said, suddenly nervous.

'Hello.'

Neither of them spoke.

'So . . .'

'Where are we going?' Jenny asked.

'To see some people. I'm not really sure who. Cimron didn't tell me much, so . . .'

'Okay.'

'I mean they could be . . . well . . . anything.' He sighed. He would have to explain. Well, some of it at any rate. 'I don't know how much you know about me—'

'All of it. Trust me.'

Richard pulled up short.

'What, everything?'

'You were going to tell me about the Weirding?' Jenny looked at her feet. 'Well, there's no need. I know.'

'Oh. Good. That's good. That makes things simpler.' He walked round and opened the passenger door for her. She was about to get in but stopped, the car door between them.

'You weren't really planning on taking me out for dinner, were you?' she said, in resigned tones.

'Okay,' Richard looked away shamefacedly, 'dinner wasn't my main reason for asking you.'

'I thought as much,' she sighed and got in the car. Richard walked back around and got in next to her.

'I'm sorry,' he said. 'We can go out afterwards, if you like.'

'You don't have to.'

'But you got all dressed up for it.' Richard shot a glance over at her. Her expression was unreadable.

'Not that dressed up.'

'You look nice though,' said Richard, and knew as he said it that it was the right thing to say. She beamed at him and appeared to relax.

'Thanks,' she said, and Richard felt things were going to be all right.

CHAPTER 17

BLOOD AND GUNS

The tall Georgian house was at the end of an extended close, heavily shrouded in sycamore trees. Their leaves were just beginning to colour for autumn but hadn't yet worked up a full burnish. Two weeping willows hung long grey strands over the gate and black wrought-iron fence outside and were beginning to shed. The path was overgrown with weeds poking through the paving. It was hard to see where they began and the scrubby lawn, choked with tall grasses and dandelions, ended. The few flower beds, up against the house, were almost bare, their only occupants a few rose bushes of a red so dark it could almost be black and two hard to identify spiky white shrubs which might actually have been dead.

Jenny paused just inside the gate.

'What is it?' Richard asked.

'Honesty.'

'What about it?'

'Over there.' Jenny smiled and bent down to where a

spindly sort of plant was growing. Stiff and skeletal with papery white leaves, Richard had assumed it was dead. 'It's supposed to be good luck.'

'Really? Do you think they'd mind if we took a sprig?'

'I doubt it.' Jenny looked up at the house. 'I'm not sure if this place is even occupied.'

Richard glanced at the windows. He couldn't see any movement within. Despite it not being quite dark yet, all the curtains were closed, and thick, black tape showed round the edges where they met the frames. The blue paint was flaking off the door, and the hinges looked rusted shut. Richard had to admit to himself: Jenny was right. It didn't look occupied at all.

'Well, it's definitely the address Cimron gave me,' he said, stretching out a tentative hand to ring the doorbell. It was stiff but still produced an impressive clang which echoed through the house.

'Well, at least that's working,' said Jenny. 'Still some signs of life.'

'I think it may be the only one,' said Richard as the sonorous chimes failed to produce any response. He tried again. This time, after a few moments' pause, they heard footsteps in the house that sounded as if they were coming from a long way away. A key grated in the lock, and in fits and starts, the door ground open a few centimetres on the chain.

'Yes?' a voice emanated from the other side. Richard stepped back off the doorstep and craned his neck trying to make out some shape in the gloom on the other side of the frame.

'My name's Richard Lampton,' he said, when nothing more was forthcoming. 'Cimron sent me. She said you might be able to help.'

The shadows gave a small grunt from beyond the portal, and the door shut again. Richard heard the rattle as the chain came off, then the door swung back. The figure who opened it stepped backwards into the shadow of the hallway before Richard could get a proper look at him in the light. He was shorter than Richard but stockier, wearing something large, black, and misshapen. His hair, too, was black, greasy, and fell in his eyes, keeping his face permanently half-concealed.

'Hi,' said Richard. The man didn't reply and instead stalked off down the passage. Tentatively, Richard followed.

'Are you sure about this?' whispered Jenny, hovering on the front step.

'No, but I'm not sure we have any option now. It'd be rude of us to just bolt.'

Jenny frowned, still hesitant, but followed Richard into the house and shut the door behind her.

The hallway was narrow and murky. The light fittings on the walls flickered like old-fashioned gas lamps and illuminated barely anything. The wallpaper was peeling in places, and both that and the carpet were of a dirty paisley pattern in brown, green, and mustard yellow. They looked very much as if they had been put in round about 1960 and not been cleaned since. Dark oil paintings—muted brown landscapes and indistinct portraits—hung on the walls in heavy gilt frames. The place smelled thick with dust and undisturbed air. Their guide led them down the hallway, past a flight of stairs leading up into darkness, and into a back kitchen.

The air in the grubby yellow room was fogged with

smoke. A haze of it hovered near the bare bulb in the ceiling, rising up from its three occupants. They were women, painfully thin with high, sharp cheek bones. Two stood over by the blacked-out window, while the third was sitting with her feet up on a small Formica table. All three were adding to the cloud by means of black, gold-ended cigarettes. They had been chatting amongst themselves but fell silent when they saw Richard and Jenny. Three knife-like gazes were trained on the two of them, and though none of them looked more substantial than autumn leaves, for some reason Richard felt like a rabbit faced with a room full of foxes.

'What is it, Andrei?' asked the one sitting at the table in a voice which had just a touch of a Slavic lilt to it. She, too, was very pale, a pallor which was highlighted by pixie-short black hair and a very dark plum lipstick. She wore tight knee-length leather boots, denim shorts with jagged, cut-off edges, and a man's white shirt.

The man who had brought them in shrugged and muttered something indistinct. Richard was no expert, but he thought it might have been Czech. One of the women by the window, whose long blonde hair cascaded down past her waist, threw another comment across the room in the same language. The third, who had yet to speak, turned her head to hide a smirk.

'Ana . . .' the one at the table said in tones of reproach. 'They are guests in our home.'

Out of the corner of his eye, Richard saw Jenny flinch at that and wondered, with a chill, what else they could have been. Behind them, the man referred to as Andrei shuffled out.

'Who are they then?' asked the third—a petite, auburn-haired figure in a black biker jacket and short, red halter-neck dress.

'Um, my name's Richard Lampton,' Richard began, but as he turned to introduce Jenny, she shook her head and instead held out her right hand, wrist slightly bent. She was wearing a signet ring. Richard wasn't sure how he'd managed to miss it before, but the woman at the table had glanced over it, and she withdrew her hand before he had time to see the device. He wasn't entirely sure there was one. Following suit, he held out his own ring for inspection. The woman nodded, then leaned forwards, drawing a chain, like a set of dog-tags, from around her neck. Another gold band dangled from its links, and she passed it over.

'I'm Nadya,' she said, as Richard cast an eye over the stylised rose symbol in the gold, 'and this is Ana and Irina. What is it that you want here, Richard Lampton?'

'I'm not quite sure,' he replied, passing the ring back. Nadya sniffed and tucked it back into her shirt. Over by the window, Irina hoisted herself onto the counter-top, kicking her heels against the cupboard underneath. She stubbed out her cigarette, then immediately reached for the packet on the windowsill and lit another.

'You know those things'll kill you,' remarked Richard. Irina laughed as if he had said something genuinely funny.

'I like this one,' she said in her lilting tones.

'Why don't you two sit?' Nadya suggested and kicked a chair out from under the table. It skittered across the floor towards Richard. As it did, he noticed a large, black-stained bandage over her knee. He sat down. Jenny pulled up another chair for herself next to him.

'Is there anything we can get you?' Ana asked, waving a vague hand at the kitchen. 'Drink, perhaps?' Without waiting for an answer, she reached up to the shelf behind her and took down an earthenware jug, into which she began pouring vodka and tomato juice in roughly equal measures.

'Erm . . . no thanks,' said Richard.

'Suit yourself,' shrugged Nadya. She took the glass handed to her, but did not drink. 'So what do you want?'

'Cimron sent me. She said you might be able to help?'

'Help? With what?'

'I need to kill the Lampton Wyrm.'

The atmosphere in the room suddenly changed. It took on a stiffness, an alertness that hadn't been there before. Irina threw out a question in the same language that they had used before. Nadya checked her with a start.

'You'll need to speak to Makar,' she said.

'Makar?' Richard's brow furrowed at the prospect of yet another mysterious stranger. Nadya signalled to Ana, who rose and slid round behind Richard and Jenny and out of the kitchen. As she passed, Richard heard the cold whisper of fabric as her long gypsy skirt grazed the floor, but her footfalls themselves were silent. He was beginning to feel decidedly uncomfortable with this encounter.

'What are you doing battling with dragons?' murmured Nadya once Ana had disappeared.

'I didn't really get a choice.'

'Nonsense. There is always a choice.'

'It's hunting me, and it won't stop until I'm dead. I don't call that much of a choice.'

'There is still a choice. You could run. You could lie down and die.'

'Who would ever choose that?' asked Jenny sharply.

'And what would you know about it, little girl?'

snapped Nadya. 'What business have you with killing?'

'I could ask you the same.'

'I don't think you'd like that answer,' smirked Irina. Nadya's expression hardened. She lifted her tattered jeans, exposing the bandage on her right thigh. Black pus oozed through the gauze, and the skin on either side of the bandage was turning a pale, bruised green.

'Don't mock me,' she said. 'And don't mock the choices you're given. Sometimes flight or death are better options. This wound will probably never heal. Many of my friends, my brothers, were not as lucky as I. I wonder if you understand, truly, what you stand to lose by choosing the fight.'

'I'm counting on it being less than if I don't,' Richard replied with a firm tilt of the head. Nadya raised an eyebrow and swung her leg back under the table.

'I hope you're right,' she said. 'For your sakes.'

'Nevertheless, it was well said.' A thick, dark voice with the same strong eastern-European accents emanated from over Richard's shoulder. He hadn't heard anyone come in. He tried to turn round, but there wasn't enough space. Instead, a tall figure slid silently past him and into the kitchen. This man, like the three women, was thin and pale and was wearing faded black robes which hung off him like a flag taken out of the wind. He walked round the table, bent down, and kissed Nadya on the forehead. She looked up at him and smiled, then allowed him to lift her out of the chair in a movement as smooth as poured cream. He held out an arm and Irina hopped down off the counter to join them.

'Makar,' she smiled.

'My dears, you should go,' he said, accepting her embrace. 'From the look on this man's face, I fear this conversation will mostly be shop-talk, and you know how that bores you.' He took each woman's hand in his, raised it to his lips, and gently ushered them both out of the room before turning back to his guests.

'Have my women offered you hospitality?' he asked. 'Drink? Smokes?'

'Yes, and we're both fine, thank you.'

'Good.' Makar slid into the seat that Nadya had just vacated. He moved with the silky grace of an old-fashioned movie starlet and economically as a cat. Like a predator, when he was still, he was still, not a move wasted. 'Now,' he continued, 'what may I do for you?'

'Um . . .' A sucking void of silence filled the air across the table. Now that it actually came to it, Richard wasn't sure what he was asking for.

'Cimron sent us,' said Jenny, glancing over at Richard for confirmation. 'She said you might help us. We need to fight a Wyrm.'

'I need to fight it,' Richard corrected. 'But, yes.'

'I see.' Makar leaned back, steepling his fingers. 'You need weapons.'

'Yes. Yes, I suppose I do.'

'You wish to buy a gun?'

Richard was taken aback. He hadn't expected . . . but then what had he expected? He wanted to kill the Wyrm; how had he planned on doing it? With a flaming sword? A magic wand? His bare hands? That would be ludicrous. As if reading his mind, Makar continued, 'It used to be the silver blade, or the lance of Holy Flames, or the bow and arrows of phoenix feather, but such things are hard to come by in these days where magic does not rule as once it did.

And gunpowder and lead fill a creature as full of holes as one could wish.'

'Right. Yes.' Richard found himself coming over all business-like. It simplified things. 'A gun.' The word tasted blunt and final in his mouth. 'What have you got?'

'I have very, very old Soviet connections. In a week, perhaps a month, I can get you anything you need,' replied Makar in slow, silky tones.

'A month?' Richard looked across at Jenny. 'That should be enough time, shouldn't it?'

'If not, I still carry some small stock here.' Makar, still looking across the table at Richard, stood and backed away into the kitchen. He bent down and took a small black box from one of the cupboards under the counter. 'This is Polish made,' he said, bringing it over to the table and opening it to display the contents.

'A handgun?' Richard looked into the box at the matt black metal. 'You're expecting me to go after the Wyrm with a handgun?'

'No. Of course not. There is a pair in that box.'

'A pair of handguns?' Richard wasn't entirely sure if that had been a joke.

'I still would not counsel you to hunt the creature,' continued Makar. 'Not alone and not with these. I can get you better, but it will take a little more time. Though these are hardly powerless. Look.' He passed Richard the small cardboard box which held the bullets. '9mm hollow points. Expanding slugs. Luger rounds. Do not try and use the Russian ammunition.'

'Why?' asked Richard, still unsure what a Luger round was. 'What happens?'

'In the best case, the gun will simply not fire. If you

are unlucky, it might explode in your face.'

'You don't have anything more stable?'

'These are very stable. And you may use them with either hand. I could get laser sights for them as well, but I believe you will be aiming at a very large target.' He smiled. It looked odd on his face, not as if he were making a joke at all. Richard tried to smile along.

'How much do you want for them?' he asked.

'That depends. Do you truly intend to kill this beast?'

'I'm going to have to. It's that or be killed myself.'

'That is good.' Makar closed the box and pushed it halfway across the table, but didn't take his hand off the lid. 'Then what I ask of you is this: when it is dead, I wish for one of its fangs. Can you do that for me?'

'One of its fangs?'

'The teeth of a dragon are powerful things. I would consider one more than adequate reimbursement.'

'And if the Wyrm kills me before I can kill it?'

'Don't talk like that!' Jenny snapped. One of her hands impulsively flew across the table top towards Richard's. She squeezed it once, then dropped it, as if caught doing something she shouldn't.

'Thanks,' Richard glanced over at her, then gave her hand a quick squeeze in return. 'But it is something I have to consider.'

'I wish you wouldn't.'

'He would be a fool not to,' returned Makar. 'Only an imbecile fights dragons and does not entertain the possibility of failure. Though, should that be the case, I shall consider your debt to me cancelled.'

'Why would you take such a gamble?'

'I prefer to think of it as an investment. One that I believe may pay great dividends someday.'

'All right then,' Richard held out his hand across the table. 'I think we have a deal.'

'Excellent.' Makar extended his own palm. His hand was cold and limp, like a perished elastic band. Richard picked up the box from the table, and the silent man who had answered the door showed them back out again.

'I'm glad that's over,' Jenny said, shuffling her feet against the pavement.

'Me too,' Richard sighed. The box under his arm felt heavy as a black hole, sucking the world into itself. 'I have had just about my fill of weird people for today. And weird things. And guns. I have no idea where I'm going to put these, by the way. Where exactly do people keep things like this?'

'Locked boxes?'

'I figured that much.' They mooched down the street back in the direction of the car. 'So where to now?' Richard asked as they approached.

'What do you mean?'

'I was supposed to be taking you out somewhere or something?'

'I did say you don't have to.'

Richard sighed thankfully. 'Good, because I'm dead beat. How do you feel about heading back to my place and sharing a pizza?'

Jenny's look of apprehension suddenly melted into a shy smile.

'Pizza sounds perfect,' she said, climbing into the car.

CHAPTER 18

THE KEY

Helen didn't even look up from her book when the magpie landed on her drawing room window ledge. The curtains blowing at the window showed that it was already opened just wide enough to let the bird hop through, and a small bowl of shelled peanuts sat on the coffee table by the piano.

'Come in,' said Helen, though the magpie had made it quite obvious that it was going to come in anyway. It fluttered over the sill and made a casual bee-line for the bowl. 'I suppose that means your master isn't far away?' she asked it. The bird, already wolfing down the nuts, didn't even look up. Helen put the book to one side, unfolded herself from the sofa and, without rushing, crossed the room to the French windows and unlocked them, allowing the Baron to make his entrance. She padded back to her seat while he hastily pulled back the glass to let himself in. Three more magpies had appeared to squabble over the peanuts.

'That's all they're getting,' Helen said, watching the

piebald birds fight over the bowl. 'So they'd be best to share. What with your birds and Kate's birds and every other type of wretched animal that I've had to make nice to this week, I'm running low on appropriate sustenance.' The Baron flicked his wrist and they quietened down somewhat.

'Winged menaces aside,' he said, taking the seat by the piano, 'I need a word with you.'

'Evidently.' Helen didn't look up from her book. 'You don't strike me as the type to make personal calls.'

'I'll come to the point. What did Kate bring you the last time she was here?'

'You mean you've been hanging round at the end of my drive for a glimpse of her half the nights this last month and you don't know? You disappoint me.'

'Not half as much as you disappoint me, Helen. And as you should know, that's not the wisest of ideas. I thought you were cleverer than that.' At that, Helen put her book to one side, and her eyes narrowed.

'Idle threats will get you nowhere. You'd be best remembering that I don't owe you a thing.' Helen stood up and went to close the French windows. The Baron hadn't fastened them properly and one door had blown open.

'How much?' he asked as she paused, her hand on the catch. She didn't need to ask him what he meant, and she didn't feign shock. Just quietly named a sum.

'That's an awful lot for a small piece of information,' he said. She returned to the sofa with a dainty shrug.

'Evidently this is worth a lot to you.'

'Very well.' The Baron reached into a coat pocket and drew out a small leather pouch. He tossed it gently at her. 'It's unmarked gold,' he said as she caught it. 'Check the weight—it ought to cover it easily.'

'And how do I know it won't disappear in the morning?' asked Helen, throwing it back to him. 'I know you. I'll take a proper cheque, if you please.' The Baron sighed and brought out a cheque book.

'Pen?' he asked, leaning on the coffee table. Helen handed one over. 'I just want you to know,' he said deliberately as he wrote out the cheque, 'that I don't like you. Not one bit.'

Helen smiled. 'You don't have to,' she replied with candour. 'In fact, I'm almost glad you don't. It makes things simpler.'

'Fine.' He tore the piece of paper out of the book and handed it over to her. 'Tell me.'

'It was a bracelet.' Helen tucked the cheque neatly into a pocket. 'An ouroboros—a snake biting its own tail. I determined for her that it was a key of the Weirding but not what it opens.' She retrieved the pen as well, screwed the lid on, and dropped it into a drawer in the coffee table. 'I don't suppose that's something you could enlighten me about, is it?' She looked up. The Baron's face was fixed in white hot fury. The smile vanished from Helen's features as well. She suddenly felt a sense of overwhelming dread, as if the house of cards she had built was missing one crucial card at the bottom and the whole thing was on the edge of collapse.

'You will have heard, I imagine,' said the Baron in a steely voice, 'of the sorcery which keeps the Lampton Wyrm caged, chained to Penshaw Hill like a djinn in a lamp? The sorcery built on my blood, bound to my will? It is a complicated thing that I would never have entered into were it not as a favour to a family I loved. Every lock must have its key. So yes, I know exactly what that bracelet opens.' Helen blanched. 'Now,' continued the Baron, 'my next question—and listen very carefully, because much depends on your answer—where is the bracelet now?'

'I . . .' Helen's voice had sunk to barely a whisper. 'Kate told me to send it to Richard Lampton.'

Richard woke to find Bobble perched on the back of the sofa, staring down at him in his makeshift bed with an expectant look.

'Morning,' Richard mumbled, still sleepy, and sat up. He glanced over at the clock; it was almost nine. 'I suppose I should be glad you let me sleep in?' he asked the bird. Bobble cawed softly but insistently and launched himself across the room to the kitchen table. Richard swung his legs round and off the sofa, almost treading in the remains of last night's pizza boxes. Trying to remain quiet, he gathered them up and carried them through into the kitchen, where Bobble, by this point, was already jumping up and down on the fridge.

'Have you never tried leftover pizza?' Richard asked. 'Food of the gods, I promise you.' He picked a few wafers of pepperoni off the top of one of the remaining slices and offered it to him. Bobble looked at it quizzically for a moment, then pecked at it. After the third piece, he seemed to have decided this new food would make an acceptable substitute for sausages and bacon and began to wolf down the bits that Richard put to one side for him. Richard himself made short work of the rest of the pizza, then disposed of the boxes and tidied up the rest of the living room.

That done, he filled the kettle and stuck his head round the bedroom door to see if he could offer Jenny a cup of tea. She was still asleep, in an old T-shirt he had lent her, one arm thrown out haphazardly from underneath the covers. She looked so warm and comfortable and safe that, for just a moment, Richard felt an urge to snuggle up next to her, like kids at a sleepover. He dismissed the thought as quickly as it had crossed his mind and shut the door quietly, hoping to let her sleep.

Back in the kitchen, Bobble had managed to retrieve one of the pizza boxes from the bin and was rooting around inside it in the hope that some more pepperoni had magically appeared within.

'Oh, stop that,' Richard murmured, flicking the kettle on. 'You've finished it all. I'll make some more sausages for you later, if I really must.' Bobble let go of the box, and it clunked back down onto the tiles. An answering clunk came from the door, and a brown padded envelope fell through the letter-box onto the mat. Leaving the kettle to boil, Richard wandered over and picked it up. It was heavy for such a small package. He tore it open and tipped out the contents into his hand. It was a silver bracelet in the shape of a snake biting its own tail. There was no note. In his palm, the green eyes flashed as if in recognition. Bobble, perched on the fridge, eyed it back with a greedy glare. Richard felt lightheaded, as if the world was standing still, holding its breath. He lifted the bracelet and slipped it over his wrist. The hard metal seemed to bend to let his hand through and then gripped his left arm tightly like a real snake would, just above the joint of his wrist. The eyes flashed again. He could hear a hum, just on the edge of perception, almost like a song . . .

'I have to go out,' Richard said dreamily. He moved unseeing to the cupboard beside the fridge where last night he had stashed the guns, took them out, tucked one into the waistband of his jeans, the other in his pocket, and walked out the front door without looking back.

The kettle boiled and then turned itself off.

Bobble's frantic cawing woke Jenny up. She opened bleary eyes to find the little bird flapping around the bedroom in a state of panic. She sat up in bed and looked round for the cause of the disturbance. Bobble fell silent and flew down to land on her shoulder. She could feel him quivering by her ear. No sound came from the rest of the house.

'Richard?' she called, swinging herself out of bed. No one answered. Opening the bedroom door, she could see that the living room was empty. So was the kitchen. She stepped out and gave the bathroom door a push. That was unlocked and empty as well.

'Richard?' She stood still for a moment, trying to catch the sound of movement. Nothing. The house was silent save for the faint gurgle of the central heating turning itself off. Keeping the door open, Jenny retreated to the bedroom and tugged on her clothes in a rush. She hoped that by the time she was dressed, Richard would have re-appeared, but the kitchen was still empty when she returned. Even worse, the front door had been left ajar.

Her insides ran cold. She bolted for the door and gazed

down the drive to the road. Richard's car was gone. Something had happened, she could feel it. The table was almost bare. No note, only a padded envelope, open and empty. Bobble was still perched on her shoulder. The house was so still she fancied she could hear his tiny heartbeat next to her ear. She sat down with a bump at the table.

'Oh, God,' she said to no one in particular. She felt like her bones had turned to water. She knew there should be something she ought to do, someone she could phone, but she couldn't get up off the chair. All she could focus on was the breeze creeping in through the open door, making the thin layer of dust on the floor dance. Spirals of sand caught by the wind began to swirl and flick into patterns, twister-like. The breeze began to pick up, and before she realised it, a wind was filling the kitchen. Higher and higher off the floor the dust danced until the patterns flew up around her ears, and then suddenly, the wind was still. For a second the dust hung in the air, then it fell away, and the Baron was standing in front of her. His gaze quickly took in the kitchen, Jenny's forlorn look, and the absence of Richard.

'Damn. I'm too late, aren't I?' he said.

Richard sat in the car parked at the side of the road at the bottom of Penshaw Hill. He had turned the engine off and rested his hands on the steering wheel. He felt giddy and dazed. He knew he must have driven there, because he remembered doing it, but he couldn't remember the sensation of driving. It was as if he had been a passenger inside his own head, looking out through his own eyes but not able to control a thing. He opened the car door and almost fell out onto the rough dirt. He sucked in great gasps of the cold Northumbrian air, waiting for it to clear his head, but as he leant back on the bonnet, he only felt more detached. It was like being drunk and floating or hanging suspended in water.

Currents of wind played against his skin. He could hear the long grass whispering to the hedgerows, and he knew that if only he leaned in closer, he would be able to understand what they said to each other. Above him, flags of cloud were racing past in the wind. A wistful, longing feeling had settled itself on his chest. Something was pulling him up the hillside, up the narrow dirt track through the pale September grass. He stepped forwards, and the snake bracelet, cool against his wrist, gave an approving squeeze.

So that's what it was. Richard's head cleared for a second. He stopped and pulled back his sleeve. The bracelet lay there on his arm, all innocent-seeming. He knew, without having to try, that like the ring, he wouldn't be able to take it off now. He wasn't even sure that he wanted to, but he eyed the cold metal with a new wariness. It had been drawing him to this place, perhaps to his death, but the knowledge that he had been led, and how, made his last shred of self-preservation wake up.

He turned back to the car. He could leave now. If he concentrated, he might be able to resist long enough to drive away. But why should he? Richard leaned through the window and picked up the guns which he had dropped on the passenger seat. They felt sturdy enough. This day would always have come, and wasn't one time as good as any other? Carefully, he fed the bullets into the magazines, thinking as he did so how each little metal charm could spell death or preservation. Each breath in seemed terribly precious, now. If he could make sure to keep breathing, keep clicking the rounds into place, that was one more breath on this earth, one more second alive, one more chance to live. Until finally both guns were filled. Sixteen rounds to a magazine, two magazines to each gun, sixty-four shots in total. He hoped it would be enough.

The morning sun came out from behind a cloud and warmed the back of his neck. Richard began to make his way up the hill. The dull grey shadow of the monument loomed large in the morning light as he took heavy steps towards it. Then suddenly it was in front of him . . . and it was deserted. There was no Wyrm.

He approached, still cautiously testing the ground beneath him as he stepped. Seventy feet of stone loomed above him—dull, smoke blackened columns, six feet wide, holding up cornice and pediments. Seven along the side, four along each end, and a gaping hole above, leaving the temple floor open to the sky. Still no sign of the Wyrm. Richard hoisted himself up onto the plinth. The air felt thick, and it was hard to pull himself up. He stood there on the lip for a moment, gazing through the open temple to the other side of the hill and the yellow-green fields drying in the morning sun.

· "'If it be now, 'tis not to come; if it be not to come, it will be now; if it be not now, yet it will come . . .'" whispered Richard to himself under his breath, the fragments of the old poet's words resting like feathers on his lips. Briefly, he wondered what would happen to Bobble. He stepped forward into the temple.

The air in front of him sprang back to let him through;

a reflective soap-bubble sheen burst as he passed between the pillars. Like the other secret places of the Weirding he had visited, as he walked into the temple, the world warped and bent around him. Inside, the sky darkened, and spreading nimbus clouds smothered the sun. The air was filled with the crackling green glow of St Elmo's fire. Everything seemed to have expanded, a crooked mirror of the world, and he wasn't quite sure how big anything was any more. He stepped backwards, feeling for the pillar and the way out but ran up against something which felt sticky and sparking. The green fire was forming itself into tangles, blocking the gaps between the pillars. He couldn't get out. Above him, the clouds began to twist and spiral. Flashes of electricity crackled and spat in the blackening swirls. Richard drew the gun from his waistband, and it all went dark.

'He's gone to fight the Wyrm, hasn't he?' said the Baron matter-of-factly.

'I don't know.' Jenny sat at the table shivering, Bobble cuddled up to her ear. 'He was gone when I woke.'

'And he didn't say anything about where he was going?'

'Not a word. Not even a note.'

The Baron wasn't really listening. He was sweeping round the kitchen, searching for something. The brown envelope which had been sitting on the edge of the table had fallen and drifted into the table leg. He pounced on it and raised it to the light.

'Just as I feared,' he said. 'Helen's handwriting. Did

you see him open this?'

'I told you, I didn't see him at all this morning.'

'We're too late,' he said. 'She's sent him the key; and worse, I know who put her up to it.'

'Key?'

'A snake bracelet. Forged by Richard's father and myself. It's the key that opens the monument and releases the Wyrm. Once Richard steps onto the temple floor wearing that bracelet, no one can get in or out again until either he kills the Wyrm or it kills him.'

'No . . .' Jenny's stomach turned over. 'We've got to stop him.'

'I'm not sure we can.' The Baron rubbed his forehead with finger and thumb. 'He could already be at the monument by now.'

'Then we've got to get up there.'

'I have to get up there,' corrected the Baron. 'I am the one who was supposed to protect that family since ancient times. I should be there. You may not wish to see the outcome.'

Jenny stared at him, fire in her gaze.

'I need to see it, no matter what.'

'If that is your wish.' The Baron held out a hand and pulled Jenny into a rough loop of his arms. At his whistle, the winds sprang up again around them, and the kitchen faded into sand.

CHAPTER 19

THE SOUND AND THE FURY

Richard couldn't see a thing. The darkness was so complete that it made no difference if his eyes were open or shut. And then he heard it. A quiet susurration, like sandpaper or the scrape of scales on stone. Richard stopped breathing. He felt around behind him until he found the pillar and then pressed his back against it, staring at the darkness as if he could will himself to see through it. He heard nothing. Then it came again, closer this time. Richard found he had to breathe again. It sounded too loud. His chest felt tight. For a moment, he thought he saw a shape, black on black, and he realised the darkness was lifting. The crackling lighting he had seen before was returning. Tendrils of green flame began flashing across the sky.

The blackness paled, and in the dull light Richard could see something moving on the other side of the temple. He thought for a moment that one of the pillars had fallen over, and it took him a moment to realise that the long, black mass was rising and falling in regular breaths. One end of it extended out to the right over the side of the plinth and looked like it was wrapping itself round the hill. He couldn't see how many times. The other end swooped up, out through the empty roof of the temple, and ended in a familiar pointed head.

His brief glimpse of the creature in the river three days ago had not prepared him for this. Evidently it grew like a weed, because it was big—far bigger than he remembered it being—and drawing the darkness around itself. It seemed to be part of the night. Its head was about a metre long from nose to neck, and he couldn't see where its tail ended. The stench of the creature was thick and acrid, its body glistened in the weird green light with an unholy slickness. The monument was so quiet that the silence was terrifying in itself. Richard tried to breathe slowly so as not to make a noise. The smell coming off the Wyrm stuck in his throat, making him wheeze.

Then it moved. Just a small shifting movement, inching itself forwards a little as the head swayed above. Searching, Richard realised, for him. The stone beneath the Wyrm's huge coils hissed as they scraped across it. Then silence. Richard, fighting to keep his hands still and feeling as if his chest had shrunk, couldn't stop thinking of the tale of the first Wyrm. And Bollbrook and the knights like him who had been killed and eaten. And the fact that he, Richard, had taken none of the advice that had saved his ancestor from sharing their fate. And then he realised none of that mattered any more, because the Wyrm had just turned its massive head and was looking directly at him.

A sense of rushing winds. The howling whisper of storms and shrieking of high gales and a constant buffeting from forces unseen. Jenny clung to the Baron's waist, burying her head in his chest to avoid the flying sand. Tiny particles of gritty gold lashed her cheeks, fought their way into the corners of her eyes and mouth, up her nose, and stung just about every patch of bare skin she had. She tried to breathe through the fabric of the Baron's shirt, inhaling his distinctive wet-forest scent. Bobble, still perched on her shoulder, had no such luxury and huddled against her ear pathetically. Then the rushing feeling passed, and the sand dispersed. Jenny shook the particles from her hair, feeling dried out and weathered. Bobble fluttered like a dog shaking itself dry and gave the Baron a meaningful squawk.

'Don't you talk back to me,' he muttered, dusting himself down. 'Bad mannered little corvid.'

'I can't see Richard,' said Jenny, looking around. They were standing next to Richard's car, and above them the monument loomed, unassuming. 'Perhaps we got here in time, perhaps he's left already?' Even as she said it, Jenny knew she was wrong. She felt something off-key about the monument. An eerie green flicker and a feeling of pressure surrounded it, which only got worse as they walked up the hill towards it. Up close, they could see the barrier drifting ominously around the pillars.

'Don't touch it,' said the Baron, grabbing Jenny's hand as she reached for the space between the columns.

'Why?'

'Because I honestly don't know what would happen if

you did.'

'Oh.'

Jenny's face caught the Baron's eye.

'Don't look so bloody worried,' he said. 'He's not dead yet.'

Richard might not have been dead, but the distinction was feeling academic. The Wyrm was staring at him. It hadn't moved, not even blinked. Had it even seen him? It didn't matter anyway: he was transfixed to the spot. He was still holding the gun in one hand, dangling uselessly by his side. Slowly, trying not to attract the creature's attention, he raised it to chest height. The Wyrm blinked, and as fast as he could, Richard whipped the gun forward and squeezed the trigger. The bang that broke the silence was like a foot thick sheet of ice breaking, and in that moment, he thought the Wyrm had hit him. The recoil sent him thudding into the pillar behind him. His wrist took most of the force, and he barely held onto the gun-stock. The bullet went badly wide, barely catching the creature's snout, and not enough to penetrate the skin. It hissed like a cat and peeled back its lips to flash its huge teeth and a dark, forked tongue. Richard swore violently and grabbed his wrist, which was now an explosion of pain. Holding the gun in both hands, he took aim again, but before he could squeeze the trigger, the Wyrm lunged.

Richard threw himself to one side and landed painfully on his shoulder. The Wyrm crashed into the pillar, leaving a fault line crack. It reared back and screeched like tortured metal. Richard scrambled to his feet and raised the gun once more. He got off three rounds before the Wyrm dived at him again. Richard lunged back towards the cracked pillar and rammed up against it, hard, but held himself together enough to fire, this time directly into the back of the Wyrm's neck. The shot connected, and the expanding slugs did their work, spattering Richard with gore. The Wyrm howled and lashed its head round towards the shot, crashing into the side of the pillar. The shock almost knocked Richard over. Before he could take advantage of the Wyrm's head right next to him, it had withdrawn and loomed back out of his reach. Richard edged to one side, trying to take aim again, when something barrelled into him from behind. The Wyrm's tail had flashed in from the side and knocked him sprawling on his face. His hands flew out in front of him and he landed flat on his stomach. He dropped the gun. It shot out in front of him, skidding over the stone.

Richard swore again and rolled over, but the Wyrm was thrashing about above his head, the vast loops of its snake-like body heaving across the temple floor. Richard reached for the other gun and, still flat on his back, took aim for the beast's head. Three shots went wide, but two seemed to connect, before he had to roll out of the way of the creature's flailing bulk. Inside the Monument, the size of the creature hampered its movement. Richard, in a moment of optimism, felt glad that he wasn't having to fight a smaller, more agile Wyrm, then remembered that even if he did survive, he would have to face a new one sooner or later, of unknown dimensions. He ducked one furious swipe of the beast's thick coils, and ran up against another segment, dense as a tractor tyre. He fired rapidly at close range. The expanding bullets chewed through the serpent's mass, chopping it almost in two. But even as he watched, Richard saw the fleshy fibres start to knit themselves back together. He shot again, and they retreated, but he knew it wouldn't last. High above him, the Wyrm screamed as dark, stinging blood spattered the stone. It angled its head, to get Richard in its gaze, then lunged, fangs first. Taken off guard, Richard barely managed to dodge the attack in time. As it was, he caught a whiff of the creature's breath and gagged. The reek was foul, like a rotting oil slick. But he had no chance to catch his breath, as the Wyrm lunged again. This time, he was ready for it and had his gun raised.

He shot five times. All five bullets punched into the skull of the creature, tearing holes in it the size of fists. One lucky shot hit the jaw, dislodging a fang. But it kept on coming. Its open maw crashed into Richard's left shoulder with the force of an iron bar. Richard would have cried out, but the blow had knocked the breath out of him. Several of its teeth had dug into his flesh, taking soft chunks out of his arm, and the broken fang had just missed his face. He was gasping and choking all at once, and a stabbing pain in his shoulder was making him retch. Somehow he staggered to one side. The Wyrm's head was still lying where it had hit him, its huge eye, bigger than his palm, still burning faintly with an inner green flame. Richard stared into the eye, less than a foot away from him. For a moment, everything was still. Man and beast waited. The creature heaved its head, trying to lift it. It snarled weakly, tailing off into a shrill whistle. As Richard watched, the holes his lead slugs had made began to heal over, and the eye started to glow fiercer.

'I'm sorry,' Richard said at last and emptied the rest of

the magazine into the creature's skull.

Outside the monument, the Baron and Jenny stood watching as the green barrier between the pillars flashed and shimmered. Shapes would appear on it: a writhing Wyrm, Richard raising a gun, Richard on the floor, spurts and spatters and unformed images. They could hear no sound, save the crackling hiss of the barrier itself. After a time, Dawlish arrived, closely followed by Kate. No one asked why or how they knew to come here. The Baron merely looked askance at Kate when she appeared, but if he had anything on his mind, he didn't say it.

'Nothing to be done but wait,' he said, instead. 'Unless anyone has any bright ideas.'

'I just wish he'd said something,' Jenny sighed. 'Not taken off without a word.'

'And what would you have done if he had?' asked the Baron, more distracted than unkind.

'I don't know. Told someone else, probably.'

'He did tell me, though,' said Dawlish in a half-whisper. 'When we went to visit Cimron. He said he'd have to kill it.'

'We all knew that,' put in Kate. 'Whether it was today or three months from now. He needed to get it done. And better sooner than later.'

'Don't blame yourself,' added the Baron comfortingly, dragging his gaze away from the monument only to give Kate a pointed glance over Dawlish's head. 'If anyone's to blame, it's certainly not you.' Kate didn't seem to notice, as she was staring at the green glow separating the pillars.

'Shh . . .' she said as Dawlish started to say something further. 'Listen . . .'

'I can't hear anything.' said Jenny.

'I know. How long's it been?'

The Baron looked at his watch.

'Either way, this should have been finished by now.'

'What do you mean, "either way?"' asked Jenny, horrified.

'The barriers only come down when either the Wyrm is dead, or—'

'Please don't say it.'

'The barriers are still up, though . . .' She peered as close as possible to the crackling green as she dared. 'I wish I knew what was going on in there.'

Richard staggered to the far side of the temple, trying to get away from the bloody pulp of minced Wyrm-head in front of him. He had kept shooting until nothing was left of the creature's skull but sodden, fleshy fragments, none bigger than a playing card. He would have turned on the rest of the corpse, but the sight of the dark, wet mound made his stomach turn, and his already painful wrist was aching from the gun's recoil. Besides, it didn't seem to be regenerating any more. The stench was getting worse, though.

He thought of how his ancestor had studied the thing after he had killed it and decided they must have had no sense of smell in those days. Something wet was stinging on his forehead. He wiped it with the back of his hand, which came away dark with blood. His stomach heaved, and he vomited until there was nothing left to void.

Enough is enough, he thought, as he sat with his back to a pillar, face hot and heavy, hands and arms aching. His left shoulder, where he had landed on it badly, was already starting to bruise and stiffen, and his right wrist was all-over pain. Why wasn't the green fire lifting? He wasn't sure how this was supposed to go, but he was fairly sure that he ought to be able to go now. He was still holding one of the guns; which one, he no longer knew nor cared. As hard as he could, he threw it away from him.

CHAPTER 20

THE STRANGEST CUP OF TEA

ut of nowhere, a hand reached for the gun and caught it in the downward curve. Richard looked up. A woman stood there, a woman wearing long, flowing white robes. She seemed familiar, but Richard couldn't think straight enough to remember exactly where from.

'Congratulations,' she said as she approached, and the green light shone eerily on her long, dark hair.

'No,' Richard replied. 'Don't . . .' He felt blurry and sick.

'I won't have a chance later,' came the tentative reply. 'Are you ready?' She looked him up and down, brow creasing. 'You don't have a sword. Funny, I thought you'd have a sword.'

'Ready for what? I . . .?' He crumpled back on himself, slumped with his face in his hands.

'Richard!' The woman surged forwards, arms out towards him but checked herself just before she reached him.

'Richard, are you hurt?'

'Yes . . . no . . . I . . . Who are you?'

'You are hurt,' she said with a tremor in her voice. 'You're bleeding.' Richard glanced down at his shoulder. His shirt was a ragged mess, one sleeve ripped along the seam and hanging by a thread. It was stained beyond repair with blood, both the blackish, oily blood of the Wyrm and his own, a brighter crimson, seeping through. The woman knelt beside him and deftly parted the cotton remnants, exposing the wound. It wasn't as severe as Richard—and it seemed, she—feared. She let out the breath she was holding. 'It's not deep,' she sighed. 'You'll be all right. But you need to wash it. Here.' Like a magician, she reached into a sleeve and drew out a goblet of white wood, brimming with water. Richard blinked.

'Where did that come from?'

'Shh . . .' She began to pour the liquid over his shoulder. It stung, but Richard didn't pull back, and after a few seconds a soothing coolness began to spread through his aching muscles. He rolled his shoulder a few times. The stiffness was easing.

'Thank you,' he said, still staring and confused as the chalice disappeared back into the folds of the woman's robe. 'To what do I owe . . .?'

'To somebody else's mistakes.' She drew her eyes away from the mess of Richard's shirt and seemed to study his face with a rueful smile. 'You look so like him. Like all of them. And yet you're not. You're different.'

'Different?' Richard met her dreamy, distant gaze for a moment, then shook his head and leaned back. 'I think you've got the wrong Lampton.'

She seemed to give this thought serious consideration.

'No,' she said after a moment. 'Actually, I think I've finally got the right Lampton.'

'Why? Whatever you're thinking, you're wrong. I'm boring and ordinary and out of my depth.' He closed his eyes. 'And I'm tired.'

'You just slew a dragon.'

'Blind luck and stupidity.'

'I meant it's natural to be tired,' she replied patiently. 'And this won't be helping.' She reached out for his arm. Richard looked down. The snake bracelet was still glinting there, cold and dead now. The strangeness that had animated it was gone, and it felt lifeless against his skin. Heavy. Gently taking his hand in hers, the woman slipped the bracelet off his wrist. Her hands were soft against his skin and gentle as summer rain. Richard felt lightened. It was as if she had taken away a leaden cloud that had been hanging over him since he put it on, and a cool breeze had blown through his head, sharpening his thoughts.

'There,' she said. 'Has that helped?'

Richard nodded. 'Now, please,' he asked, 'what's going on? Who are you?'

'I'm not really anyone,' she replied, tucking the bracelet into her sleeve. 'It doesn't matter now anyway. It's almost over.'

'Almost over?'

'Yes. Almost. There's just enough time for a cup of tea, I think. And there's a few things we need to discuss.'

'I think I can,' said Dawlish after a moment. 'Find out

what's going on inside, I mean.' She was standing at one corner of the monument watching Bobble, who was fluttering around one of the corner pillars.

'How?' asked Kate, still peering at the green barrier.

'Because there's a door here.'

Everyone stared at Dawlish.

'A door?' asked the Baron. 'Where?'

'In the pillar. Did you guys not see it?' Dawlish put a hand up against the stone where, sure enough, there was a door. It was at an odd angle, smoothed and curved with the grain of the pillar so the crack was barely visible, but now that it had been pointed out, it did seem to have been staring them in the face all this time. 'If I can get in using my keys, then perhaps I can find a way to see what's happening to Richard,' Dawlish continued.

'Daw, don't do anything stupid,' said Jenny. 'It's not safe.'

'Neither is crossing the road. I've done worse and come out of it all right.'

'But—'

'Look, Richard is in there, risking his life. Yeah, sitting around here moaning about it sounds like a really good plan to me. Do you want to know what's happening in there, or not?' Before anyone else could gainsay her, she reached into her pocket for the keys and fitted the silver one into the lock.

'Having difficulty?' the Baron asked, as she struggled with it for a few seconds.

'It won't turn at all.' She shook out her stiff hand. 'I'd expected difficulty but . . .' At that point, Bobble fluttered down from his perch on Jenny's shoulder and landed on the haft of the key where Dawlish had left it in the lock. The key immediately clicked round.

'Did we know he could do that?' asked Kate, as the others looked on in surprise. 'I didn't know he could do that.'

'I'm sure we'll wonder about it later,' said the Baron with a shrug. 'For now, let's not look the gift horse in the mouth?'

Dawlish snorted. 'I must have loosened it for you,' she muttered, shooting a dark look at the bird who fluttered up to her shoulder. She rolled her eyes and returned the key to her pocket.

'This is all we've got, right?' She paused with her hand on the door and looked back at them.

'I think it might be, yes.'

'Right.' She took a deep breath. 'Just wanted to make sure.' And she pushed open the door and was through it before another word was said.

'A talk, perhaps,' replied Richard, 'but I think the tea will have to wait 'til we get out of here.' He glanced up to where the green light still crackled between the pillars.

'I don't see why.' The woman lifted a hand and made a plucking motion in the air, and as she brought it down, she was holding a mug of steaming tea.

'How did you . . .?' Richard gaped.

'Here, take it.' She proffered the mug. Richard reached out and then almost dropped it.

'It's hot!' He repositioned his hands so as not to burn them. 'How did you do that?' She didn't pretend to misun-

derstand him, just sat back on her heels and plucked another cup from the air for herself.

'There are some people in this world who have the
power to imagine things differently,' she said, taking a sip.

'Doesn't everyone?' Richard decided to chance the tea
as well. It was hot and sweet and tasted slightly of oranges.
The woman shrugged.

'The world doesn't pay attention to most people. You
and me, on the other hand—when we believe something,
reality listens, bends itself just a little. We are the people
whose dreams come true.'

'My dreams certainly don't come true,' scoffed Richard. 'If that were the case, I wouldn't be here, for a start.'

'Indeed? Didn't you want to be a hero?'

'No. And I'm not.' Richard took another sip of the tea.
'My dreams are much simpler than that.'

'Yes, indeed.' A faint flicker of a smile crossed the
woman's face. 'They once were about a little girl called
Jenny.' She bent her head to drink, leaving Richard with
his mouth hanging open.

'I'm sorry?' he gasped, shaking his head. 'Spell that
one out for me, because I need to be absolutely sure of
what you just said.'

'You were a lonely child,' the woman replied, her
voice gentle. 'It was understandable that you would want
someone to play with. Many children have imaginary
friends. Jenny was yours.'

'But she's real.'

'That's what I'm trying to say. When you imagine
things, they become real, if you want them badly enough.
You could call it faith, or you could call it magic. Either
works.'

Richard had thought he had lost the capacity to be surprised after the last week. He wasn't entirely glad to be proved wrong. But thinking about it, he really shouldn't have been surprised. He had known there was something odd about Jenny; so touchy yet so eager—she'd been waiting for him to remember her. The things she liked, the clothes she wore, even the way she spoke had the ring to them of something far away and long ago, something that ought to have been outgrown stretched to fit.

'She's hanging on,' he said. 'What for?'

'For you,' came the reply. 'You never imagined she'd grow up, so in some ways she hasn't. She can't. You outgrew her, and now she doesn't know how to be her own person.' She sighed. 'It is the curse of Dreamers that we can create but not destroy. Our mistakes don't fade away; they stay with us forever.' She sounded like she spoke from experience.

'What mistake did you make?' Richard asked. Her face fell.

'I'm so sorry,' she said, shaking her head.

'What? You can't tell me? Won't?' An anxious, sinking feeling grew low down in the pit of Richard's stomach. Whatever she was about to say, he knew he wasn't going to like it at all.

'You never meant to leave Jenny like she is. I never meant for . . .'

'Tell me.'

'I dreamed of a hero who would come and slay a dragon,' she said, closing her eyes as if for some blow. 'But there were no heroes and there were no dragons. So I made one.'

'You dreamed of me?'

'Worse. I dreamed of the Wyrm.'

It was like an explosion had gone off in Richard's chest. He was burning with frustration and pain. To have spent so long in the dark, then been taken into such a trial of fire was ordeal enough, but to be confronted with the person responsible—offered tea!

'You?' he asked, surging to his feet in white-hot incredulity. 'You did this? All of this?'

'Richard, I'm sorry—'

'Damn your sorry!' He threw the mug of tea across the monument, where it smacked into one of the pillars and shattered with a crash. The woman backed off, still looking at him steadily.

'I know you must be angry—'

'My uncle . . . my father! My whole family! And what? You think you'll make it right with tea and a biscuit?'

'No, I—'

'Well, you can't! Nothing can make up for that!'

'I thought Kate would have—'

'What has she got to do with this?' Richard threw his hands up. 'No, don't tell me. I don't want to know. I don't want to know any of this any more. I've had enough!' He could feel it bubbling up inside him, a desperate need to be somewhere else, away from all of this madness, all of this pain. 'I wish . . . I wish I could be back there, at home, in my own home, in my own bed, before all of this . . . nightmare!'

'Richard—'
'Just GO AWAY!'
And with a sudden in-rush of air, Richard vanished.

Through the door, Dawlish and Bobble found themselves in a circular white room. A thin layer of dust coated the floor and a white spiral staircase running round the walls—the only features in an otherwise bare room. The staircase looked like it ran all the way up to the top of the monument. She started to climb. Bobble flew beside her, gaining height in increments as she did, until they reached the top, where the stairs opened out onto a small platform. A door stood here too, which sprang open to her touch. Stepping through it, Dawlish found herself on a small balcony running round the empty space at the top of the pillars where the roof should have been. In the dim light she could see the body of the Wyrm sprawled in pieces below her. The faint sound of voices came drifting up towards her: two people, arguing. Her gaze darted around, and her heart leaped as she caught sight of Richard. He was still alive!

'Damn your sorry!' Below her on the floor of the monument, Richard threw something—it looked like a mug of tea—into a pillar, where it smashed into hot liquid and fragments. In front of him, a woman was backing off, as if confronted with a wild animal.

'I know you must be angry—'

'My uncle . . . my father! My whole family! And what? You think you'll make it right with tea and a biscuit?'

Something was terribly wrong. Dawlish had no idea who the woman was or what she was doing here, but she trusted her gut, and right now it was screaming that down there, something was collapsing like a tower of cards.

'I thought Kate would have—'

'What has she got to do with this?'

Kate? Dawlish frowned. Yet another secret she wasn't privileged to know. What had she got into this time? Below her, Richard threw his hands up. 'No, don't tell me. I don't want to know. I don't want to know any of this any more. I've had enough!'

Something was definitely wrong. It was as if the air was struggling, bending round him like ripples in water. Dawlish watched, terrified yet fascinated, completely frozen, as Richard continued to yell.

'I wish . . . I wish I could be back there, at home, in my own home, in my own bed, before all of this . . . nightmare!'

'Richard—'

'Just GO AWAY!'

And with a sudden in-rush of air, Richard vanished.

Dawlish was stunned for barely a moment, horrorstruck, then pelted back through the door and down the stairs, fumbling with her keys as she did so. Bobble was fluttering round her head, frantic but silent, as if he, too, knew how much hung in the balance. They reached the bottom of the stairs, and Dawlish dashed straight for the door, jamming a key into the lock. Bobble clutched at her shoulder, the key turned, and they stepped through. Only as she pulled it out, and shut the door behind her, did Dawlish realise that she wasn't holding her silver key, the one she knew and trusted, but the black one she had never figured out. She turned around, and all around her the blackness closed in.

'She's been in an awfully long time, hasn't she?' asked Jenny back on the hillside. 'She has? I'm not just imagining this?'

The Baron checked his Rolex.

'You're imagining it,' he said, but Kate caught the look on his face. A shadow had passed over it, and he tugged at his earlobe. Sure signs he was concerned.

'I'm sure she's fine,' she told Jenny, not believing a word.

Blackness. It was so thick that Dawlish couldn't see her own hands in front of her. She couldn't hear a thing, couldn't speak through the stifling dark that hung like a velvet shroud in the air. She floated there, feeling only Bobble's claws digging into her shoulder and the floor beneath her feet. She felt sleepy, drifting off into eternity. Sensations became numbed, dulled. The pressure of the bird on her shoulder was lessening. This was the end. Everything was slipping away. And then a bright light and a door.

CHAPTER 21

THOUGHT AND MEMORY

Dawlish felt like she had fallen into the night sky. The room beyond the door was in darkness, but dotted around, motes of light like stars were drifting just out of reach. On the edge of hearing was a low murmuring, like a conversation happening several rooms away. She heard a fluttering from behind her, and in a few wing-beats, Bobble landed on her shoulder. He shoved his beak gently against her ear in what she assumed was a gesture of reassurance. The air in this place felt dry. Cool and still, but not stale. It was difficult to tell in the weak light, but the room seemed to extend quite far in all directions with no indication of where any direction might lead. She began to walk forwards.

Her feet made no sound on the stone floor, and the bobbing points of light were disorienting. She didn't feel like she was moving at all. She strained her ears, trying to hear something, anything, that might tell her where she was and that she wasn't alone, but all she could distinguish was the muttering and, faintly beyond that, a high singing note of silver bells. It felt like wandering in a dream.

In the distance ahead of her, the lights were getting more numerous, or at least more clustered together, as if crowding round something. She quickened her step, and soon, amongst that cluster she could see a figure standing transfixed by a point of light hanging still in front of his face. It was Richard. Bobble seemed to catch sight of him at the same moment as he instantly took off, gliding across the empty space between them to land on Richard's shoulder.

Richard couldn't be certain that he wasn't still drunk. The room was spinning like one of those fairground rides that stick you to the walls with G-forces, and all he could do just at that moment was cling on to the bed and hope that it would stop soon. His mouth and throat were dry and tight, his tongue sticky and gummed-up. He felt as if there was a steel band round his skull, over his eyes, squeezed just too tight so that whenever he moved, he could feel just how heavy and dull his head was. Each noise was louder than ball-bearings rolling around in the taut, hollow space where his brain used to be.

He tried to sit up and regretted it instantly. He felt dizzy and sick. The muscles over his ribs were cramping and aching, each movement a further jab in his side from last night's stiff alcoholic fingers. He flopped back down on the mattress as carefully as he could. Instead, he tried opening his eyes. Just for half a second, as the flash of light sent shards of pain stabbing through his temples, but that limited glance let him ascertain that he had made it home, and he was lying in his own bed. A bed that was warm and comfortable and yielding as cotton wool. It was like lying on a cloud. He drifted back to sleep.

'Richard!' Someone was shaking him awake. He blinked. He was standing in a darkened room filled with drifting motes of light, like fireflies floating in the black. One of these spots hung in front of him: a glowing Christmas bauble. Reflected in its sides, he could see himself lying in bed. A bed that was warm and comfortable and yielding as cotton wool . . . He could feel the softness of the downy quilt and the terrible banging in his ears, the steel band around his head . . . The woozy sickness and the way the morning sunshine felt like needles poking at the corners of his eyes . . .

'Richard! Richard look at me!' He felt a stinging slap on the side of his face, and he looked away. A girl was standing there with a furious expression, her black hair showing gingery at the roots.

'Dawlish?'

'Oh, thank God.' The girl sighed. 'Don't look at it. Just don't.' Richard could still see the glowing sphere out of the corner of his eye, could still feel it drawing him in. He tried to focus on Dawlish instead. Trying not to look at it herself, she took off her coat and flapped at the orb, sending it scudding away into the darkness.

'Gone,' she said. Richard shook his head to clear it of the last vestiges of the hangover. As unlikely a rescuer as she was, Richard was glad to see the girl, however she'd managed to get here. He wasn't even entirely sure he knew how he'd got there. The last thing he remembered was standing in the temple, talking to some woman who had appeared, and being filled with an all-consuming wish to be back at home in his bed, before all of this mess had begun. Before he had to know, had to think about it. Then the world had shifted . . . and here he was.

'What was that thing?' asked Dawlish, gesturing in the vague direction of the mote of light. 'Why were you staring at it like that?'

'Staring? Is that all?' Richard's brow creased. 'It had sucked me in. I could feel the bedsheets. I was thinking the same thoughts. I was back there.' Dawlish's eyebrows flew up on strings.

'They're memories?' she asked, awestruck.

'I don't know. Maybe?' Richard shrugged. 'I mean, I guess so. I can't see what else it could have been. But how?'

Dawlish smiled.

'I think I know where we are. But I never thought it could be real. Not even Kate or the Baron have been here. It's only ever been theorised to exist. It's just too cool to be anything more than a story. Come on.' She started forging forward into the darkness. 'I need some proof.'

'What sort of proof?' asked Richard, tagging along behind.

'I'll know it when I see it,' Dawlish replied.

Time didn't seem to pass the same way, wandering through the vast expanse with no markers to say how far they'd gone or which way. Richard couldn't tell if they'd been walking for five minutes or five hours. It was a strangely disconnected place, distanced from any form of reality—even the strange new world of the Weirding that he'd come to recognise. This was something altogether different, a total remove.

After a time, their eyes managed to adjust to the eerie twilight, and they began to pick out shapes in the distance. Silhouettes and shadows that never resolved to anything distinct. The floor beneath their feet was made of some sort of mosaic. Black and white tiles of different shapes and sizes, picking out a pattern of clocks and hourglasses. Dawlish spent some time studying it but didn't seem to find what she was looking for. Here and there they came across a door hanging in mid-air and apparently leading nowhere, but Richard doubted that was really where they led. He didn't feel like trying any of them to find out.

'How did you find me?' he asked, breaking the hush.

'What?'

'How did you know where to look? How did you even know I was lost?'

'Jenny was staying at yours, remember?' said Dawlish, exasperated. 'You left her there. Then people figured out where you'd gone, and when I got there you were trapped in the monument with the Wyrm, and I went after you and . . . yeah. All of that.' She made an expansive gesture that still failed to clarify anything for Richard.

'Okay, so . . .'

'I don't really know, okay. It was a mistake.'

'You didn't mean to come and find me?' asked Richard, confused.

'No, I mean, I didn't mean to use the black key.' She took the two keys out of her pocket and dangled them in front of him to illustrate. 'I saw you talking to that woman, and then you just vanished. And I was trying to get back in a hurry, and I put the black key into the lock by mistake, and then I opened the door, and I was here. Luckily, you were, too.'

'That was quite a risk. Even if it was by accident.' Richard stopped walking for a second and looked directly at Dawlish. 'Thank you,' he said firmly.

'For what?' Dawlish walked on a few steps before she noticed her companion had stopped. She turned to look at him, puzzled.

'For saving my life. I think.'

Dawlish snorted. 'Don't be stupid.'

'No, I mean it.' Richard gestured back the way they had come. 'If you hadn't come after me, I would still be stuck there, staring at that memory like a lemon. Who knows how long I'd have been trapped.'

'You could still be. We don't know if there's a way out of here yet.'

Richard didn't reply at first, just took a few more steps to catch up with her.

'Still. Thank you,' he said again when they were once again walking side by side. 'I'm glad you did come.'

'Wait . . .' Dawlish stopped, peering into the distance. 'What's that?' she asked, pointing. Up ahead of them, one of the shapes in the darkness was beginning to resolve. Bobble, who up until that point had been surprisingly subdued, suddenly took off with a sharp squawk and sped off in its direction, leaving Dawlish and Richard no choice but to follow.

They didn't have far to go. When they caught up with Bobble, he had landed on the floor in front of two towering statues of cold, black marble. Both depicted a figure of a raven. Bobble was crouched in front of them, head bent and wings spread in a gesture of submission.

'It is . . .' breathed Dawlish in reverent tones. 'It's the Halls of Muninn.'

'As in Huginn and Muninn?' asked Richard. 'The two ravens of Odin? What were they . . . Thought and Memory?'

Dawlish blinked. 'You know something?' she asked, aghast. 'You?'

'I read early history at university.' Richard shrugged. 'One of my professors had a thing for Norse mythology. Is it really so surprising that I know things?'

'In a word, yes!'

Richard gave her a withering look and was about to ask if he could rescind his earlier thank you, when a tortured grinding came from the statues as the head of the one on their right swung round to fix them all with a stony glare. Richard froze in shock, and even Dawlish was rattled enough to instinctively grab his hand. The statue opened its beak and uttered a series of gravelly croaks. Dawlish, pale as a sheet, shook her head.

'Do you understand it?' asked Richard. 'What's it saying?'

'I'm not sure. It's old speech . . . Something about a welcome?'

'Reassuring, I suppose?'

'And it has what we seek.' She looked up at him, blankly. 'I don't think I'm understanding right. We're not looking for anything, are we? Except possibly the way out.'

'That could be it?' shrugged Richard. 'Whatever it is, I think we should take it seriously. It's a safe bet this thing knows more than we do.'

'Don't look a gift raven in the beak?'

'Something like that.'

Again, the statue gave a resounding croak. Richard looked at Dawlish for a translation.

'The way out is in the dark beyond them,' she said. 'But it's talking about a price . . .? Toll . . .? Forfeit . . .? I don't know that word.' On the floor in front of them, Bobble turned his head back and let out a few squawks of his own.

'Does he understand it any better?' asked Richard.

'The Jackdaw word is closer to "compulsion" he says,' replied Dawlish, shaking her head. 'But from them that could have a number of meanings. Something they have to do, or something they can't resist taking.' She threw her hands up. 'I'm not a scholar. It's your choice. What do we do?'

'I don't know. Do you think there's another way out?'

'Probably not.'

'Then I don't see that we have a choice. Bobble? Can you tell it that we agree?'

'Aak.' Bobble obediently croaked at the statue, then hopped backwards a few paces as, immediately in front of the plinth, a shape began to coalesce out of thin air. Out of the mists formed a thin, flat-topped pedestal with a shallow indentation in the top, like an old bird-bath. The motes of light which still surrounded them seemed to sense the pedestal's appearance and began to crowd round, but a gesture from the statue stopped them. They hung still in the air, looking more like a star-field than ever, except for one. One memory, golden and effervescent, sidled forwards then sank, dreamily as a sunset, into the depression on top of the pedestal. Richard took a step closer, but Dawlish reached out a steadying hand.

'Are you sure?' she asked. 'Remember the last one.'

'I don't think it's going to be the same.' Richard glanced over at the statue. 'I don't think that's my memory.' He squeezed her hand and stepped up to the plinth, where the memory had melted into a shimmering golden mirror in the stone bowl. As he approached, the ripples on the surface began to spread. The memory grew, overflowing the basin and running in sparkling rivulets over the side of the pedestal, over the stone floor, then shooting up, surrounding the three of them in a shining dome, 'til everything seemed to melt away, and they were staring at a scene none of them recognised.

They were standing on the hill in the shade of Penshaw Monument. The Northern sky had shaded to a deep blue velvet, punctured here and there with the last of the summer stars. The final shreds of the day's warmth were steadily being pushed back, and a sharp tin edge to the wind spoke of September's arrival. In the dark and the chill, the huge pillars atop the hill were shot through with the same green crackles of light that Richard remembered pulsing across their surface from before. Like a pillar herself, the woman stood waiting a few feet from the plinth which formed the base of the columns, white robes whipping round her ankles. Richard drew a sharp breath. It was her.

The green light flared and died like a candle flame

SIGIL of the WYRM

blown out, and in the afterglow, a man stumbled heavily out from among the tall stones. Richard felt Dawlish clutch his arm in recognition. It was his Uncle Tom. One hand was wrapped around his side, pressed to his ribs, while the other, groping in front of him for support, let fall the long steel blade he had been clinging to. It dropped to the stone floor with a dull clang. In a few steps, the woman was there at his arm, supporting him as he crumpled forward like a dropped cloth.

"Is it done?" she asked, propping him up on the damp grass against the plinth. "Tom? Is it done?"

Tom coughed. "My shirt's wet," he said in a matter-of-fact voice. He tugged at the side straps holding his vest together. "I don't think the Kevlar made much—Ah! Damn it!" He winced as he peeled the black material aside. Beneath his hands, a dark pulsing stain spread up and across his chest. Richard felt his own chest tighten.

"You're hurt . . ." The woman's brows furrowed, and her eyes flashed with pushed-down panic.

"No, I'm dying," Tom replied. He gave another damp cough, "And I'd really rather not be. Look, there's a phone in my car. Driver's side door pocket. Call someone?"

"We had a plan; you have to—"

"You have to call someone. First. Before it's too late."

"Then . . ." For a moment she looked about to argue, but then nodded. "There is still time. The important part is done." She stood and hastily swished away through the wet grass.

'What is she doing here?' hissed Dawlish.

'I was hoping you could tell me,' replied Richard. 'And what was that about a plan?'

He turned back to the scene at hand. Tom was sitting,

gazing across the countryside below, the lights of the city twinkling and growing fuzzy in the distance. He tried to wipe the blood from his hands.

"I've called Kate," the woman said as she returned. "She's on her way. Now, before it's too late . . ." She knelt and looked imploringly at the broken figure. "Please. You know what you have to do. Where is your sword?"

He shook his head.

"It doesn't matter now. I'm sorry. Kate won't be here in time."

"You can't know that. We need to finish this."

"I am finished. Even if I tried . . . it's already moved on." He uncurled his fingers, and Richard could see the little gold band of his signet ring nestling in his palm. "The ring's off. I've not got long." The woman wrapped his hand in hers, closed his fingers again on the ring.

"There's still time. What if you're wrong? We could end it, here and now, forever. Like we planned."

"Stop." His free hand reached out limply for her face, came to rest on her shoulder. "Even if it would work, I'm not doing it. Not with my last moments. I couldn't face it."

"And I can't face doing this all over again." Her face looked young, fragile, as if it would crack.

"Richard's not like me. He doesn't know you, doesn't know any of us. Listen, you've got to—" he crumpled as a spasm of pain shot across his features. "You've got to take the key. Get it to Richard. Perhaps . . . he can . . . be the hero you've always wanted."

"But he doesn't know me, doesn't know—"

"Then don't tell him. Trust me, it'll be easier if . . . if he doesn't know you." His breath was now slowing, coming thick and rasping now. "Easier . . . easier if he doesn't . . .

doesn't love . . ." Tom's hand dropped from the woman's arm. The harsh wheeze died on the wind, and Richard felt the first spots of rain begin to fall.

'Richard . . .' Dawlish was looking at him.
'I don't know . . .' he said in a daze. 'I don't know what all of this means. I wish I did.'
'Are you all right?'
'I don't know.'

Distantly, they heard the sound of a car pull up. The engine cut out and the door slammed shut. Out of the darkness, a figure emerged. Even at this distance, Richard recognised Kate's swaggering walk. Her hair was falling down around her shoulders, and her clothes looked rumpled, as if they'd been slept in.

"What exactly is so urgent that you had to—" she broke off as she saw the slumped form at the base of the monument. Her face turned ashen. "No. No, no, no, no, no, no . . ." She ran straight past the woman in white and slid to her knees by the limp body of Tom Lampton. "No!" she declared, shaking him. "You are not dead! You are not allowed to die! Damn you, Tom, damn you, you're not . . . you're not supposed to . . ." Running out of steam she slumped back on her heels. Richard had never thought he would see Kate cry, but when she looked up he could see tears smudging their way down her face. She wiped them away with the heel of her hand.

"This is your fault," she said with bitterness. "You should have just left well alone. Wasn't it enough for you, what you've already done to his family?"

"I'm sorry."

Kate was on her feet in a flash. She took three steps over and landed the other woman such a slap across the face that Richard felt his own cheek sting in sympathy.

"You dare to say you're sorry? You dare?"

"It's true. It was never meant to be this way. I never meant . . . I'm sick to death of this . . ."

Kate's eyes narrowed.

"Yes, but it wasn't your death, was it?" she spat.

"It was supposed to be!"

Kate's expression changed at that. She took a step back, her face registering surprise and a faint flicker of approval.

"What went wrong?" she asked in a more level tone.

"I don't know. He was dying, and he couldn't . . . We had planned . . ."

"You planned for him to kill you and complete the terms of the curse." Kate finished for her. She nodded slowly. "Why?"

"Because I made a mistake. I should never have inflicted the curse on them. There's always a price. And I'm sick of watching others pay it."

"The price of heroism is making the hard choices."

"And this was my choice." The woman sank onto the wet grass.

"No," Kate sat beside her. "It was his. And he chose not to end his life with killing a friend." She shook her head ruefully. "Lampton boys. Soft as clarts, the lot of them."

They sat in silence for a few minutes on top of the hill. Kate lit a cigarette and they watched the blue smoke twist and curl in the drizzle and starlight. A screech pierced the night from a hunting owl diving in for the kill.

"What are you going to do now?" Kate asked as the noise died away.

"Try again?" she had an edge of quiet despair to her voice now, raw and bitter. "I have lived too long, Kate. I'm ready to die."

Kate shrugged.

"Yes, but is Richard ready to be the one to kill you?"

"I don't know. I've never met him." She sounded exhausted. "I suppose I should make myself known, and—"

"No, you won't," interjected Kate. "You won't go anywhere near him. We know where that path leads." She cast a pointed look at the foot of the monument. "Besides, this one is different. He'll need a lot more than just talking to."

"Then you'll have to do it."

"Me?" Kate squawked, looking thoroughly taken aback. "No. Ask someone else. I'm not the right person for this."

"Then who?"

"Robin," she replied quickly. It took Richard a moment to realise she meant the Baron. "He's got that way with people, he could—"

"No." The woman seemed to have rallied and was speaking now with authority. "It can't be him. Because he's . . . what was that phrase you used? 'Soft as clarts?' And because he knows what this is." She reached into her robe and pulled out the now familiar snake bracelet with its glittering green eyes. Richard realised he hadn't seen her take it from Tom's wrist.

"What is it?" asked Kate.

"If you knew, you wouldn't give it to Richard. And he needs it if this plan is going to work."

"Dangerous, is it?" Kate's eyes seemed to sparkle as she glanced over the gems.

"No more so than this." The woman handed Kate the Lampton signet ring. She took it gently and once more Richard saw shining wet beads try to escape the corners of her eyes.

"Poor Tom . . ." she whispered, fingering the gold band.

"Make sure Richard gets them," the woman continued. "Please. He has a little time, but not much. A week at the outside." She ran a hand through her hair. It was the most human gesture Richard had seen from her. "You'll have to judge when he's ready. You're right—I can't meet him, not until the right moment. But this is my last chance to put this right. Promise me, Kate," she implored. "Promise me you'll see it come right?"

Richard watched, waiting for Kate's reply, but the vision began to dissolve like ripples in water, and he found himself back in the Halls of Muninn, Dawlish clutching his arm, before either of them could hear the answer.

CHAPTER 22

SACRIFICE

N o!' Richard tried to grasp for the fading memory but didn't know how.

'Richard—' Dawlish put a hand on his arm.

'It's gone . . .'

'I think that's all we needed to see.' She shrugged, back to her usual sarcasm. 'Show's over, movie's finished. Time to collect our popcorn and go.'

In front of them, the raven stretched and tucked its wings away. If a statue could be said to have emotions, Richard would say it looked satisfied.

'Is that it?' he demanded. 'Are we done? Can we go?'

In the darkness behind the two statues, a door leading to nowhere, still slightly fuzzy, was beginning to coalesce. Richard took a step towards it when suddenly the other statue—the one which had been silent all this time— ground into life.

Bobble had flown up to the top of its plinth and was bobbing and fluttering deferentially in front of the giant bird. It had been patient, and now swung its great head round to look Richard in the eye. In his head, Richard heard the voice of Huginn echo.

'*Richard Lampton?*'

'Thought,' whispered Dawlish. 'Should have known he'd be telepathic.'

'*Before you go, your bird has come to me begging a boon. He wishes to walk the Wooden Path. Do you accept his service?*'

Richard's brow furrowed.

'The Wooden Path? What is that?'

A rumble like an avalanche came in reply, and Richard took a second to realise the raven was laughing.

'*Soon will he show you. Now you must simply accept his sacrifice and service.*'

'Sacrifice? What?' Bobble fluttered to the floor in front of the statue and bent his head. 'Is this what you want, little guy?' Richard asked, frowning. Bobble looked up at him and nodded once.

'*Son of Lampton, Heir of the Wyrm, do you accept?*'

'If that's what he wants, but what—'

Before Richard could get his explanation, Huginn bent his great beak and plucked out the last remaining tuft of down from the top of Bobble's head. The little bird screamed. Richard lunged forward and gathered his diminutive companion up in his arms.

'Was that necessary?' he snapped at the raven.

'*The price that is paid proves the worth of the giver. The struggle makes the success all the sweeter.*'

Richard nodded, accepting the point.

'I liked that bit of fluff,' he sighed, gently stroking Bobble's head with a finger. Bobble snuggled deeper into the crook of his arm.

'*So did he,*' replied Huginn, sounding almost paternal. '*Had he not valued it, why would I? That is what it is to be a hero.*'

'Come on.' Dawlish tugged at Richard's sleeve. 'Let's get out of here.'

Richard was forced to agree and followed the girl between the two stone columns towards the bone-pale door. He shot a glance back over his shoulder at the statues.

'*We will see you again, Son of Lampton,*' whispered the gravelly voice of Huginn in his head.

The door sprang open to Dawlish's key. The blackness on the other side swirled with menace.

'Take my hand,' Dawlish instructed. Richard did so. 'Well, here goes nothing . . .' And they stepped into the dark.

The door in the side of the monument clicked and swung open, and Dawlish tumbled out onto the grass. Jenny caught her before she fell.

'Daw? Are you all right? What happened? What's going on in there?'

'Easy, give the girl a chance to breathe!' the Baron cautioned. 'Dawlish?'

'It's all right, I'm fine, just let me up . . .' Dawlish coughed and stumbled to her feet. 'Where's Richard? And Bobble?'

'Richard? You got him out?'

'He was right with me . . .' All eyes followed Dawlish's to the base of the pillar where the door still gaped open. After a minute, Bobble tumbled through in a ball of spluttering feathers. But there was still no sign of Richard.

'Shoot,' whispered Jenny to herself.

Richard emerged from the stifling black on his own. Dawlish wasn't there and neither was Bobble. He was standing in a circular white room, featureless, save for the door behind him and the spiral staircase that wound its way invitingly up the walls. Richard took a deep breath and grasped the banister. At the top of the stairs, the door to the upper level of the monument waited. He stepped through and found himself looking down on the gory remains of the Wyrm. It seemed to be fading away. Dissolving at the edges. The woman—the Dreamer—was not with it.

'You're back?' The woman looked up from where she was staring, despondent, over the balcony. 'I thought you were gone for good.'

'So did I.' Richard approached and leant backwards on the railings next to her.

'I didn't mean to scare you off,' she said.

'I'm sorry I broke your teacup.'

She smiled at that and made a dismissive gesture. 'I can make another one.'

'So can I, apparently.' Richard sighed. 'I thought, back then, that you were gloating or that you'd come to kill me.'

'With a cup of tea?'

'Stranger things have happened.'

'I imagine it has been an odd kind of week,' she said

with a rueful look. Richard rolled his eyes.

'Understatement of the century.'

They sat in silence, he thinking over everything that had happened, how all of it had been leading up to this moment, and she probably contemplating the same.

'I think,' she said at last, 'you know what I'm going to ask you now.'

Richard nodded. 'Muninn showed me what you were trying to do with my uncle. You made sure you were the first living thing I saw once the Wyrm was dead. You're going to ask me to kill you.'

'I'm asking you to break the curse.'

'That amounts to the same thing.'

'I'm afraid it does.' Her voice held no resignation so much as pity, and not for herself. 'It's a terrible thing to ask you, I know.'

'I just wanted to be rid of it,' said Richard. 'It's too much of a burden. But then I saw Tom and what he was trying to do. The only way to finish this is to go through it, not back away. He died for this. It meant so much to him that he was willing to kill the woman that he loved—' the Dreamer started at that, but Richard carried on, '—the woman he loved to make this right. For me. So I didn't have to carry this burden. He was a good man.'

Richard looked at her again, this ancient woman, still little more than a child in some ways, who had so captivated his uncle. She seemed light as thistledown, with porcelain skin, hair the colour of age-blackened oak and eyes like ocean depths.

'This thing is bigger than me,' he said. 'It may be my curse now, but it carries weight. I have a responsibility to see this through.' He gave a wry laugh. 'If I can end it now,

I could be a hero.'

She smiled, and it was a shaft of starlight in the gathering gloom. 'I'd settle for you being a good man.'

'They're supposed to be one and the same.'

'I used to think so,' she said. 'Now, I'm not so sure.'

'You know . . .' Richard stretched, affecting nonchalance. 'I've thought about it, and it may not be you who has to die.'

'Why is that?' She gave him a puzzled look.

'The moment I knew the thing was dead,' speculated Richard, 'well, in that moment I took a long hard look at myself. It changed me. And I think it was the first time I'd ever really "seen" myself.'

She smiled and shook her head. 'Thank you for trying,' she said, 'but you and I both know that's not how it goes.'

'A sacrifice has to be meaningful. I don't even know you, but I'm the last of the Lamptons. The line ends with me. If I die—'

'The Wyrm wins.'

'But it will have nothing to do, no one to chase, no reason to return.'

'Or nothing to stop it.' She stretched out an arm and took his hand in hers. 'Perhaps it isn't your sacrifice to make,' she said. 'I should be the one to die, and at your hand. You have so much to live for, and I am prepared.' Her free hand flexed on the railings as she steeled herself. Richard gripped the hand she had offered tightly.

'Your sacrifice or mine,' he said. 'Either way, we have to make sure.' And with that, he reached out and pulled her to him. He had half a second to register the shock in her eyes, the smell of her hair reminding him of a summer's green fields, as he took another step towards the balcony, closed his eyes, and jumped.

They fell together, twisting in the air, not enemies any more, all sins forgotten, just holding on. Richard felt the pinch of her fingers in his shoulder blades, his own twisting into the fabric of her gown. He could see the whites of her eyes grow larger like a frightened horse, hear, close by his face, her painful gasps for breath in the rushing air. The moment before the impact stretched out into the distance beyond the end of time.

They hit the stone together, he on top, she beneath. She didn't even cry out, there was just a crack and a sudden limpness, and Richard felt the ripples echoing across the boundaries of worlds. The breath was knocked out of him and his mind and nerves shrieked the dying shriek of the Wyrm. Then nothing. Just the feeling of cold flags and be-neath him . . . He stood up too quickly and tripped, fell away from the body, scrambled into the corner as far away from it as possible. A wave of horror and revulsion hit him. Something heavy was sitting on his chest, and he couldn't breathe.

'Oh, God,' he whispered, 'God, no, this isn't . . .'

This was different. Not a life and death struggle with a monster which he had been drawn into against his will. This was a calculated dealing of death, a choice he never remembered making. His hands no longer felt like they were part of him. He no longer felt attached to himself.

Moments which felt like hours passed. He couldn't

stop staring at the body. He shut his eyes, saw the imprint of the temple floor and the huddled shape, so still, on the back of his eyelids. Opening them, it was still there. With care, he crawled closer. She looked younger now. More fragile. Softer and less alien, but the spark of what she had been was gone. She was just a girl, and he had killed her. He stared down into those dead eyes that were already filming over. He touched the side of her face with his fingertips.

'This isn't . . . isn't what I wanted,' he said. 'It should have been me. That would have been the proper way to break the curse. I'm not a killer, I never meant . . .

'I wish there could have been another way,' he said at last. 'And I'm sorry.' His throat was burning, and his eyes were hot and prickly. He bent his head and rested his forehead against hers. 'I'm truly sorry.'

He felt a warmth beneath his hands and on his face, then a sigh-like breath. He opened his eyes. She was gone.

The green, crackling wards sputtered and died. The onlookers on the hill—Kate, the Baron, Dawlish, and Jenny—surged forwards to see. For a moment, Jenny saw a knight stooped over his sword, praying, but then that image faded and it was only Richard, kneeling with his head bowed, as if a weight had been lifted from his shoulders and he hadn't quite noticed yet.

'Richard!' she called, and he looked up. His eyes were too bright, and they had a faraway look in them, as if he wasn't looking at her but something behind her on the hill.

She didn't care; she just ran to him and caught him in her arms.

CHAPTER 23

THE END AND THE BEGINNING

He was here in her house after so long. Jenny bustled with the kettle, the business of making tea, trying not to look at him or stay still long enough for him to speak to her. He had caught hold of her on the hill like a drowned man would driftwood. It had seemed natural that, as the others went their own ways, she would go with him. Even Bobble, after the initial volley of squawks when he and Dawlish had re-appeared, had flown off with the other jackdaws. Now Richard was sitting on her sofa, on her actual sofa, in her actual house. And she was making him tea. He hadn't said a word.

The kettle boiled, and she tipped out the hot water over the teabags into the good mugs. The spotty ones, of which she still had a whole set. She was about to fish out the tea-bags when she suddenly thought that maybe the teapot would make a better impression. Hurriedly she got it out, tipped the tea, teabags and all, into the pot, then added some extra water to be sure. She took the cups and the milk to the table in front of the sofa, sat down, then had to get up again in a rush to fetch the teapot, left unaccountably on the side.

'Tea?' she asked him.

'This mug's hot,' he said, cradling it in both hands.

'Sorry. I forgot about the teapot.'

He glanced up and looked at her deeply for what probably was the first time.

'Yes,' he said, 'some tea would be nice.'

She felt his gaze on her as she poured out. 'What?' she asked as she handed him the cup.

'Could you pass the milk, please?'

She did.

'I know who you are,' he said, out of the blue.

'Well, of course.'

'No, I mean, I know what you are. Where you came from. Only that sounded rude in my head.' Her breath caught, and she felt the blood rushing to her face.

'Well . . .'

'It does sound rude, doesn't it? I'm sorry.'

'No, no it's not that.'

'Yes, it is, look . . . I should have realised. It may have seemed like a trivial detail from way back when to me, but I shouldn't have forgotten it, because it was life and death to you, and I'm making it worse, aren't I?' A tear slowly edged its way down Jenny's cheek. 'I should just stop talking.'

'It was so long ago . . .' she sniffed. 'It shouldn't matter. I've got a life now; who cares about all that stuff?'

'But it obviously does matter. You call it a life, but you haven't really moved on since we were children, have you? You still wear the same kind of clothes I remember you in. You like everything that I liked as a child. I can't see anything in this flat that doesn't remind me of then. And I'm still talking when I promised I'd stop. Sorry.'

Jenny still couldn't look at him. She was just staring at the surface of her tea, not even crying.

'I just want there to be something I can do,' Richard said. He sighed and put the mug of tea back on the coffee table. 'I could invent a personality for you, see if it would stick, but then in some ways you'd always belong to me. What if I decided I wanted to remake you? I don't want that for you. You deserve to take charge of your own life. I've had enough of manipulation, even for the best of reasons. I won't go down that route.' He passed a hand over his face. 'I want you to be your own person, not just a part of me that's been left unfinished. You're not a . . . handbag . . . you're you; you just don't know it.' She looked up at him, and he saw that even her eyes were grey and washed-out looking. Her hair was falling in her face. He reached over and brushed the loose, mousey strands behind her ear. Then he leaned forwards and gently kissed her.

'Handbag?' she asked, when their lips parted.

'Yes, I'm sorry. It was the first thing I could think of.' He leaned forwards to kiss her again, but she pulled away.

'No, don't . . .'

He flushed and drew back to the other end of the sofa. 'Sorry, sorry . . . I shouldn't have . . . I mean . . . that was probably taking advantage, and . . . sorry. Just, sorry.'

'No, no it's not that. It's what you said about belonging to people. I don't think I want that either.' She smiled, and her face started to light up. 'I've spent so much time obsessing, I need a change of pace. I don't think I want to be so hung up again over any man.'

'I haven't scarred you for life, have I?' A worried frown crossed his face.

'No, I just . . . Now I come to think about things, about what I want, not what I think I ought to want . . .' She threw her hands up. 'I don't know. Heck, I could be gay.'

He looked up at her and saw that her eyes weren't grey at all. They were a warm honey-brown. And her hair, which until today had been a nondescript mousey kind of tint, was now the shade of hazel nuts in autumn.

'I mean, I don't know for certain,' she continued. 'Everything's all still so new, and I'm not completely sure what being gay feels like.' She took a deep breath. 'I'm not sure what I want to be,' she said, her smile spreading as colour came into her face for the first time, 'but I know it's up to me to decide now. Thank you.'

'I wouldn't thank me just yet,' said Richard, still marvelling at the transformation. 'It's not an easy path.'

Jenny shrugged. 'That wallpaper's going to have to go as well,' she added, glancing round the flat. Then she gave a broad grin and topped up their mugs of tea.

The Baron was sitting on the bole of a tree when Kate found him, leaning back against its trunk, eyes closed, as the evening sunlight lanced down around him through the leaves. He was wearing a green tunic with coffee-coloured breeches and high-topped brown boots and looked rather like a tree himself. She crunched towards him through the leaf-litter.

'Hello, Robin. Nice to see you're busy,' she said.

'I thought you said you'd never be back here,' he said, squinting up at her through half-closed eyes.

'Never say never.'

'How about forever, then?' he suggested.

'Oh, I never say that either.' She moved out of the light and sat next to him on the moss.

'You said it once. 'Til death us do part, remember?'

'And there was a death, and we were parted.'

'But does it have to be forever?' He put out a hand to touch her knee, and for once, she didn't flinch or pull away. 'I'm sorry. I know you don't like me to speak of her, but I can't help thinking that she wouldn't have wanted this for us.'

'No. She wouldn't have. But every time I look at you, I see so much of her, of the person she would have grown into. She looked so much like her father.'

'I thought time would lessen the pain.'

'It will.' She grit her teeth. 'But not yet.'

She took his hand and squeezed it in her own. For a moment they were quiet. Even the birdsong seemed dimmed.

'But she isn't the girl I've come about,' said Kate when the silence became too much.

'So you're not just here for me. Will I ever learn to stop hoping?'

'Hopefully not,' Kate smiled.

'Then I shall live forever in hope.' He raised her hand to his lips and brushed them against her fingers. 'Helen told me about what happened,' he continued, releasing her. 'About the bracelet and where you got it from.'

'You sound like you're judging me for what I did.'

'I'm judging you for not telling me,' he replied pointedly.

'I'm not beholden to tell you these things any more.' She sighed, staring up into the branches above. 'And anyway, you would have found out sooner or later.'

'I like hearing these things from you, you know.' He paused to judge her expression, but it remained impassive. 'But it seems Helen wasn't who you came to talk about either. Who, then? Jenny? I thought she and Richard were sorting things out?'

'No.' Kate took a deliberate breath. 'It's about Dawlish.'

'Dawlish?'

'She saved a man's life today.'

He inclined his head. 'That she did.'

'I don't think she's even realised it. I think in all the excitement, it's completely passed her by what that means.' She leaned back against the tree, her hand still in his lap, and let her head fall to rest on his shoulder. He made no mention of the fact but stretched out his own hand to cover hers as he continued.

'It means she's grown up. She can hold her own in this world.'

'And she's earned her soul back.'

'Oh, she's already done that.' The Baron let his head fall to the side, resting gently on Kate's curls. 'She's done that a few hundred times over, down the years. This just makes it official.'

'You've never set much store by the letter of the law. Nor, for that matter, the subtle distinction between mine and yours.'

'You're one to talk.'

Kate shifted and reached into her jacket pocket to

bring out a small velvet ring-box. She set it down on the Baron's knee.

'What's this?' he asked.

'Open it.'

Inside was a silver ring. Thin strands of metal looping themselves round an opalescent stone, glowing with an inner fire that didn't seem to belong to this world.

'I had it reset a while back,' Kate whispered. In the distance, they could hear the soft scrunch of boots through fallen leaves.

'It's Dawlish though, isn't it?' The Baron's soft smile spread back across his face.

'It is. Shall we give it back to her?'

The tramp of footsteps on the forest floor grew closer, and a voice pierced the gathering dusk.

'Hey guys. You wanted to see me for something?'

One week, thought Richard as he let himself back into the house. Was that all it took to change a life? Turn it upside down and then back again? Everything had happened so fast, his head was still spinning. And now it was over. More than anything else, he felt a sense of loss. The pumping adrenalin had left him fizzing, and the sudden cessation of stimulus was making his stomach burn. The question kept presenting itself: what was he going to do now?

A whole world had opened up to him and just as suddenly closed again. He had discovered an arch nemesis and defeated it, lifting a curse that had lain on his family for generations. He had met with dragons and princesses, rogues and ravens. Seen places no one would ever believe if he told them. Kissed the damsel in distress. Been an absolute idiot and maybe a hero. And all in the space of seven days. How could he go back to work on Monday after all of that? Automatically, he began to fill the kettle for a cup of tea. The window above the sink was open, and Bobble was sitting on the sill.

'Hey, there,' said Richard with a warm smile.

'Aark.'

Richard glanced out of the window. The tree outside was full of jackdaws watching, waiting for something.

'You're leaving?' he asked Bobble. 'To follow that path that Huginn mentioned? Is this goodbye from you, too?' Another bolt of sadness caught him in the chest. He knew that Bobble would be better off with his own kind, but he had grown quite attached to the little bird. It felt like the loss of a friend. As if reading his thoughts, Bobble fluttered up to his shoulder and snuggled up against the side of his face. Richard scratched the top of his head, where the downy feather he had been named for had once been.

'I'm gonna miss you, little guy,' he said. Then Bobble hopped off his shoulder and back to the windowsill. Poking his head out, he called three short notes to the assembled jackdaws, who took off together as if they had been dismissed. Bobble turned back to Richard and looked at him expectantly.

'Aren't you going with them?' Richard asked.

'Aark.' Bobble looked out of the window, then back to Richard, then fluttered to the top of the fridge where he started trying to pry it open. Despite himself, Richard couldn't help but smile.

'All right, I get the hint,' he said, secretly relieved. 'I

guess that means you're staying.'

The cheering smell of cooking sausages began to fill the kitchen. Richard finished making his cup of tea and sat down at the table. He started to thumb his ring absently. The gold felt like a part of his hand. Glancing over to where Bobble was sitting on the worktop eyeing the sizzling pan, he smiled. He was still the Lampton heir; he just had to figure out what that meant now. Something told him this was not the end.

ACKNOWLEDGMENTS

So many people have contributed to the making of this book in so many ways that it would be impossible to thank them all, but honourable mention must go to a few:

Firstly, to all of my incredible publishing team at The X, in particular Penny, Sarah-Beth and Merilyn. Thank you for believing in me, and for all the hard work you've put in to make my dream a reality.

All of my loving family: my Mum and Dad, for every bedtime story and trip to the library, and for their continuing support, my sister, who has always had my back, and my Gran, who sadly never got to see the final draft, but who was always on the other end of a phone when I needed her.

My friend and fellow author, Russell, for all the tips and pointers.

My friends, old and new, but especially Nik, Sandy and Casper, my very first readers and my motivation to keep writing.

My fiancé, Paul, for love, support, and much needed prodding when occasion demanded.

And last, but not least, to you. For reading, and hopefully enjoying, this book. I couldn't have done it without you.

A.J.

ABOUT THE AUTHOR

Born and raised in the wilds of Northumbria, A.J. Campbell was brought up on a diet of stories and local folklore, of which the Legend of the Lampton Worm was a perennial favourite. She eventually left her home town to study English and Creative Writing at the University of Warwick and now lives in Hampshire, (which she persists in calling the "wrong" end of the country), with her fiancé and a succession of dead houseplants. At weekends she can often be found dressing up and pretending to be other people, immersing herself in the lives of fictional historical characters—or as it is better known, "LARPing". She makes her own costumes and has a weakness for detective stories.

ABOUT Xchyler PUBLISHING

Xchyler Publishing strives to bring intelligent, engaging speculative fiction from emerging authors to discriminating readers. While we specialize in fantasy, Steampunk, and paranormal genres, we are also expanding into more general fiction categories, including several manuscripts in the developmental phase. We believe that "family friendly" books don't have to be boring or inane. We exert our best creative efforts to expand the horizons of our readers with imaginative worlds and thought-provoking content.

At The X, we pride ourselves in discovery and promotion of talented authors. Our anthology project produces three books a year in our specific areas of focus: fantasy, Steampunk, and paranormal. Held winter, spring/summer, and autumn, our short story competitions result in published anthologies from which the authors receive royalties.

Upcoming themes include: *Worldwide Folklore and the Post-modern Man* (Fantasy, Winter 2015), and *The*

Brothers Grimm (Steampunk, Spring/summer 2016).
Visit http://www.xchylerpublishing.com/site.cfm/Submissions/Anthology-Submissions.cfm for more information.

Other Xchyler Publishing titles you may enjoy:
On the Isle of Sound and Wonder by Alyson Grauer
Hohenstein by Didi Lawson
Forte by JD Spero
Vivatera and *Conjectrix* by Candace J. Thomas
The Vanguard Legacy series by Joanne Kershaw
The Accidental Apprentice by Anika Arrington
The Grenshall Manor Chronicles by R. A. Smith
Shadow of the Last Men by J.M. Salyards

Look for these upcoming releases from Xchyler Publishing:

Bindings and Spines by R.M. Ridley: the second White Dragon Black novel, a return engagement for paranormal PI and magic addict and practitioner, Jonathan Alvey.

The Mage and the Magpie by M. K. Wiseman: Liara finds herself banished from her village and the kindly priest who raised her and thrust into the protection of a mysterious mage. Thus begins her quest to develop her inborn magical talent and discover the identity of the wizard who sired her.

Kingdom City: Revolt by Ben Ireland: Paul Stevens leads the revolt against the Kingdom City dictator responsible for his wife's death. With his children gone missing, he must choose between saving what may remain of his family or the fledgling rebellion on the verge of collapse.

Dragon Moon by Scott E. Tarbet: the Chinese set

their sights on the moon and heat up the space race while the unsuspecting Russian and American governments focus their attentions elsewhere in this near-future techno-thriller. The cost of failure: worldwide hegemony under a totalitarian regime.

Made in the USA
Charleston, SC
28 June 2015